G000021580

MADELEINE

EMMA NICHOLS

Britain's Next
BESTSELLER

First published in 2018 by:

Britain's Next Bestseller
An imprint of Live It Publishing
27 Old Gloucester Road
London, United Kingdom.
WC1N 3AX

www.bnbsbooks.co.uk

ISBN: 9781791321628

Also available in digital format

Other books by Emma Nichols

To keep in touch with the latest news from Emma Nichols
and her writing please visit:

www.emmanicholsauthor.com
www.facebook.com/EmmaNicholsAuthor
www.twitter.com/ENichols_Author

Thanks

Without the assistance, advice, support and love of the following people, this book would not have been possible.

DC Joy. You are a star, reading and re-reading, stating the blindingly obvious, and then accepting that I will still do my own thing anyway. Thanks chicky.

Valden. You were on my mind with this story! I knew you would get it, and thank you for your valuable comments, as always. I am delighted you loved it, loved it, and loved it some more! Bless you my darling.

Mu. Thank you for your on-going support, creative ideas and especially your cover-designs. You are so talented, and nailed it again. Thank you, my love.

To my wonderful readers and avid followers. Thank you for continuing to read the stories I write. I have loved writing this book, which is written in a different style than my other work, a style that I hope reflects the post-war period in which the story is set. I hope you love it.

With love, Emma x

Dedication

To the post-war women, who fought for our liberation and freedom. Sadly, that fight still continues today, but we wouldn't be where we are now if it hadn't been for those who took up the fight before us.

1.

Génissiat, France 1947

Claudette gazed skywards, her eyes weary, the light fading as she ambled towards *Restaurant Vietti*. The rain clouds had passed in a brief moment, leaving a spongy feel to the lightly dampened path, the wetness insufficient for the soil to stick to the well-worn boots that weighed heavily with every pace. The day had seemed endless and the work, as always, arduous, but even more so on this, her first day. She had vowed to pace herself, not to feel that she needed to prove herself, but railway work was a man's work – she'd heard it often said enough – and she found herself doing more, working longer, demonstrating her strength to the eyes boring into her back. The sniggering had stopped soon enough, though the subsequent silence in her presence and whenever she moved past a chattering group of men, told her all she needed to know. She wasn't welcome, didn't fit in. Never would. She had skipped lunch, her stomach groaning, overhearing the men describe in great detail the sumptuous meal they had stopped to consume. They were cruel, rigid in their beliefs, and bigoted. Yes, very narrow-minded. She nodded her head, affirming her thoughts, and inhaled deeply, her pace slowing to a stop. She had hoped the war would have changed things, but it hadn't. If anything it had made matters worse – men reasserting themselves into a world they left behind, one that had changed in their absence but without their approval.

The pervasive scent of ferns springing to life, the musty earth, and a subtle sweet-floral smell drew her from her musings. The rain did that, brought nature to life. She breathed in the fresh fragrance, gazed at the sky again. Dusk was approaching earlier these days, with the transition into autumn, but the sun still held warmth, and it would be another two hours before it dived behind the mountains. She removed her jacket, slung it over her shoulder and continued to amble.

Something was reassuring about the near-silence inside the wooded parkland, and she wondered if her Papa had walked this path before her. A smile crept into a yawn, and she rubbed her eyes. He was right; this was a beautiful part of France. She rolled her shoulders, eased the tension held in tired muscles and wondered, momentarily, where the tightness had gone. She squinted into the sky expectantly, but it looked the same. Being in nature always seemed to affect her in this way, give her cause to question the essence of life, but there was something intangible here too, soothing and calming. Ethereal. A large boulder resting under the canopy of an old oak tree caught her attention, and her feet followed her eyes to the edge of a lake. The water, motionless; a black mirror settled into a bed of ferns and foliage. She dipped her boot, humoured by the ripple that danced across the surface, obscuring her reflection. Folding her jacket neatly, she pressed it against the boulder, sat and leaned her head back, her eyes closing, her mind stilling. Aware of a distant dog barking, children's laughter, and birdsong; she sighed as she drifted. Settling her body against the smooth hard surface, her lips parted slightly, and her breathing slowed.

'Help! Help! Help!'

Claudette jumped to her feet before her eyes opened fully, her ears locating the panicked cries, her heart pounding in her chest. An urgent groan escaped her as she squinted across the lake.

A young child, a girl, grappling frantically at the side of a small boat seemed to be struggling, unable to reach the boy's hand. The girl's head dropped under the water, re-surfaced. The high-pitched screams echoed across the water. The boy leaned over the boat, reached out again, trying to find the small hand, shouting instructions. Fingers slipped through fingers, and the girl submerged then resurfaced again.

2

Wading, diving, Claudette punched her arms through the water, adrenalin driving her the short distance at a swift pace. Lifting the girl with ease, the boy shaking, wide-eyed and silent, she heaved the small body into the boat. The girl was staring at her, and she tried to smile reassuringly. Then the girl started to sob uncontrollably. 'It's okay,' Claudette said, her heart racing. She had no idea how to handle children. None whatsoever. 'You're okay. It's okay. I'm going to get in the boat,' she said, nodding at the girl and then the boy, seeking an affirmation. The boy stared, the girl continued to sob. She climbed in. 'Where is the oar?'

The boy pointed to the stick resting on the bank.

Merde! She lowered herself back into the water and moved behind the boat. Arms pushing and legs kicking, she eased the craft to the bank and stepped out of the water. Reaching her arms out, the young girl climbed into them, and Claudette lifted her to the ground, thankful that the sobs had ceased. She dropped to her knees, assessing the girl.

The boy jumped out of the boat and stood, his eyes downcast, scuffing at the loose soil at his feet. She gazed up; he looked pale.

The girl threw herself at Claudette and wrapped her arms around her neck in a vice-like grip. Claudette froze at the unexpected contact then softened, enfolding the child in a reassuring embrace. 'You're safe now,' she said. The girl clung on tightly.

The boy kicked at the soil.

'My name is Claudette, what's yours?' she said, addressing the boy.

'Albert,' he mumbled, his gaze still firmly directed at his feet.

The girl's grip eased, and wide eyes studied Claudette's face intently. 'I'm Natty. I'm six, and he's ten,' she said. Claudette's lips curled, and Natty beamed a smile.

'We'd better get you home,' Claudette said. 'You're soaking wet.'

Natty twiddled with Claudette's now off-white shirt in her fingers. 'You're all wet too,' she said.

Claudette laughed. 'Yes, I am.'

Albert stared at her. 'I'm sorry,' he said.

Claudette stood, placed her hand on his shoulder and squeezed. 'Where do you live?' she asked. She smiled, hoping to draw him from his concerns.

He gazed down the path. 'The restaurant,' he said, pointing down the tree-lined route from the lake. He still wasn't smiling.

'Ah, right. Well, that's good because I'm really very hungry,' she said. She beamed a grin at him, and his mouth twitched.

Natalie grinned back at her. 'I'm hungry too,' she said, her hand finding its way into Claudette's.

Claudette frowned at the unfamiliar sensation against her palm. The fragility she would have expected with something so small and delicate also held the quality of strength and determination she associated with something far more robust. She held on firmly. 'Right, lead on,' she said.

Albert led.

'She's going to be cross,' he said as they walked.

'Who is?' Claudette said.

'Maman.'

'Ah, yes.' Claudette nodded and reached out her hand. He seemed to relax with the comforting touch. 'Do you come to the lake often?' she said.

He kicked a stone across the ground as he walked. 'Maman said we're not allowed to go in the boat,' he said, his voice broken.

'Ah, I see,' she said, squeezing both their hands, falling effortlessly into step with Natty's shorter pace.

'I'm cold.' Natty said.

Claudette stopped, studied the straggly fair hair and chattering teeth. She glanced over her shoulder. Merde! 'I left my jacket on the rock,' she said.

'I'll go and get it,' Albert said.

'It's the other side of the lake.'

He shrugged, released her hand, and ran back along the path, heading for the track leading around the water's edge.

'We'll wait here for you.' Her words followed him, and he raised his hand in acknowledgement before dipping out of sight.

'I'...m c...o...l...d,' Natty said again, her eyes watering, her lips a shade closer to blue.

Claudette crouched, pulled her into her chest and kissed the top of her head. The tiny arms wrapped around her, gentle sobs snuffled into her chest. 'You're okay,' she said, lost for anything more reassuring to say.

Natty stopped snuffling suddenly and pulled out of the embrace. She stared at Claude intently. 'Are you a man?' she said.

Claudette released a short puff of air in a splutter. 'No. Claudette is a girl's name. Though I prefer to be called Claude,' she said.

'Maman calls me Natty. My real name's Natalie.'

'That's a pretty name.'

Inquisitive eyes scanned Claude. 'You've got no breasts,' Natty said, staring directly at her chest.

Claudette chuckled, aware of the rough damp cloth that had been rubbing against sensitive skin. 'My shirt hides them,' she said, wondering if that was the right response to give to a six-year-old.

'Maman's got big breasts.'

'Oh!' Claudette gulped, her throat constricted, and a brief coughing fit challenged her breathing.

Natty stared wide-eyed, studying her further. 'Why is your hair short?'

'Because I like it that way.' Claudette looked down the track to the lake, willing Albert's return.

'It's like a man.'

'Yes.'

'Why?'

'Why what?'

'Why do you have it like a man?' Natty reached up and pulled at the short hair around Claudette's ear.

Claudette retracted. 'Do you always ask a lot of questions?'

Natty nodded. 'Maman says it's good to ask questions.'

'Ah, right. And what does your papa say about that?' The smile on Claudette's face was met with nonchalance and a shrug.

'He's dead.' Natty said. She turned her head towards the path and started waving.

Claudette took a moment to follow Natty's gaze. She stood, took a deep breath and released it slowly, relieved that Albert was running towards them with a beaming grin on his face.

'Here,' he said, puffing and holding out the jacket. His smile thinned his lips and revealed brilliant white teeth. He would be a handsome man in a few years.

'Thank you.'

Claudette glanced at Natty. 'Do you want to wear it?'

Natty grinned, and the tip of her nose and cheeks glowed. She held out her arms enthusiastically. 'Can you put it on me?'

Claudette guided the short arms into the long sleeves, wrapped the jacket around the slender frame and buttoned it up. Natty looked down at the cloth hanging from her body.

Claudette tried to roll a sleeve up, but it slipped down immediately. She shrugged. 'Shall we go home?'

Natty reached up, and Claudette clasped the sleeve-covered hand, fully aware that the other sleeve was dragging in the dirt as they ambled along the path.

2.

'Mon Dieu!'

'Maman,' Albert said, his shoulders slumping. He averted her fierce glare as they approached the house and Madeleine closed down on his personal space.

'Albert, what on earth happened?'

He winced.

The woman's eyes darted to her daughter, who stood stiffly, attention on her brother. The woman reached out and pulled Natty into her arms. 'Are you hurt?'

Natty shook her head. 'I just fell in the water,' she said, in a voice that was noticeably quieter than when she had fired questions at Claudette.

'What have I told you about playing next to the lake?' she said to her son, thrashing an arm towards him. 'Allez! Go to your room. Maintenant. Now!'

Albert's eyes caught Claudette's briefly, with a look that said, please don't tell her about the boat, and then he turned towards the restaurant and ran.

Claudette stared. The passion emanating from this slender woman, in a wrap-around dress that perfectly accentuated her figure, caused her muscles to tighten and she found herself standing to attention next to Natty. She cleared her throat, forced her shoulders to relax and held out a hand. 'I'm Claudette,' she said.

The woman's eyes eventually shifted from her daughter to the outstretched hand and then settled on Claudette's smile. 'Bonjour, Claudette. I am Madeleine,' she said, shaking hands.

The grip was firm and warm. Claudette cleared her throat again, acutely aware of the tingling sensation that had caused the hairs on her arms to rise and her skin to prickle.

Words escaped her, and all that came out of her mouth was a mumbled groan. She stared. She couldn't help herself.

'Madeleine Vietti,' Madeleine said.

The words pulled Claudette from her stunned inarticulate state, and she rubbed clammy hands down her trousers. 'Sorry, I, umm.' Madeleine's eyes were assessing her, and her racing heart was making words even harder to find.

'You are soaking wet,' she said.

Claudette hadn't expected Madeleine to reach out and touch the shirt on her arm, or the electric response that shot through her body, or the groan that she fought to suppress. 'Umm.' She looked down. Her shirt had dried a little, but her trousers hung heavily from her hips, and when she wriggled her toes she could feel the pools of warm water that bathed her feet.

'We need to get you out of those clothes,' Madeleine said.

'Umm, I'm fine, thank you. Natty got very cold.' Claudette could feel heat rising to her cheeks.

Madeleine stilled, her hand resting on Claudette's arm, her eyes fixed on Claudette's face, and then a smile formed that softened her features. 'Yes, Natty too,' she said, removing her hand and raking her fingers through her hair.

Claudette swallowed, absorbed by Madeleine's movement that seemed suddenly self-conscious, and smiled. She touched the burning spot Madeleine had left on her arm.

'I'm hungry.' Natty flapped at her mother's dress, her gaze shifting between Madeleine and Claudette. 'Can Claude stay for dinner?' she said.

Madeleine frowned.

'It's okay, I...,' Claudette started.

'Of course, she must stay for dinner. I think we owe... Claude...' She paused, her tone shifting, 'a lot of dinners, don't we?' She crouched down, smiled broadly at her daughter and

9

tugged the wild, wet locks around her ears. 'Let's go and get you changed,' she said, reaching for Natty's covered hand.

'You will join us for dinner?' she said to Claude.

There was no option to refuse. Claudette nodded.

'So, Natty, what happened?' Madeleine said as they walked.

'Albert got the boat out on the lake and I fell in the water and Claude rescued me and I got cold and Claude wrapped her coat around me and Albert went for her coat and we talked, and Claude isn't a man, you know.'

Madeleine released a sharp noise and flushed. 'Ah right,' she said.

Claudette lowered her head, heat prickling the back of her neck.

'Claudette's a girls name and she likes to be called Claude and she likes having short hair like a man and her shirt hides her breasts...' Natty continued without pausing for breath.

Madeleine turned her head to catch Claudette's attention. 'I'm so sorry,' she mouthed, her cheeks glowing, her eyes struggling to hold Claudette's gaze.

Claudette couldn't stop the grin forming or the repressed chuckle that caused her eyes to water. She cleared her throat. 'We had a good chat,' she said.

'So it seems,' Madeleine said, her gaze intense, penetrating.

Claudette broke away first, butterflies dancing low in her belly. She had never felt more self-conscious than she did at that moment, and there was nowhere she could hide. The flap of a jacket sleeve brought her attention back, and she took the small hand beneath the cold damp cloth and squeezed. Natty dragged her along the path with one hand, her mother holding the other.

'I can't thank you enough,' Madeleine said, as they approached the farmhouse to the rear of the restaurant. She opened the door and stepped into a large living room. Natty released both hands and ran across the threshold pulling at the jacket.

Claudette bent down and undid the buttons, fighting with the thrashing arms that suddenly wanted free of the encumbrance.

Released, Natty ran to the stairs. 'Albert, Albert,' she said, climbing the steep wooden steps with hands and feet.

Claude scanned the room as Madeleine went to the back of the living room, past a dining table and through a door. Red poppy-print dotted on beige wallpaper lined walls that met natural wood flooring, mostly covered with a sizeable Persian-style rug heavily patterned in shades of red, beige and blue-purple. A black and white photograph of Madeleine caught her attention, and another of the children, in a polished-silver frame on the mantelpiece above the fireplace. Claude stepped closer. She guessed the one of Madeleine had been taken before the children were born; she looked younger, her smile radiant. Her eyes shone as if captivated by excitement. Claude gazed with wonder, a soft smile forming as she pondered what might have made Madeleine so happy. The look suited her. There was something carefree about the smile that gave the impression of a light-hearted spirit. Claude lingered on the shape of her and the way her hair fell softly around her shoulders, her features fine like porcelain with high cheekbones. Delicate. Elegant. The slender fingers resting lightly on the back of a chair in the image caused her to wonder at the tenderness of their touch and her mouth parched. She looked across at the picture of the children, taken maybe a year or so ago and there was the noticeable absence of any photograph of the children's papa. She turned as Madeleine came back through the door, the dryness in her throat, their eyes meeting, and heat moved through her in a wave.

'Here,' Madeleine said, holding out a short glass of milky white liquid.

Claude caught the quizzical gaze, and the aniseed aroma reached her senses before the glass made it into her hands. 'Thank you, but you don't need to...'

Madeleine raised the palm of her hand. 'I insist. You are a guest in our house. You saved my daughter's life, and I can never thank you enough. Whatever you want to eat or drink, or if you need a place to stay or anything, you are always welcome here. I, we, are indebted to you,' she said.

'Umm, thank you,' she said and sipped at the pastis. Fire scolded the back of her throat, and she winced.

Madeleine straightened her dress and turned towards the room she had just come from. She stopped at the door. 'I need to feed the children,' she said. 'The restaurant is open if you would like to eat there,' she added, indicating with her eyes. Her gaze then settled on Claude, and she smiled. 'Or you could join us here? I need to go to work in an hour. The children will go to bed then,' she said. 'Would you like a bath, and perhaps a change of clothes?' she said, sizing up Claudette. 'I have something that will fit you.' She nodded her head as she spoke.

Claudette smiled. She rambles just like Natty. 'Thank you,' she said. 'I will be honoured to join you.' Madeleine's eyes seemed to darken, or maybe it was the just the light changing with the distance across the room. 'A bath would be very welcome,' she said. A shiver rose within her as if on cue, and then heat flooded her cheeks. Madeleine's smile carried genuine affection. It didn't help.

'The honour is ours,' Madeleine said. 'The bathroom is upstairs, the first room on the left. I will bring some clothes up.' She headed toward the back of the house.

Claudette finished the drink and placed it on a side-table before climbing the stairs. The aroma from the kitchen followed her, and her stomach reminded her that she hadn't eaten since breakfast. She took the stairs two at a time and found the bathroom. Closing the door, she leaned against it gathering her breath. Her heart raced, and the image of Madeleine's shapely breasts and soft mouth was firmly lodged in her mind's eye. Worse still, she had no desire or intention to erase it. Merde! Merde!

A light tapping sound on the other side of the door caused Claudette to jump out of her skin. Pressing her hand to her chest, she watched as the door opened. Her eyes tracked down.

'Maman said to wear these,' Natty said and threw a scrunched-up ball of clothes at her then disappeared from view, and clomped down the stairs.

Claudette appraised the flower-patterned dress and dark blue cardigan. Non, non! The last time she had been seen in a dress, she would have been Natty's age. She closed the door, turned on the taps, and started to undress. She stepped into the shallow water, realising how chilled she had become, the water feeling hotter to her feet than was justified by the temperature. She washed quickly, stepped out of the bath, dried, and put on the dress and cardigan. The fit was perfect. She pinched the fabric between her fingers; she could have sworn the scent of Madeleine came to her, and the fresh smell of soap. Glancing into the steam-frosted mirror, she didn't recognise the alien being staring back at her. Picking up her damp clothes she descended the stairs.

'You look pretty,' Natty said through a mouthful of food, her legs swinging beneath the table.

Albert turned his head and looked in her direction, grunted his approval, and then turned back to his meal, shovelling hungrily.

Claudette could feel the cool air on her partly exposed chest, and as Madeleine appeared from the kitchen carrying two plates of food, heat coloured the flesh and rose swiftly up her neck.

'You do look pretty,' Madeleine said, nodding at her daughter. Then the widest smile highlighted faint laughter lines, and her dark eyes seemed to sparkle at Claude. 'Please, take a seat; you must be starving,' she said. 'I'll take your clothes and dry them on the stove.' She held out her hands to receive the garments.

Claudette's cheeks still blazed, but something about the playful and welcoming nature of her host relaxed her more than she would have expected, in her state of dress. She handed over her trousers and shirt and sat in front of the plate stacked with meat and potatoes, the aroma wafting under her nose causing her stomach to grumble loudly.

'You look like a girl now,' Natty said, through another mouthful of food.

Claudette ruffled her hair. 'Is that so?'

'Hmmmm.' Natty's attention went back to her dinner.

Claudette took a mouthful of gravy-soaked potato, and moaned in silent pleasure.

'Would you like a glass of wine? Madeleine said, stepping from the kitchen with a glass and half-carafe of white wine.

Claudette nodded, raised the back of her hand to her full mouth and swallowed. 'Thank you,' she said.

Madeleine placed the glass and carafe in front of Claudette and sat at the head of the table. She glanced from Albert to Natty and then settled on Claudette. 'So, what brings you to Génissiat? I haven't seen you here before,' she said.

Claude swallowed. 'I work on the railways. Today was my first day. I'm staying at the guesthouse in town.' Madeleine was staring at her with raised eyebrows, and she couldn't tell whether the expression was one of surprise or impressed amusement.

'Ah!' Madeleine continued to assess Claude with something akin to compassion. 'And how did Gustave take having a woman in his workplace?'

Claudette lowered her gaze, toyed with the fork in her hand. 'You know him?' she said softly.

'Oh yes. Everyone knows Gustave. He might not be the most forward thinking man in the village, but his heart is big, and he is well respected,' she said, with a slight tilt of her head.

Madeleine's smile warmed where it touched, and Claudette felt that touch in all the wrong places. 'I didn't see much of him,' she said, her thoughts drifting to the cold shoulder and mumbled displeasure she had endured for the best part of the day.

'He will be in for dinner later. They all will.' Madeleine's head tilted back and forth as she spoke, the tints in her hair catching in the low light. 'Come on, eat up,' she said, addressing her children.

Claude continued eating, her fork moving slowly.

'I need to get to work shortly,' Madeleine said. 'You're welcome to stay here for as long as you like. The kitchen here is linked directly to the restaurant kitchen, and so between us we keep an eye on these two. My sister will come in if you need to get away, but you may want to wait for your clothes,' she said.

Claude felt the gaze as if it were penetrating the thin dress and caressing her. Her skin prickled in a wave down her back and she sipped at the wine.

'Can we stay up with Claude?' Natty said, pushing her plate away and making a move to rise from the table.

'What do you say, mademoiselle?' Madeleine said, stopping her in her tracks.

'Please can I get down, maman?'

'Can I get down too?' Albert said.

'Yes. You have half-an-hour before bed.'

Albert groaned.

15

'What about Claude?' Natty said in a pleading tone, her body rocking from side to side, presenting her best puppy-dog eyes.

'I'm sure Claude has better things to do than babysit you two.' Madeleine smiled. 'And remember you have school tomorrow,' she said.

Claudette shrugged, sensing that Madeleine was being polite. 'I have to wait for my clothes,' she said. 'I can stay until they go to sleep.'

'Yeah!' Natty squealed. 'I can show you my doll,' she said excitedly and ran to the stairs.

Albert slumped in the living room chair to the side of the fireplace, picked up a book and leafed through the pages.

'Please don't feel obliged. Natty will keep you here all night,' Madeleine said.

Claudette felt a warm melting feeling spread through her. The sensation had her heart racing, and the foreign feeling was both disconcerting and enticing. With a broken voice, she said, 'It's fine. I intended to dine here tonight, and I seem to have done that already.' She smiled, glanced at the empty plate, and frowned at the tone in her own voice. Thrust out of the moment, a lump of hard plastic landed in her lap.

'Her name's Marie.' Natty said.

Claudette stared unblinkingly at the pink, naked doll with a painted face. 'Where are her clothes?' she said.

'They got lost.'

She wished she hadn't asked. Natty's bottom lip started to quiver and her eyes glassed over, tears poised with what appeared to be well-rehearsed imminence. 'We will have to make her some new ones then,' Claudette said, without thinking.

Natty squealed loudly and skipped around the room, 'Claude's going to make some clothes for Marie,' she said to

Albert, pulling at his leg. He grunted, his eyes on his book, his foot easing her away from him.

Claudette wondered if she had imagined the display of upset, curiously amused by Natty's instantaneous transition to joy. Turning her head, she realised Madeleine was watching her and felt another rush of heat. She held her gaze and smiled.

'Can we make clothes now?' Natty said, reaching for the doll.

'Natty, don't be rude,' Madeleine said.

Claudette reached out, cupped Natty's chin in her hand and looked into her eyes. She will break hearts when she's older, she thought. 'I need to get the materials,' she said. 'How about we measure her up?'

'Maman, where is the measure?' Natty turned sharply to her mother, the doll hanging from her hand by one leg.

'In the sewing box.' Natty's feet had moved before Madeleine finished the sentence. 'Be careful of the needles,' she said. Natty already had the box open, her tiny fingers searching eagerly inside.

Claudette watched Madeleine watching Natty thankful she wouldn't be trying to sew with unsteady hands. Next time she came around, she would have better self-control, she promised. She considered the idea of visiting again, and immediately thought about staying away from the mother of the children she had rescued. Catching Madeleine's warm gaze on her as she wrestled with her thoughts, her stomach twisted. Her lips tried to form a smile and failed, Madeleine's brows shifted in question.

'I can get some clothes from the market,' Madeleine said, mindreading Claudette's apparent distress.

Claudette smiled. 'No. Sorry, I was lost in thought,' she said.

'It looked awfully painful!'

Claude felt the dark eyes assessing her with kindness, seeking answers. Honest concern for her, a complete stranger, landed in her chest with a thud. If Madeleine were aware of her desires, her inclination, she would throw her out. She would need to leave town and her job. She would never see Madeleine again. The dull ache lingered under her ribs, tightening as she processed the reality. 'Everything is fine,' she said. She took a deep breath and turned her attention to Natty, who was doing battle with the tape measure that had unravelled in her hands. Turning to Madeleine again, she smiled, hoping her desire didn't reveal through her eyes. A knotted tape measure landed in her lap.

'Can we measure Marie now?' Natty said, looking from her mother to Claudette and back again.

'Of course.' Claudette ruffled the wavy locks, the minor distraction coming as a welcome reprieve.

'I'm sorry, I need to go to work.' Madeleine said. She hesitated. 'The restaurant is through the kitchen.' She pointed.

'We know, maman,' Natty said with confidence beyond her years.

'We'll be fine,' Claudette said. 'Won't we?' she said to Natty.

Natty nodded, a beaming smile on her face. She threw her arms around Claude's neck and squeezed tightly.

'Half-an-hour and then bed,' Madeleine said.

'Aww!' Natty complained, squeezing tighter. Albert tutted.

'Your clothes should be dry by then,' Madeleine said to Claude.

Claude felt caressed by Madeleine's eyes again. 'Thank you,' she said. The air seemed thick with tension. In a low voice, she said, 'Perhaps I should leave.'

'No!' Natty said, strangling her.

Madeleine was shaking her head. 'No, you are welcome to stay. But they need to be in bed in half-an-hour. I'll pop back then.'

Claudette nodded, easing Natty from her neck. 'Do you hear your maman? Half-an-hour,' she said.

Natty looked at her mother. 'Oui, maman,' she said, picking up the doll and tape measure.

'We will be fine,' Claudette said. 'And I know where to find you.' She eyed the kitchen door.

'If you're sure?'

'Can we measure now?' Natty said.

'You two go to bed when Claudette tells you.'

'Oui maman,' the two voices chorused, both with their attention on other things.

Madeleine left the room, Natty telling Claudette how to measure the doll, Albert with his head in his book, Claude confused.

3.

Claude released a long breath, eased out of the dress and put on her trousers and shirt. She sighed. The slightly damp cloth was warm from the stove and the familiar sensation of the material against her skin comforting. She winced as she put on her boots, the cold wet instantly chilling her feet. Forty-five minutes had passed since the children had gone to bed. She stared into the silence emanating from the top floor of the house, tenderness radiating through a smile that mirrored her thoughts. Playing dolls with Natty had been fun. They had measured Marie and designed the outfit on a piece of paper. She had promised to go to the market and Natty had insisted on a red dress and black trousers for the doll. Albert had read from his book, and they had talked a bit about her work on the railways. He had gone to bed full of questions and a sparkle in his eyes.

'Hello!'

She jumped at the voice. She hadn't heard the kitchen door. Catching Madeleine's intense gaze, her heart raced, and a simple verbal response wouldn't come.

'Sorry, I'm late,' Madeleine said, looking towards the stairs. 'Thank you for staying.'

Claudette cleared her throat. 'They went to sleep quickly,' she said.

'I can't thank you enough. I hope they were...'

'They are wonderful children.'

Madeleine's gaze shifted in the silence between them. Her eyes searching, she released a deep sigh.

She looks tired, Claudette thought. 'It must be tough bringing up two children on your own,' she said, her voice quiet, immediately regretting being so forward. 'Natty told me about... your husband.'

20

Madeleine nodded. 'She likes you.'

'She's smart. They both are. Albert's got a keen interest in engineering, and Natty's really creative.' She smiled, recalling the dress design conversation and Albert telling her in great detail how the steam train worked.

Madeleine leaned her head to one side a fraction and her brows furrowed as she gazed at Claude. 'How did you come to work on the railways?' she said.

She drew in a long breath and released it. 'I used to work in a tank factory during the war.'

Madeleine's frown disappeared, replaced by wide eyes.

'I am good with vehicle repairs and maintenance. My father is an engineer and businessman, and he taught me from a young age. It came naturally, I guess. His factory got converted during the war, and we repaired and built tanks for a while. When the war ended, I started working on cars again, as a foreman, but I've always loved the railways. My father...' She paused, held Madeleine's gaze. 'My father is very well connected, and he talked to a friend of a friend, and I got offered this job. It's only labouring, but I hope one day to manage people again,' she said, watching Madeleine's response. Heat surged through her, and her cheeks responded; the brief silence and Madeleine's gaze, painful.

'How old are you?'

'Twenty-three,' she said, her eyes darting from the penetrating stare. She could tell Madeleine was quite a bit older and the appeal caused the tips of her ears to tingle.

'Hmmm. It must be tough, your work.'

Claude noticed Madeleine's eyes display the same shade they had earlier in the evening. There was a quality and depth that she couldn't quantify, effortlessly reeling her in. 'It is very physical, but I am as strong as most men,' she said, standing slightly taller as she spoke.

'I'm sure.' Madeleine said, exploring the length of her. Her eyes shone, and faint lines appeared at their outer edges as she smiled.

Claudette felt restless unease with the mix of emotion rushing through her, the dancing in her stomach and the heat that flowed in waves, in the presence of this woman. She hoped her reaction wasn't too noticeable. She could find no logic that explained her instantaneous and intense response to Madeleine. Lord knows she had spent the best part of the forty-five minutes playing with the children consumed by the strength of her feelings and trying to find some explanation. She had always been sceptical about love-at-first-sight, having never experienced anything remotely close. But as Madeleine looked at her, and the sense of awareness they seemed to share, it was the only explanation she could find. Merde! She struggled to find her voice. 'I had better go,' she said, transfixed by an intensity that was slowly becoming unbearable.

'Yes.' Madeleine said, her voice quiet, contemplative. She followed Claude to the door. 'I can't thank you enough for what you have done. You saved my daughter's life.'

Claudette didn't think of it that way, but she had needed to act swiftly. 'I'm glad I was at the lake,' she said. Madeleine's eyes wandered again, and she sensed there was something she wanted to say. 'I'll see you tomorrow,' Claude said, unlatching the door.

The words found a vacant stare. 'Hmm?' Madeleine said.

'For dinner, at the restaurant,' Claudette confirmed.

'Ah, yes, of course.' She smiled. 'I look forward to seeing you then,' she said. 'And you are always welcome to eat here of course. Anytime. We owe you that much at least.'

Claude blinked as Madeleine made a move towards her. She stiffened at the light touch of Madeleine's lips on her cheek then wondered if Madeleine had felt the fierce heat radiating from her skin. Even she could feel her cheeks burning, and the sensation of Madeleine so close, albeit briefly, had fired up an ache that filtered through every part of her. This woman with an apron fitting tightly around her slim waist, and flour dusting her forehead. She smiled. She had never seen anything so beautiful; so gracious, and so very, very arousing. 'Good night, Madeleine,' she said.

'Good night, Claude.'

Claude closed the door softly behind her and stepped into the dark night, the slight chill, though refreshing, causing her skin to tighten. Her heart racing, her hands shaking, it took a while for her breathing to settle as she walked along the main road into town. Baffled. Bemused. What a strange affair. The last few hours had passed like a whirlwind, and the experience seemed quite surreal. She wanted to grin broadly, but an overwhelming sense of sadness occupied her. The desire to return to the restaurant and be close to Madeleine was overpowering and unrelenting. Yet, her affinity for women would be a position that Madeleine wouldn't or couldn't possibly condone. And, then again, there was something in the way Madeleine had looked at her too, as if they had seen, felt, shared something intangible together. Whatever it was that had connected them deeply, that something would need to remain unaired. She stopped and rested her hands on her hips, took three deep breaths and watched the lights emanating from the restaurant windows. The attraction was stronger than anything she had ever felt, and the further she moved away from the house the more drawn she felt.

*

Closing the door to her room, she stood replaying the thoughts that had occupied her as she walked. It would be perfectly reasonable for everyone to be up on each other's business in such a small town, entirely different from her own upbringing in Lyon. But she had met Gustave Blanc, the railway's site manager, earlier in the day and he didn't strike her as a man with a big heart. He had been forced to take her on; she knew that before she arrived, and he had made his position very clear. His eyes had narrowed, the skin on his face tight, the creases deeper, as he had dictated her orders almost through gritted teeth. She knew a disapproving glare when she saw one. Only in the presence of the men did he smile. Around her, his lips remained thin and his eyes piercingly dark.

It will have irked him that her father held a position of power about which he could only dream. She had seen his kind before. Wielding authority that he didn't really have, revered by a small but significant group. She imagined him charming the ladies, women like Madeleine, and him always being there to rescue a damsel in distress, though she suspected that any rescuing he did came at a price. She definitely wasn't one of those women. She didn't need rescuing.

She had expected him to send her to the furthest point from the stock of steel-rails and piles of stones dotted along the track, and he hadn't let her down. She had missed the morning break because he had asked her to run an errand. Only when she had looked up had she seen the others downing tools and heading off-site for lunch. Then in the afternoon, he had ordered her to work with a group of three other men. He had walked around, chatting frivolously, laughing with the others, and she had sensed him watching her, judging, waiting for her to make a mistake; looking for a reason to have her dismissed. Of course, she would never give him one.

She had learned how to deal with men like Gustave Blanc, working in the factory during the war. You cannot show weakness, her father had said. Maybe it was her appearance that threatened them, or just as likely her knowledge and capabilities, and particularly her physical strength. She was equal to any man she had worked with and had learned that most didn't take too kindly to that fact. They seemed to be okay with other women, women they could bed, women who wore skirts and dresses. Of course, she had to challenge them when they tried to cut corners doing their job. Not to do so might endanger lives, and she couldn't live with the consequences of doing nothing. Standing up to them, not being bullied. There was always a price to pay for that, but she had concluded a long time ago it was a price she was willing to pay.

She rubbed the back of her neck, tired from the long day. The small room felt damp, unlike Madeleine's house that was warm and homely. She hadn't given much attention to the guesthouse accommodation when she arrived. The heavily patterned wallpaper and single bed with patterned blanket looked like hand-me-downs, thrown together without consideration for the aesthetic impact. A small mahogany-wood bedside table, scarred across its surface wedged tightly against the bed, her battered brown-leather suitcase next to it. The room would be dark even in daylight, she thought, the bed squeaking loudly as she perched on it. She picked up her book from the table, rested back against the pillow and tried to read.

She hadn't been aware of the point at which her eyes had closed, the thumping outside the room waking her rudely. Lifting the book from her chest, she placed it on the table and sat, noticing the first signs of dawn appearing through the thinly curtained window. The regular pounding of heavy boots on wood alerted her to the time of day. She yawned, stretched and eased off the bed. It squeaked objectionably, and she almost wanted to respond. She hated this room already; the space that would be home for as long as she worked here. She walked to the bathroom on the landing, splashed cold water on her face and headed down the stairs. If she didn't get to the dining room early, the meagre breakfast offering would be gone.

The chattering in the room silenced as she entered. She took a croissant from the basket and poured a cup of coffee. Standing by the bay window, she gazed out, oblivious to the resuming conversations. Water slid in erratic movements down the glass; condensation on the inside, rain on the outside. She studied the clouds, thick, static. It was going to be a wet day. Her thoughts drifted, and she could feel Madeleine in the sensation sweeping through her, the silent moan on her lips, and the weakness that affected her legs. The seductive image; dark eyes, soft, penetrating, flustered at times, lost in an inner world at others, wouldn't shift. Madeleine was deeply fascinating, addictive even. She moaned, the sound hitting her ears, eyes on her from around the room. 'Going to be a wet day,' she said. The last of the croissant struggled past the constriction in her throat, and she stared out the window waiting for the room to settle, her heart thumping, and the impression of Madeleine etched deeply.

4.

'Where's Claude?' Natty said, running into the kitchen. 'Did she get the things yet?' She waved the plastic doll by the arm as she spoke, her enthusiasm drawing a soft smile, Madeleine's unhurried gaze resting on her.

'She went to the house where she is staying,' Madeleine said.

'Why can't she stay here?' Wide eyes suggested it was blindingly obvious what should happen.

'She has her own place to stay,' Madeleine said, feeling the heat rise from her chest to her cheeks, reminded that images of Claude had distracted her thoughts on more than one occasion the previous evening as she worked, to the point that her older sister Maude had asked her if she were unwell. Unwell wasn't the term she would use to describe the less than subtle tremors that seemed to linger with her imagination. She had stirred several times during the night with the most shocking and titillating dreams, and the first picture in her mind as she had woken, was the vision of Claude as she approached the house in wet clothes, Natty wearing the oversized jacket holding her hand. The surge of anxiety that had stormed through her at that first sighting of Claude had dissipated quickly, replaced by something akin to admiration. Or, was it something else? Adoration? Whatever it was, Claude had an uncanny way of making her feel good.

'Why?' Natty said, swinging the doll, gazing intently at her mother.

Madeleine dropped down to Natty's height, swept the unruly hair behind her daughter's ear and kissed her on the nose. 'How about eggs for breakfast?' she said, hoping to distract attention away from the handsome stranger on both their minds.

'Why?' Natty said again. 'Why can't she stay with us? She could sleep with me, there's lots of room in my bed.'

Madeleine released a chuckle, pressed her hand to her mouth and turned to face the stove. Even she wouldn't want to share a single bed with her wriggly daughter. 'Egg?' she asked again, reaching for the pan.

'When will she bring Marie's things?' Natty said. 'We measured her arms and her legs and around her waist and her chest and her neck and her head and Claude is getting red material for her dress and black for the trousers,' she said, pointing to each body part measured as she talked. 'And, we have a sewing machine she can use, maman, and then I can help her,' she continued. 'I can pin,' she said, seeking her mother's approval.

Madeleine turned her head from the sizzling egg in the pan, soft loving eyes holding her daughter's attention. 'You are such a big girl,' she said. 'I am sure Claude will need your help.' The beaming grin coming back at her took her breath away, and then Natty turned and ran into the living room.

'I'm going to help Claude make the clothes for Marie,' she was telling Albert. 'Maman said I could.'

Madeleine placed the plates on the living room table. 'Come and eat,' she said.

Albert was there in a flash and stuffing egg and baguette in his mouth at a rate of knots. 'Merci,' he mumbled.

'Did you have a good time with Claude?' she said to him.

'Oui.'

'What did you talk about?'

Albert flashed a look that said, why are you asking me questions? 'Trains,' he said, shovelling more bread and slurping at a glass of water.

'Good,' she said. It was the only word in her vocabulary at that moment, and even it came out as two syllables. Struck speechless by the sensations that seemed to have consumed her, she went into the kitchen. Another surge flashed through her, and she leaned against the counter edge, overcome with faintness. Maybe she was going down with something?

Taking a deep breath, she regained her composure, challenged her thoughts as foolish idolising and vowed to behave like the grieving widow she was expected to be. She didn't feel like a grieving widow though. Truth be told, she never had. The initial shock of knowing Raoul had died in the war had caused her heart to race for the briefest moment, but then she had quickly settled to the idea of being a single parent and continuing to run the restaurant alongside her sisters. She had been happier. Natty had been too young to remember her father, though Albert was a different case altogether. She sighed, her heart heavy. Albert. Had he suffered for the lack of a father figure? She had always refused the many men who had sought her company, unwilling to settle for a replacement for Raoul, but perhaps she had been wrong to do so. Determined to ensure the children weren't spoilt to make up for his absence, had she been too hard on him? Her expectations were high, but then again, Albert would be a man soon enough.

Why was she even thinking about a father figure right now? How had her thoughts shifted from Claude to the men who had tried to worm their way into her life? She didn't think of Claude that way, worming her way into their life. On the contrary, for some inexplicable reason she already thought of Claude as a good friend and a part of their lives, and so it seemed did Natty. Maybe it was the fact that she was deeply indebted to her. Perhaps it was the way she effortlessly engaged with the children and received their unreserved respect. Natty had gravitated towards Claude in a way she had never seen with anyone else, even with her sisters, and Albert had been willing to talk to her, and he had never spoken honestly to anyone. Maybe it was her gentle manner or the quiet confidence with which she carried herself, slightly detached in some respects, yet yielding in others.

The fluttering in her chest was new and somewhat perplexing. Heading into Christmas was a busy time for the restaurant, and with the opening of the dam coming up she couldn't afford time off work with illness. Puzzled, she splashed her face with water, entered the living room, and ushered both children to the bathroom to clean their teeth. 'Transport will be here in five minutes,' she said.

Albert thumped up the stairs.

'Maman, will Claude be here when we get back from school?' Natty asked.

Madeleine cleared her throat. 'No, she will be at work. Now go, up the stairs,' she said, gently pushing Natty up the first three steps.

As soon as Madeleine released her, Natty stopped climbing, turned her head, and gazed with wide eyes. 'Will she come for tea?'

'I don't know sweetheart. When she comes to the restaurant for lunch, maybe I can ask her,' Madeleine said, the words coming across with more composure than she felt.

Natty grinned widely. 'Make her come for tea, maman,' she said. Determined steps carried her to the top of the stairs.

Madeleine continued to stare up to the first floor, listening to the ritualistic sounds of brushing teeth, spitting, and the clanging of brushes in the sink. Albert descended quickly and grabbed his coat from the peg by the door. Madeleine reached for the small jacket and presented it to the open arms as Natty reached the bottom of the stairs. Kissing them both on the top of their head, she ushered them out the door and into the rain.

Grey-black smoke pulsed from the back of the waiting truck. The driver beeped his horn and waved, as he did every day. 'Have a good day; work hard,' she said vacantly and waving.

'Bye maman.' Natty said, wrestling with the satchel over her shoulder that hung past her knees and clattered against her legs.

'Bye,' Albert said, breaking into a run.

'Wait Albie,' Natty said, her short legs working hard to keep up with him.

Madeleine watched until they had joined the other children in the back of the truck. She closed the door and stood, immobilised by the sudden realisation of emptiness. Yes, she was curious to find out more about Claude. No, what was she thinking? Claude was Claudette. And Claudette was a woman. And she didn't have those kinds of thoughts about other women

She wiped at puffy eyes, brushed her hands down her apron, and marched through the house into the restaurant kitchen.

'Morning,' Antoinette said. Her younger sister's voice was as cheery as her smile.

'Morning.' Madeleine frowned.

'Is everything okay? Are you okay? The children okay?' Antoinette's voice seemed to rise with each question, her eyes focused, widening, appealing to Madeleine.

Madeleine forced a tight smile.' We're all fine,' she said. 'Just tired.' The yawn appeared naturally, supporting her words and loosening her jaw in the process. She did feel tired, but that was nothing new. The long hours at the restaurant, the children, and maintaining the house always took its toll. That said even with Raoul, little had been different.

'You need a break.' Antoinette's lips formed a thin line as she shook her head. She dropped the rolling pin to the work-surface and pulled Madeleine into a tight embrace; floury hands leaving their mark.

Madeleine sighed. The intention behind the comforting hug didn't reach her as it would normally. She just hoped her sister hadn't noticed the difference. 'I'll start on the soup,' she said, pulling out of the hold and brushing down her apron.

They worked in silence, the soup bubbling and plopping in the background, knives tapping rhythmically on boards, footsteps padding on the stone floor as they moved to and from the pantry and stove. The familiar aroma of onions and herbs started to waft, steam hovering in the dense kitchen air.

'Gustave was asking after you last night, after you had gone,' Antoinette said. She stood with her knife poised, studying her sister's response.

Madeleine's eyes narrowed.

'I'm sure he wants to be your escort,' Antoinette said.

Madeleine pondered the idea of Gustave Blanc escorting her anywhere and shuddered. She had guessed some time ago that he had eyes for her. He would run his hands through his hair and tweak his moustache, then clear his throat before speaking to her, his tone compassionate, his words sincere. He would ask after the children, tell her she looked elegant and ask if she needed any help. Maybe she should give the idea some thought. It would at least be an appropriate distraction from Claude, and Albert did respect him. 'Maybe I will go to a dance sometime,' she said, immediately questioning the abruptness of her decision.

'He's very handsome,' Antoinette said.

Madeleine studied the faraway look in her sister's eyes, her smooth cheeks flushed from the heat of the stove. Of the four sisters, she had always been the dreamy one. Maybe one day she would find her prince. 'You think so?' she asked.

Antoinette cupped her mouth with her hand. 'He's got such beautiful eyes. When he looks at you, it's as if he's caressing you gently.'

Madeleine's frown deepened. That would be a good description of how Claude made her feel; not one she would associate with Gustave. A wave of heat rushed through her, and she fumbled with the knife. Bringing her focus back to Gustave and going to a dance with him, the sensations that thoughts of Claude provoked disappeared and her tiredness seemed more palpable. She sighed, rubbed the back of her hand across her eyes. 'Why don't you go out with him?' she said.

Antoinette gazed in her direction, her eyes unfocused. 'He doesn't think I'm attractive,' she said.

'Well, then he is a bigger fool than I thought,' Madeleine said. 'You are beautiful.'

Antoinette sighed, picked up the knife and started to chop.

'Morning,' Beatrice said, easing herself and a crate loaded with baguettes through the door. 'The delivery just arrived.' Puffing, she glanced from at her sisters. 'I'll unload then,' she said, acknowledging the tension in the room.

'I'll help,' Madeleine said. She wiped her hands and followed her sister out the door.

'I'll make coffee,' Antoinette said, picking up the kettle.

By the time the kettle boiled, three stacked crates of bread sat on the floor next to the small round table in the kitchen. It would be sufficient for the three hundred hungry workers who would show up for lunch. This afternoon a second delivery would arrive, ready for dinner. It was the same every day.

The women sat, sipping at hot coffee. 'So, what did I miss?' Beatrice said.

'Nothing,' Madeleine said.

'I was saying Madeleine should date Gustave,' Antoinette said.

She was back to her usual self, but it didn't make the thought of Gustave seem any more appealing to Madeleine.

'Hmm,' Beatrice said. She broke off a piece of bread and dunked it in the drink. The wrinkles that formed around her tight lips reflected her thoughts about the man. She had known

Gustave since they had schooled together. 'He's too old,' she said. 'You need someone younger, more interesting,' she said.

'He's mature,' Antoinette said, in his defence. 'Sophisticated.'

Beatrice sniggered. 'He's old and bigoted,' she said.

'He would be a good father-figure for Albert,' Antoinette said.

Beatrice harrumphed and dipped another piece of bread.

Madeleine shrugged. 'Maybe,' she said. Of all the options in town, he was undoubtedly the most eligible, and wealthy, and at forty years old he was only six years her senior. She released a deep breath, placed her cup in the sink and stirred the pot of soup before removing it from the stove.

'I'll get more wood,' Beatrice said, easing up from the chair with a grunting noise and making her way to the backyard.

Antoinette rose from the table, and Madeleine stepped towards her, arms open. 'I love you,' she said, pulling her close and kissing the top of her head.

Madeleine studied her. Antoinette had always been the sensitive one; the one who saw the best in everyone. She hoped she would find a kind, loving man one day. Antoinette deserved that much at least.

5.

'Lunch!'

The word passed swiftly along the track, work grinding to a sudden halt, shovels dropped or thrown onto the mountain of gravel, from which the stone-bed of the railway line was slowly being constructed.

Claudette stood, pressed her thumbs into the muscles in her lower back and swept the rain from her face. She had an hour to get into town, to the haberdashers, and back again. She studied the sky; cold, wet drips landing on her face. The rain wasn't going to let off any time soon so it would be a trudge. An image of Natty's wide eyes pricked at her conscience and she set off towards the road in the opposite direction to the other workers. Not that they would notice, or care.

'You not eating?' The man's voice caused her head to turn.

She recognised his face, handsome in a rugged way. She couldn't place his accent, but he wasn't from this region and may have even been from a neighbouring country. He had been one of the few who didn't seem to have an issue with her doing men's work and the only man who had moved to her side and risen to his full height of over six-feet, studying the foreman quizzically when he had approached her and asked questions. Although he hadn't spoken, his presence had sent a message to Gustave, who had mumbled incoherently and walked towards another group of men. 'I need to go to town,' she said.

'Would you want me to bring you something to eat?'

She nodded. 'Thank you.'

He lifted his chin, pursed his lips. His light-blue eyes held warmth and compassion. Then he turned towards the restaurant and started running to catch up with the others. She watched for a moment, wondering whether Madeleine would be serving the food. The somersault in her stomach sent a flood of warmth to her chest that then dropped lower. She pulled up the collar on her jacket and strode towards the centre of town, mumbling.

*

Madeleine set the large pot of steaming soup on the serving plate, groaning with the strain. She watched Maude position the baskets of sliced baguette on the tables and set the ladle, before returning to the kitchen.

The routine was the same every day, and to the outside world, the operation seemed to run seamlessly. Even during the rationing years, the four sisters had managed to serve a hearty meal at lunch and dinner. It was one of the reasons they had been asked to provide for the dam and railway workers. The companies paid well too. The *Barrage Génissiat* was scheduled to open this side of Christmas, and the number of dam workers increased daily. During the war they had regularly served a hundred covers for each meal, now it was closer to three hundred.

Madeleine glanced at the torrential rain patting the misty window. The men would be soaked. Claude would be drenched too. She had a sudden urge to rush to the house, collect up a towel and hand it to her when she arrived for lunch. Her eyes skittered around the room as her mind presented a series of images. Her pressing the towel to Claude's wet body and then caressing her face, the warmth of her hands against Claude's cold skin, and then the material covering the muscular frame, registering an altogether different sensation on her fingers as she flicked open the buttons and then...

'They're coming up the road,' Antoinette said, loading more plates onto the stacked pile.

Madeleine jolted, shifted her attention to the soup and gently stirred. Does Claude like ham and vegetable soup? Her heart racing and feeling slightly giddy, she stared at the door. 'I'm ready,' she said, praying Claude wouldn't be the first to appear, then hoping she would.

'Beatrice, where's the pie?' Maude said, laying out the spoons for the crème anglaise and the serving-slice for the desert.

'It's coming. You're so impatient, Maude,' Beatrice said. Her cheeks flushed and she puffed as she approached the counter. At first glance, it seemed as if the sizeable oblong tray lay precariously on her ample bosom. She plonked the large serving plate down, vapour sneaking through the tiny holes in the pastry and filling the room with the scent of apple and cinnamon. She waved a large knife menacingly and began to cut.

'Sixty.' Maude said, pointing at the pie.

'I know.'

'You did fifty-four last week,' Maude said.

Beatrice glared. 'I most definitely did not,' she said, her pitch rising.

'You did. I counted them myself,' Maude said, hands on hips.

'I did not.' The shade of Beatrice's face was reaching puce. She huffed and turned towards the kitchen.

'You did. We nearly ran short.' Maude said, her finger still pointing, her lips silently counting.

'Did not.'

The door swung open and male voices descended on the ensuing argument. Madeleine's breath stopped in her chest, then continued at the sight of Gustave heading towards the hotplate. 'Good day to you, Monsieur Blanc,' she said.

'And a good day to you, Madame Vietti,' he said. His eyes lingered on her for too long and his moustache twitched with the curl of his lips, revealing tobacco-stained teeth. 'You are a blessing on the eye on this rather wet day,' he said. His smile broadened, and his eyes peered at her. 'A sumptuous feast again today I see,' he said.

Madeleine released a breath as soon as his eyes shifted to the soup. She picked up a bowl, the pace of her movement causing it to dance in her hand. With the bowl under control, she ladled the thick soup to the brim in the hope that his attention would stay with the filling of his already well-fed belly.

'Thank you, Madeleine,' he said taking the bowl, his fingers lingering too close to hers. 'Smells delectable.'

'Help yourself to bread,' she said, averting his gaze, reaching for the next bowl.

She continued to serve, dish after dish. Antoinette replaced the empty pot with a full one. The rumble of men's escalating voices filled the room. The second pot emptied and a third pot appeared. She hadn't had time to look up since serving Gustave, but when her eyes rose from the hotplate, the space in front of her was empty. A dull ache registered and a sigh dropped from her lips. Where was Claude? Had Natty scared her away? Surely not! Had there been an accident?

She cast an eye over the faces in the room. They would have been talking if there had been an incident, and she wouldn't have missed Claude. Gustave's beaming grin, directed at her, caught her attention and she shuddered again. She smiled with as much warmth as she could muster, but it was a long way short of her usual amiability. She had always thought fondly of him, even though she hadn't seriously considered him a suitor, at least, not until her confused musings last evening. Seeing him now though, the thought of his fingers so close to hers on the bowl, she couldn't think of anything more frightful. She frowned. How had she not realised before? Even earlier when Antoinette suggested that she allow him to escort her, she hadn't been aware of her true feelings towards him. Considering him as potential suitor had been based on what? Need?

Definitely not! She was more than capable of looking after her family and the business. Desire? Yuk! His close proximity and the way he smiled had elicited a sensation that was far from comfortable and even further from lustful. No, she realised with absolute clarity, there was nothing about him that was physically attractive. Want was it then? No, she didn't want Gustave in her life. What about Albert? Did he need a father?

'Excuse me?'

Madeleine looked up. 'Hello, can I help you?' she said. She liked the lightness in his gaze contrasting with his ruddy complexion and a smile that revealed white teeth. He was more appealing to the eye than Gustave. He wasn't from these parts she could tell, and she didn't recall seeing him before.

'Could I get a cup of soup and bread to take to the railway, please?' he said.

Madeleine's eyes widened.

He must have noticed her reaction because his smile grew and his eyes shone. 'It's for a colleague. She had to go to town on an errand,' he said.

Madeleine's heart skipped. Claude! She could feel her cheeks flush and turned away from the hotplate, hoping he hadn't sensed her awkwardness. 'I'll get a container, she said.

'Thank you.'

She bolted into the kitchen and searched for an empty jam jar. It was the best she could come up with, although she wished she could find a bigger container, but at least it had a lid that would lock shut. She wrapped the jar in a towel that would try to hold in some heat. Returning to the restaurant, she filled the jar with as much soup as she could, clipped the lid shut and handed it over. 'Please take as much bread as you can... as you like,' she said.

'Thank you.' He grabbed a handful, wrapped the bread in a napkin and squeezed it into his pocket.

'What's your name?' she said. The urgency in her voice surprised her, as did her desperate need to know the name of the person kind enough to ensure Claude was looked after.

'Xavier,' he said.

He had an honest look. 'I'm Madeleine,' she said, holding out her hand.

He shook it, his skin calloused, his touch tender. 'Pleased to meet you, Madeleine.' He dipped his head a fraction, his eyes remaining on hers.

'Thank you,' she said, feeling the heat rise to her cheeks again. 'It's dreadful weather today.'

He nodded, turning his head to the window. 'It certainly is very wet,' he said, his expression remaining the same. 'Thank you for this.' He clasped large hands firmly around the towel wrapped jar.

'You're welcome.' The words came out in a whisper and he had exited the restaurant before she reached the end of the short sentence.

'Well, I must say, that was most exceptional,' Gustave said as he approached.

Madeleine's insides churned. It was only soup! She looked directly at him, the remnants of his meal hanging from his facial hair, and stifled a chuckle. 'I'm glad you enjoyed it so much, Monsieur Blanc,' she said.

'Good day to you, Madame Vietti. I don't know where this town would be without you,' he said.

She watched a crumb drop to the floor as his moustache twitched. The weather would likely rid him of the rest. Her smile was lacking, distracted by the soup travelling en route to the railway line, hoping it wasn't too cold by the time Claude got to eat it. 'Have a good day,' she said, turning sharply. She would rescue a piece of apple pie for Claude, for later, she decided.

*

Xavier held out the wrapped jar, and Claude accepted it with a nod. 'Thank you.' He groped inside his pocket for the bread and handed it over. She smiled.

'It's good,' he said. He studied the clouds. The rain had eased on the walk from the restaurant and a slither of sunlight had started to appear. 'Did you get what you wanted?'

Claude sipped at the soup. 'Yes. Material for dolls clothes,' she said, with a shrug of her shoulder.

'You have children?'

Claude wrestled with the soup as it travelled down her throat in the wrong direction and a coughing fit took her by surprise. 'No!'

He laughed. 'Me neither,' he said. 'Maybe one day.' His mood shifted with the brief reflection, and he suddenly looked older, his eyes darker and unfocused. 'What about you?' he said. His focus returning as quickly as it had departed, his curiosity piqued.

'It's not something I ever considered,' she said. The recollection of Natty measuring Marie for the clothes brought a rush of warmth. The sensation released the tension in her neck, and the heat continued to light up her face. She sipped at the lukewarm soup.

'And now?' he said.

She held his gaze, admiring of his perception. 'Maybe one day,' she said softly.

He nodded.

The sound of male voices intensifying, he picked up a shovel, started collecting stones and throwing them to the edge of the track.

She finished the soup, abandoned the empty jar to a position of safety, her mouth bulging with a large piece of dry bread, and picked up her shovel. She liked Xavier. With him at her side, their shovels moving in unison and something

41

intangible between them having lifted, they progressed faster than they had earlier in the day.

Gustave wandered up and down the line, his eyes searching for something upon which to challenge her. He examined her work with utmost precision, the process taking longer than it had with the other workers. She waited.

He grunted. 'Those stones need to be higher, no gaps under the rails,' he said.

The stones were as high as they could be and there were no gaps; she knew that. She nodded. 'Oui Monsieur Blanc.'

Gustave turned away and walked back up the track.

'Arsehole,' Xavier said under his breath.

She patted him on the shoulder. 'It's okay, I'm used to it,' she said.

They continued to gather and distribute the gravel, inching their way down the route, laying out the new steel rails and hammering at the metal pegs that would contain them.

Xavier stood and stretched. 'You're as strong as most men here,' he said, glancing over at the crew. Four men stood in a huddle, glancing across from time-to-time, their eyes on her then back to a member of their group. Gustave walked up to them, said something, and they jeered, laughed, and then their eyes settled back on Claude. Bastards! 'You work harder too,' he said.

She placed a hand on his arm, drawing his eyes to her. 'It's okay,' she said. 'Ignore them.' His tight smile and narrowed eyes conveyed something she couldn't discern, beyond the apparent rage that tightened his jaw. Injustice? She made a move to carry on working.

'Wait!'

'What?'

'They stop; we stop! You work too hard and will burn out,' he said.

She chuckled. 'I'm used to hard work Xavier.'

'That's not the point.'

He leaned on his shovel and smiled in the direction of the group.

She mirrored his stance, but her smile felt false. Standing, doing nothing, just waiting, an itching sensation grew within her, and her eyes flitted between the large pile of gravel and the track. Hot flames, irritating, driving her feet to move, she buried the shovel deep into the stones. She couldn't help herself, and her arms moved faster to make up for the lost time.

He shook his head, submitted to her will, and continued to work alongside her. 'You need to learn to pace yourself like a man,' he said. She couldn't tell if he was teasing, but she hadn't seen him standing to idle in the time they had worked together either.

6.

Claude reached into her trouser pocket, reassured by the feel of the sealed paper bag as she walked, her pace reflecting the light fluttering in her stomach, her thoughts with the broad grin she imagined on Natty's face as they pinned and sewed the doll's clothes together. Her heart raced as she approached the house, and she tried to breathe deeply to release the tight band constricting her chest. Even her first day on the job didn't elicit this response. She squeezed the bag tightly, stemming the tremor that vibrated through her. The curtain inside the window flickered, briefly throwing light onto the doorstep, then closed again, and the door flashed open.

'Claude's here! Claude's here!'

Claude chuckled.

Natty thrust Marie into Claude's crotch and ran into the living room, continuing to squeal. Claude stepped onto the mat and shut the door. She waited, the fizzing in her stomach rising to her chest. She blew out a slow breath before noticing Albert gazing over his book at her. He tilted his head, squinted, studied her a moment and then returned to his book with a grunting, mumbling sound. She squeezed at the bag in her pocket, praying for her heart to slow.

Natty was already exploring the sewing box.

'Come in, come in.' Madeleine said.

Madeleine! Claude's heart flipped, and she hesitated before following the simple instruction. Madeleine's dark eyes steadied on her, and she swallowed the air in her dry mouth. 'Madeleine,' she said. She thrust the paper bag at Madeleine in the same manner as Natty had launched the doll at her on the doorstep. 'Sorry!' she said, aware of her clumsiness.

'Nonsense. Come through, please.' Madeleine said, catching the bag with ease, amusement registering in the steadily growing smile.

Madeleine's gaze felt reassuring, comforting, and Claude's heart slowed. She cleared her throat. 'Natty wanted to make the clothes with me,' she said.

'Yes, she can be very insistent,' Madeleine said. She placed the bag on the dining table as passed, and entered the kitchen. 'You must be hungry.'

The thought of food hadn't occurred to Claude, but at that moment her stomach responded, and she pressed a hand there to calm the grumbling. Yes, she said to herself.

'Here,' Natty said, holding out a fistful of bits and bobs from the sewing box, a needle, white cotton reel and a bobbin.

'Natty, leave Claude alone.' Madeleine's voice emerged from the kitchen.

Claude responded to Natty's frown with a shrug of her shoulders, then smiled.

'Claude needs to eat before you do any sewing, so until then you can get on with your homework.'

Natty huffed.

'I'll eat quickly,' Claude whispered. She swept the loose bangs behind Natty's ear, lifted her chin with tenderness. 'I promise.'

Natty's eyes sparkled, and the tight-lipped objection to her mother's command disappeared. She ran to the dining table and opened her reading book.

Claude placed the doll and bits and bobs on the table next to the paper bag of goodies. 'Keep them safe,' she said, and Natty pulled the items close to her book. She wandered into the kitchen, her gaze drawn to Madeleine leaning into the oven, her dress rising above the back of her knees.

She had the sense of her hand on Madeleine's thigh, smooth silk, her mouth pressing kisses to the back of her neck, her hand slowly reaching around the slender body and cupping the ample breast, the nipple tightening at her fingertips. Deliciously inviting and so very unhelpful to her self-made promise of propriety she tried to shake the image. Some part of her had other ideas though and the sense of Madeleine warm and wet on her fingers shot into her mind.

'I just need to get this,' Madeleine said, distracted by the hot dish she was pulling from the oven.

Claude moaned. The browned pastry, gravy bubbling around its raised edges, and the erotic images had Claude's mouth watering. 'That smells delicious,' she said, her stomach joining in a chorus of approval with her thoughts.

'You like beef?' Madeleine said, placing the dish on the work surface, then lifting the boiling pot and straining the vegetables.

Entranced by the effortless flow that had four plates of food constructed in seconds, Madeleine had walked past her before she realised she could move. Alerted to her senses, Claude picked up the remaining two plates and carried them through to the living room.

'Thank you.' Madeleine took the plates and set them on the table. 'Please sit,' she said, pointing to the chair next to Natty.

Albert stared at his food, his tongue dancing across his lips, his knuckles white, his knife and fork hovering.

'You may eat,' Madeleine said.

Claude's bottom landed heavily in the seat, the steaming beef pie drawing her attention to her hunger. 'Thank you,' she said.

Natty's gaze narrowed and the smoothest ripples formed on her forehead. She shifted her focus repeatedly from Claude to her mother then lingered on Claude. 'Will you be my best friend?' she said.

Claude stopped the fork tantalisingly close to her lips, withdrew it a fraction and smiled. 'Of course,' she said. She held the pose for as long as she could resist, the fork with a will of its own finding her mouth and paralysing any further consideration of the question.

Natty stared intently at her mother. 'Claude is going to be my best friend, so she can't be yours,' she said.

Madeleine coughed the food that had been mid-swallow stopping suddenly and gripping her throat. She raised the back of her hand to her mouth fighting the choking.

'Arrêt! Natty, you're being a baby.' Albert said.

'Am not.'

'Are.'

'Am not.'

Finally able to breathe, 'Enough!' Madeleine said, the palm of a hand directed at both children.

'Are.' Albert said, allowing his cutlery to bounce off his empty plate.

Madeleine thumped the table with her hand. 'I said enough, Albert.'

'Why is it always me who gets blamed?' Albert said. He rose to his feet sharply, chair-legs dragging across the wooden floor, and stomped towards the stairs.

'Come back to the table right now,' Madeleine said.

Claude froze at the sudden, apparently unwarranted, shift in energy between mother and son. She wanted to reach out, take Madeleine's trembling hands in hers, hold her close and make everything right, but she knew first hand that people were difficult to get close to when in a fit of rage. Madeleine's jaw remained tense in the standoff, but something in her eyes touched her.

Natty nibbled at the food on her fork.

Albert stopped with one foot on the lower step. He looked between the top of the stairs and the empty chair several times before taking short steps back to the table and slumping into the seat. He crossed his arms and closed his eyes.

'Uncross your arms. That is very rude.' Madeleine said. 'And sit up properly. We have a guest Albert, and you need to behave like a gentleman.'

Albert moved slowly.

Claude watched with mute fascination. She wasn't used to dealing with children and under no illusion as to the challenges of doing so, especially as a single parent, but the sudden escalation stimulated by Albert's response and Madeleine's frustration with him, struck a chord. She gazed from child to mother, both holding their position and Albert only following the instructions because he had no choice. One day he would be able to make his own decisions though, and what then?

'Can we do the sewing…?' Natty said.

'Not until everyone has finished,' Madeleine said.

Claude felt her heart sink, along with Natty's bowing head. 'We need to gather a few more things,' Claude said, her tone soft.

Natty stared at her. 'What things?'

'Well, we need some scissors, paper, pencil, ribbon for her trousers and small buttons for her dress. If we gather all the bits together and trace out the pattern, maybe we can put it altogether another night. I have lots of time on Saturday if you would like?'

Natty regarded Claude, and her bright eyes narrowed as it dawned on her the clothing wouldn't be finished before going to bed. She huffed. 'Maman, may I please leave the table?' she said.

'Yes, you may.'

The smile fell from Claude's lips. The slight tremble in Madeleine's jaw and glassy eyes commanding her attention, her stomach churned in an entirely different way. The urge to reach out, so compelling as to cause her to freeze, she clenched her fists.

'Albert you may leave the table.' Madeleine said.

Claude sensed Madeleine working hard to control her temper.

Albert rose, picked up his plate, collected his sister's plate, and took them into the kitchen.

Claude held Madeleine's gaze with tenderness and an intangible sense of understanding, awareness of the shadows beneath tired eyes. 'Would you like me to read to the children?' she said in a whisper.

'I'm sure they would both like that,' Madeleine said. 'Thank you.'

Claude observed the colour transforming Madeleine's appearance, the tone in her eyes becoming a shade lighter, and the soft lines appearing as she smiled. She rose from the table as Madeleine stood, reached for the plate in the same moment and when their fingers made contact, her heart skipped a beat. Overcome by weakness, transfixed by Madeleine's beauty, her eyes lingered, and she struggled to breathe. She wished time would stand still, and she could hold onto the moment, but Madeleine had released the plate and turned away, leaving her stranded, the plate hot where it rested in her hand.

'I got these,' Natty said, and scattered a range of objects across the table.

Claude puffed out a short breath. 'Good! Can you make them into special piles for us for tomorrow?'

Natty gathered the bits from the table, squeezed them to her chest, and skipped away. 'I'll get a box from my room,' she said.

Claude hovered before taking the plate to the kitchen. 'Shall I take them to bed now?' she said.

Madeleine turned to face her, rubbed at moist eyes with the back of her hand, and nodded. 'If that's okay with you?' She hesitated, Claude's eyes assessing her. 'Thank you, Claude,' she said.

Claude nodded, lowered her gaze, and went into the living room.

7.

Madeleine stirred vigorously, the cocoa refusing to mix with the water, the pink-powder floating when she wanted it to dissolve. She mashed it against the side of the cup, the movement becoming automatic, thoughts occupying her awareness. She shouldn't have been cross with Albert, but his antics and apparent inability to follow instructions had escalated, and especially since the end of the war and the death of his father. He was growing up and needed to learn quickly. She reached up, massaged her neck, the tension there having taken up permanent residence. And, in fairness, it wasn't just about Albert. There was Claude, upstairs, putting her children to bed, and then there was Gustave.

She hadn't been able to make sense of her extreme visceral response to Gustave's less-than-subtle advances across the hotplate. It wasn't as if he hadn't flirted with her before, but never had she felt so repulsed by him. Then again, never had she felt so kindly towards another woman. Her heart fluttered, the spoon came loose in her hand, and a spray of dark, thick liquid formed a constellation across her blouse. Merde! Not for the first time in the last two days had her musings rendered her ineffectual. She had burned her finger badly on a frying pan wondering what it might be like to touch another woman, Claude in particular. The ineptitude was becoming a regular occurrence, leaving her incoherent in thought, emotionally exposed, and utterly confused. She rubbed a wet dishcloth at the specks, smearing them into something that resembled a ploughed field in winter. Merde! Throwing the cloth into the sink, she resumed the process of making cocoa, filling the cups with boiled water and topping them with a little milk.

She sat at the table trying to adjust to the unfamiliar sound of silence, suddenly aware of the ringing in her ears and the tension that had sustained her for too long. Resting her elbows on the table and her head in her hands, she closed her eyes. Moisture formed slowly at first and eased the burning behind her lids. As the flow of silent tears gained momentum, a hot line trickled down her cheeks, and her eyes started to ache.

Light footsteps on the stairs lifted Madeleine's head from her hands. She wiped the back of her hands across her cheeks in an almost casual manner then rested her arms on the table and cupped the mug of hot cocoa. A faint smile fought its way to the surface, too weary to muster anything more engaging, as Claude approached.

'You look tired,' Claude said.

'I am so sorry about tonight,' Madeleine said. Claude was staring directly at her again, those keen eyes assessing her no doubt. Her initial desire to look away, to hide the truth and put on a brave face, melted under the spell of Claude's silent inquisition. 'I made cocoa,' she said.

'Thank you,' Claude said.

She has a sweet smile, Madeleine thought. 'There's apple pie. You missed it at lunch, and I saved you some.' An adorable smile, she thought.

'Sounds lovely.'

Madeleine started to rise from the chair, Claude's hand appearing on her arm in an instant and immobilising her. The grip was tender and warm, and then it was gone again. The desire to be held drained the power from her legs, and she slumped back into the seat, Claude watching her intently.

'The children are asleep. Do you want to talk?' Claude said.

'I'll get the pie.' Madeleine said.

Claude nodded.

Madeleine entered the kitchen, her heart racing. She hadn't spoken to anyone except her sisters about family matters, and here she was about to talk openly to a complete stranger. Except, Claude didn't feel like a complete stranger. On the contrary, she had never experienced this kind of closeness to anyone before, not even her sisters. There was no logical explanation for the way her heart raced at the sight of her or the warmth that suffused every part of her as she watched Claude listening attentively to Natty and talking to Albert. And, how desperately disappointed she was earlier, when Claude didn't show up for lunch and how the inadequately small meal she had sent back with Xavier had troubled her for the best part of the afternoon. Natty adored Claude, and it wasn't just because she had rescued her, that much was clear. Even Albert had warmed to Claude. She fetched the apple pie and a fork and returned to the living room.

The sweet aroma of cinnamon and baked apple drifted into Claude's awareness, the plate in front of her drawing her eyes from Madeleine. 'That smells delightful,' she said.

Madeleine sat down, cupped her drink and sipped. 'I don't know where to start,' she said.

Claude straightened her back, her fork poised. 'Do you have to go to work?' she said.

'Not tonight.'

'I have all night,' Claude said, guiding the fork to her mouth.

'It may take a while,' Madeleine said, aware of the swell of tears building and her lips drawing into a smile. There was something profoundly comforting about being able to confide in Claude. She gazed at her across the table, the kind eyes, the faintest lines etched on youthful skin that accentuated their shape, and the way her lips moved when she spoke.

'Is this about Albert?' Claude said softly.

Madeleine stared at her. 'You're very perceptive.'

Claude swallowed the pie. 'He seems...' She paused. 'A little lost,' she said.

Madeleine lowered her gaze. 'He hasn't been the same since his father died.' She rubbed at her eyes and yawned. 'Raoul signed up close to the start of the war, Albert hadn't even turned two when his father died.'

'I'm sorry.'

'I'm not,' she said, her head rising sharply, eyes lingering on Claude.

Claude blinked several times in quick succession.

'Not about Raoul.' Madeleine said, shifting her gaze back to the mug in her hands. 'When Raoul left to fight in the war, he also left his gambling debts. Those included several loans he had taken out against the business. He thought being a soldier would enable him to send money home, which he did... until.' She paused, sipped the drink. 'He only came home twice; hence we have... I have, Natty. He was killed in action on the twenty-fifth of March 1943. The money dried up then too, of course. We were expecting him home for a forty-eight-hour pass to celebrate Albert's sixth birthday. Albie had been so excited; he had everything planned. They were going to fish together, and Raoul was going to show him how to take apart and reassemble his pistol. We had even managed to pool rations to make a birthday cake. Instead, he spent most of the day crying and shouting at me. It was the first time I had seen him really angry. He ran off, and we had to send out a search party to find him.'

Claude rested her fork on the plate, her gaze unwavering.

'Apparently, it was a 'friendly' landmine that killed him,' she said, a slight snigger of disgust following her words. 'The instructions they had been given about the area were inaccurate. His body is in a military graveyard, the large ones with the rows of white crosses. I've never been. It's in the north and too far for us to travel.' She looked up. 'I had fallen out of love with him long before he died, even before Natty, and it didn't seem the right thing to drag the children all the way there to look at a white cross for a man they didn't know,' she said. She shrugged her shoulders, wondering as she always did whether she had done the wrong thing. 'Maybe I should have taken Albert to his father's grave,' she said.

Claude lowered her eyes. 'It must have been difficult.'

'It was, particularly for Albie. I think it was very hard for him then, though now, to be honest, his memory of his father is vague. But, that doesn't seem to stop him misbehaving.'

Claude reached across the table and took Madeleine's hands in hers.

Madeleine released an involuntary gasp, the soft warmth of the gentle touch reaching inside her. A wave of intense heat swept into her cheeks and prickled the top of her neck and shot down her spine. She pulled away, certain she was about to have a heart attack. She hadn't experienced anything like it in her life. She stared at Claude, paralysed by whatever it was that had just happened to her.

'Sorry, I didn't mean to offend you,' Claude said.

Madeleine remained frozen, staring at the face of rejection. The heaviness in Claude's eyes, the dull expression that pulled her lips in the wrong direction, and the way her shoulders hunched as if winded by a sharp blow to the stomach. The pain of observation was far worse than the feelings that had sparked at the touch. 'No, you didn't offend me,' she said.

'It's my fault. I shouldn't have been so effusive.'

'No, it's me.' Madeleine couldn't explain her reaction; she didn't know where to start. She felt foolish for the sudden withdrawal, and guilty because Claude was blaming herself. 'I'm just not very tactile,' she said. The explanation was weak, and even more alarmingly, inaccurate. She craved adult contact, and she craved the feelings Claude's touch had elicited, but not from a woman.

'Has Albie ever asked to go?' Claude said, placing her hands in her lap.

'Uh.' Madeleine gazed without seeing, mentally readjusting to the question. 'Umm, no, never.'

'Maybe he's just trying to grow up quickly; trying to be a man,' Claude said.

Madeleine stared at her. She had considered whether Albert was just an inquisitive boy exploring the world around him, and moody with it. 'He blew up the chicken shed last year,' she said, smiling with the memory, though she hadn't laughed at the time.

Claude chuckled. Her cheeks darkened, and she raised her hand to cover her mouth. 'Sorry I shouldn't laugh.'

Madeleine joined her, laughing until tears wetted her eyes and bathed her in a sense of release. Sharing somehow made the event seem less grave, even though it had been momentous and deeply distressing at the time. 'He and an older boy from his school broke into the railway compound and stole some explosives. It was a very dangerous thing to do, and he knows that now. The other boy egged him on, and he yielded without thinking about the consequences.'

The lines that had framed Claude's face as she laughed disappeared as the severity of the event registered. 'Gosh! He was fortunate not to get hurt. It is quite a skill to be able to fire dynamite,' she said. 'He really is a very bright boy.'

'But needs to find a better way of applying his intellect,' Madeleine said.

'Yes, he does.'

Madeleine studied Claude, losing herself in thought. Claude's skin as smooth as silk, her features perfectly formed, she was stunningly handsome.

'Do you have a car? Claude said.

Madeleine's eyebrows furrowed. 'Yes, why?' Fine lines emerged at the corner of Madeleine's eyes as the smile on

Claude's face widened. There was a sense of mystery in Claude's unrevealed thoughts, she thought. 'Why do you ask?' she said.

'Do you think he might care to learn how a car engine works and how to service it?'

'You can do that?' Madeleine's eyes widened.

'Yes. I mean, I know it's not a train, but it is an engine.'

'I think he would be very excited.'

'Maybe, at the weekend, unless you have other plans?'

Madeleine smiled. 'I will be working, so I'm sure he will be very happy for the company. As will Natty!' She held Claude's gaze, aware of the shift in her expression.

'How do you all cope?' Claude said. 'If you don't mind me asking, with the long work hours.'

Madeleine sighed, her lips forming a thin line, the air releasing through her nose. 'I'm not sure we do, if I'm honest,' she said. 'The children spend a lot of time on their own, and I have to trust them. The locals also keep a keen eye on them if they are out playing, and my sisters, of course. Thankfully the restaurant is right here so I can work and be flexible, perhaps more than would be possible elsewhere.'

'Are you not sick with worry?'

Madeleine's shoulders dropped. 'I try not to be,' she said. Her voice had lost its spirit.

'Sorry, I shouldn't have pressed. It sounds dreadfully hard work. You must be exhausted.'

'Most of the time, it's fine. We have a routine. But it wasn't my idea of parenting. I thought I would have more time with them, doing interesting things, helping them learn; being there for them.'

'They are lucky to have you,' Claude said.

The intensity in Claude's gaze caused a short, sharp intake of breath and Madeleine averted her gaze. 'What about your family?' she said.

'My papa owns several car manufacturing plants across France and was often away on business when I was young. Maman died when I was four, and I am an only child. My papa's sister looked after me when he was away.'

Madeleine noticed Claude's matter-of-fact tone and nodded. 'How did your mother die?'

'In childbirth; my sister too.'

Claude's tone hadn't changed, but a sinking sensation registered in Madeleine. 'I'm so sorry, how ghastly, and you were so young.'

'I don't remember her,' Claude said.

Madeleine still felt sad at Claude's loss. She wished she felt as spirited about her own plight, as Claude appeared to be about hers.

Claude was smiling at her.

'You're very...' The word escaped Madeleine and heat started to spread from her chest, up her neck. 'Sincere,' she said. It wasn't the right word, but it was also true.

Claude's cheeks coloured, and her smile broadened. 'Death is hard to take, but it is a reality that we can't change. We are all trying to do the best we can, and I try not to judge such things as inherently good or bad.'

'That's very admirable, but surely some people are deserving of judgement? Not everyone is inherently good,' she said, her tone light-hearted.

Claude's demeanour shifted. 'How can we judge others when we are imperfect?' she said.

Madeleine pondered the wisdom and genuine belief Claude held for the words. 'So true,' she said. Claude didn't strike her as a student of the bible. 'Do you believe in God?

'No.'

Madeleine flinched, curious as to the abruptness of the response.

'At least not in the biblical sense,' Claude said. 'What about you?'

Madeleine considered the question. She had never talked about her thoughts with anyone. 'I'm really not sure what I believe any more,' she said. 'Do you think not believing in God makes life harder?' she said. It was a question she had asked herself many times since the war.

Claude's eyes glazed over, and she bit down on her lip in deliberation. 'I don't know. I think not believing in anything beyond this world can make death seem very frightening. Maybe we create God and our beliefs about what comes next to ease the burden of truth.' When she looked at Madeleine, it was as if her soul lay bare.

Madeleine hadn't realised for how long she had been staring. She couldn't imagine having this conversation with anyone else, and yet it seemed so perfectly natural to be having it with Claude. In fact, she wanted to ask more questions, debate, and explore Claude's thoughts further, but it was getting late.

'I think it's time I said goodnight,' Claude said, her smile softening the intensity.

'Thank you.' Madeleine said.

Faint lines appeared, Claude's eyes narrowing.

'For the stimulating conversation,' Madeleine said.

'It has been a pleasure for me. It's rarely I meet people who are willing to discuss matters of such importance. But I find them fascinating.' Claude said.

'Hmmm,' Madeleine said, lost in her innermost thoughts and feelings. Claude was indeed, extremely fascinating.

8.

Claude buried the shovel deep into the gravel, lifted, and carried it to the track. Sliding the contents into position she stood and stretched her back, resting for a brief moment on the handle.

'That's the spirit,' Xavier said.

She chuckled at the broad smile on his face, picked up the tool and strode towards the never-decreasing pile of stones. 'No chance,' she said, reloading and repeating the process. The clattering and scraping sound attained a monotonous rhythm that set the natural pace of their work.

'Break!'

The word filtered down the line, followed by the gradual cessation of work. Tools dropped, and cigarettes lit, pockets of male voices starting to drift.

Xavier drew down on his cigarette. 'Did you get the fabric to your friend?' he said.

She watched the smoke leave through his nose and mouth as he spoke. The habit had never appealed to her, but she was in the minority. It occurred to her, she had never seen Madeleine smoke either. 'Yes,' she said.

'That's good,' he said. He continued to smoke, seemingly comfortable with the silence between them.

She drifted in thought to the previous evening and Madeleine, the depth of conversation and how they had talked with effortless ease. There were moments when she sensed a deep affinity between them. The way Madeleine had held her gaze with a quality she had seen only once before. The way her cheeks flushed when she rallied with thought. She had seen through the veneer of the mother to the vulnerability and sensuality of the woman, and her heart had ached with compassion, and dare she say, affection.

Concern for Madeleine and the children had continued to haunt her after she left the house, and she had walked for two hours, eventually succumbing to her bed weary with worry. Madeleine wasn't like her, but the twisting in her stomach had eased as she allowed fantasy in, and with lightness vibrating softly in her heart, sleep had eventually silenced her. Awaking to reality, a general sense of unease had prevented her from eating a full breakfast and she had remained distracted by her thoughts on the walk into work.

Madeleine had apparently never taken a female lover; it had probably never occurred to her, and maybe it never would. But, Claude had never felt more convinced by her own troublesome feelings; in her heart, she had known from the first time of seeing Madeleine, and there wasn't a second that hadn't gone by since when she didn't think of Madeleine in that way. In Madeleine's presence, fire had flooded her in waves, and sparks of electric energy had stolen her breath. Dark, dark eyes had touched her deeply, and soft lips had tormented her. And, all the while, she had needed to suppress the feelings. She had never experienced the pain of such longing.

Tension rising as her thoughts shifted to the impossibility of being with Madeleine, she slammed the end of the shovel into the stones. At some point, she would have to tell Madeleine about her inclination towards women. Maybe speaking to Madeleine and being honest would help lessen the desire. What if Madeleine thought her a freak? What if she kept it a secret and then word got out? Word always got out; though at least in Paris the consequences hadn't affected anyone. Townsfolk were small-minded and often fearful of people who didn't fit in. Hell, the men she worked with were an excellent example of that fact. The idea that Madeleine might not want to see her, or let her near the children, filled her with emptiness. Though she didn't think of Madeleine as narrow-minded, she had come across ignorance before, and the fear born out of it. Fear changed people; even good people.

The clattering and scraping of Xavier's shovel drew her from her thoughts, and she noticed the inquisitive look on his face. He nodded as if to say are you okay and she responded with what she hoped was a convincing smile. Compelled by a force over which she had no control, lunchtime couldn't come quickly enough. Madeleine, what have you done to me? She slammed the shovel into the stones.

*

Claude tensed at the sight of the restaurant ahead. Butterflies danced in her belly, and a sense of dryness filled her mouth. Clammy palms clenched in the deep pockets of a coat that seemed to restrict her pounding heart.

Xavier had talked to her as they walked from the railway site, but she had barely registered a word, grunting in what she hoped had been the right places. If he had noticed her preoccupation, he hadn't said anything. She tried to swallow as they moved closer to the restaurant door.

She followed the line of men inside, the warmth enveloping her instantly, the grating of chairs dragged across tiles and the hum of male voices echoing loudly. She waited, inched forward, her sight of the hotplate obscured by the broad shoulders ahead of her, her stomach spinning.

The broad man in front of her, whose name she didn't know, took his plate and moved to the right, exposing her to the counter. She stood, the smile dropping from her lips, a sinking feeling hitting her gut.

'Sausages and potatoes?' the woman said, barely looking up. She was older than Madeleine and her hair a lighter shade, but the resemblance was clear with the same nose and same shape of the mouth, though her lips were noticeably fuller than her sister's.

'Thank you,' Claude said taking the offered plate, her voice subdued. She looked around the room at the even rows of tables and bench seats. With feet heavy, she found a space on the end of a long bench and set down the plate. Xavier took the seat opposite and immediately began to eat.

'Everything okay?' he said.

He was staring at her, two lines creased between his eyes, the food moving between his cheeks as he spoke. The low-pitched voices in the room coalesced, his with them, each individual sound indecipherable from the rest.

'Claudette!'

'Hmm. Sorry?' she said.

'Everything okay?' he said.

'Yes. Fine.' She knew she was trying to smile, but his look told her that she had failed. She picked up the knife and fork and started to eat. No matter what, she needed something in her stomach or she wouldn't last the rest of the day. A surge of adrenaline alerted her, sparked the thought that Madeleine might have been offended by the frankness of their discussion after all, and her cheeks burned, the food she had just swallowed forming an immovable lump in her throat. She filled a glass with water from the carafe on the table and sipped, searched the room again with a more than curious gaze.

Xavier's smile grew as he observed Claude continuing to eat. He didn't speak.

Giving her attention to the meal, she cleared her plate, collected a custard tart and demolished it before Xavier finished his main course. Within a few minutes, she excused herself to him and stepped outside.

She paced down the road and into the woods, long strides taking her with urgency towards the lake. Following the muddy track, she halted. He was the last person she had expected to see. His head bowed, selecting pebbles, being particular about it, too. She watched as his arm recoiled then released, the stone bouncing off the surface three times before dropping under the water. He must resemble his father, his hair fairer than Madeleine's, his build stockier. She moved towards him, eager to know why he wasn't where he should have been at this time. 'Albert,' she said. He turned his head, revealing the raw graze on his swollen cheek and a light shade of purple-blue framing his eye.

'Claude,' he said. He lowered his eyes, and his feet scuffed at the earth as she increased her pace towards him.

His voice was quieter than usual, and she sensed the vulnerability in him. 'Albert, what happened to you?' she said, crouching to meet his eyes. She drew his chin up. 'Mon Dieu! Who did this to you? Where is your mother?' His innocence pierced her heart, and she could feel the rush behind her eyes. She looked up to prevent the tears and pulled him into her chest, careful not to further injure his face. 'What happened?' she said in a whisper, his weight heavy in her arms.

'I got into a fight at school,' he said, the words struggling their way through the sobs.

She sighed.

'It wasn't my fault,' he said. 'They were being nasty to Natty, calling her a bastard child. I asked them to stop like maman told me to do before. They carried on, calling me a sissy.'

She pulled him closer, rubbed her hand along the line of his back. 'Where's your mother?' she asked softly.

'She's at work. She had to come and collect me from school.'

'Does she know you're down here?' She could feel his head shifting from side to side, his body tensing.

'Non,' he said, his voice barely audible.

He started to shake. 'It's okay, Albert. It's okay.' She held him until he stopped crying and moved away. Holding his gaze, she smiled. 'That's a nasty bruise,' she said. 'Did you put a cold cloth on it?'

He shook his head.

'Do you think you should go home, in case your mother comes looking for you? She would be very worried.'

He nodded.

'Would you like me to walk with you?'

He threw his arms around her neck, challenging her balance. 'Can you stay with me?' he said.

Her stomach twisted. 'I'm sorry, I can't. I have to get back to work,' she said, sensing his disappointment through her own, even before she finished speaking. 'I'll come and see you this evening. Would you like me to read to you?'

He nodded.

She stood, held out her hand, and he took it.

'People used to call me names when I was at school,' she said as they started walking.

He glanced at her fleetingly.

She squeezed his hand. 'I used to fight too.'

'What happened?' he said.

'I got a black eye, a lot.'

There was natural ease in the silence between them, as they continued to walk back to the house.

*

With a heavy heart, Claude went back to work. The shovel weighed heavier and the effort required was more draining than usual. She felt their eyes on her differently too, feeling her self-protection violated in some way, and leaving her naked to their insults; the words they never allowed to reach her ears. She didn't need to hear what they said to know what they thought of her.

She slammed the shovel into the stones and heaved them under the rail, fuelled by the sense of injustice. It was a feeling she knew all too well.

Albert's injuries, and the inane cruelty, had left her feeling restless with familiarity, the seed of frustration ignited, again. This was the pain of her past too, except, it wasn't in her past now. It occupied her present, every day of her life. One day, Albert would be a man, thriving in a man's world. She would never be accepted in their world. She would continue to be judged, as the children had condemned her back then, the boys who beat her, and the girls who ostracised her.

'Time!' Word travelled quickly down the track, and she stopped working instantly.

They stored the shovels, and Xavier smiled at Claude's uncharacteristic sense of urgency. 'See you tomorrow,' he said.

'Yes,' she said, She smiled, not least out of pleasure that the working day had finally come to an end.

She followed the path towards the lake, the beauty of the surroundings that would normally soothe her, evading her. Searching the ground, she stopped. Perfect. She picked up the chunky branch and went to the boulder. Leaning against the stone, she pulled out her knife, flicked the handle to release the sharp blade, and with considered movements started to strip the bark. Caressing the soft surface of bare wood, fresh and slightly damp, sensing the image in her mind's eye and translating the concept to the knife in her hand, she started to carve out a shape. Soft splinters fell and nestled in the ground. She turned the wood in her hand as if peeling a potato, the simple movement, precision with the tip of the blade, creating effortless perfection. She studied the shape, acknowledged the impending dusk, and stood. Pocketing the carving and knife, she gazed at the shimmering water, red shadows cast across its surface from the setting sun. Taking the path around the lake, she followed the track to the restaurant.

Approaching the house, she took in a deep breath and released it slowly, her feelings for Madeleine dampened in the shadow of her concern for Albert. Her knock on the door was received with Natty's squeals, bringing the twitch of a smile to her lips. Natty has a way of lightening any mood, she thought. As the door opened, she lowered her gaze to wide eyes. 'Bonsoir, mademoiselle,' she said, greeted by a grin as big as the face behind it.

Natty launched herself and wrapped her arms around Claude, pinning her in a vice-like grip. 'Can we make the clothes?' she said.

Claude swept the bangs from Natty's eyes and tucked them around her ear.

'Claude!'

Claude's stomach flipped. She looked up, struck by Madeleine's gaze and the soft smile that lingered. Her tongue seemed to lose all sense of movement. Her lips moved, but she remained mute.

'I wasn't expecting you.' Madeleine said.

Claude swallowed, releasing the muscles in her throat. 'I'm sorry, I promised Albert I would read to him tonight,' she said, suddenly aware that Madeleine might not know of their encounter by the lake earlier. Heat flushed through her as she studied Madeleine's response.

'Yes, Albert mentioned he saw you, but he omitted to tell me of your promise,' she said. She was smiling, like in the photograph, and there was a light-hearted quality in her tone as she addressed her son with raised eyebrows.

'I forgot, maman,' Albert said.

Claude looked down at the small hand, repeatedly pulling on her trousers. She crouched down and righted the nightdress on Natty's shoulders. Holding her gaze, she said, 'I still need to get the special bits in town tomorrow. Shall we make Marie's clothes on Saturday, like we said? We can spend all morning on them.' She waited, staring at Natty's eyes as they darted around.

'Can we have breakfast first?' Natty said, her gaze intense, her features stern with seriousness.

Claude grinned. 'Yes, if that's okay with your mother.' Natty's expression shifted to elation on the 'yes' and by the time Claude had finished the sentence she was skipping around the room. As Claude stood, her eyes caught Madeleine's.

'Would you like a cup of cocoa?' Madeleine said. 'The children are having one before they go to bed.'

'Thank you,' Claude said, her eyes on Madeleine until she moved out of view. Claude joined Albert at the table.

Natty had plonked herself in the middle of the floor, surrounded by bits of cloth, cotton, scissors, tape measure, needles and bobbins.

She studied him. 'How's your eye?' she said. The bruise looked darker than it had done earlier, although the swelling seemed to have reduced a little.

'Sore.'

'It looks it.'

'I have to go back to school tomorrow,' he said.

He had a dull look to his eyes, the lids too heavy for a boy of his age. 'Would you like to talk about it? Maybe, instead of reading?' she said. 'I can read another day.' His nod was barely perceptible but his demeanour lifted, and he tried to raise a smile. She guessed even smiling hurt.

'Here.' Madeleine set three cups of cocoa on the table. 'I need to go to work,' she said.

Claude held her gaze, and it occurred to her that Madeleine didn't want to leave. The sensation of emptiness, low in her own belly, told her she felt the same way too. 'I can see they get to bed, if you want?' she said.

'We'll be fine, maman,' Albert said.

'Do you think we will need black or white cotton?' Natty said, thrusting two reels into Claude's face.

Madeleine chuckled, a light, soft sound.

Claude smiled, her eyes fixed on Madeleine, wondering if she could read her mind and only half-praying that she couldn't. 'They are fine.' The words sounded broken to her, and she hoped Madeleine hadn't noticed. The broadening smile aimed at her, causing her cheeks to shine, said she had.

'Will you come to the restaurant for dinner later?' Madeleine asked.

'Yes.'

'Good. I'll see you then.'

'Yes. In an hour.'

'Hmm.' She hovered. 'I need to go.'

'Night, maman,' Albert said.

'Night, Albert, night, Natty.'

'How many buttons do we need?' Natty said, holding out her hand. 'I've got these three, but this one might be too big,' she said.

'Say goodnight to your mother,' Claude said, ruffling her hair.

'Night maman - is three enough?' she said, addressing Claude and poking at the buttons in her hand.

Claude could see the back of Madeleine through the corner of her eye as she disappeared into the kitchen and her ears pricked at the click of the door. Natty had returned to the floor, comparing the buttons in her hand to the selection in the box. 'Natty, your cocoa,' Claude said.

Natty jumped to her feet and took the cup, repeatedly sipping at the drink, tipping the cup until it was upside down on her face and empty, and leaving a brown smile that extended up her cheeks. She placed the cup on the table with a thud and returned to her task.

Claude sipped at her drink, watching Natty play.

Albert yawned and then complained at the pain in his face. His eye looked puffy, tired, his skin pale, set against the raw-red marks.

'We need to clear those away and go to bed,' she said to Natty, nodding at Albert.

She joined Natty on the floor, helping to stack the bits and bobs into the box from which they came. Natty watched her working then picked up a button she hadn't noticed before and studied it carefully. 'These are precious, and I need to keep them safe under my pillow,' she said, wandering to the stairs with them.

Albert bent down to help. 'I've got this.' Claude said, rubbing his arm gently. 'You go and get ready for bed. I'll be up in a minute, and we can talk.'

The faintest hint of a smile formed, and he too went up the stairs.

9.

'When will Claude be here? Natty said, for the twentieth time, skipping merrily around the kitchen. 'Will she be here for breakfast?'

Madeleine stopped cutting the baguette. 'Sweetheart, I don't know when she will be here or whether she will...'

A knock on the front door and the high-pitched squeal emanating from Natty as she ran into the living room stunned the words, melting the mild sense of frustration that had built with the incessant questioning. She followed her daughter, her heart fluttering, and a swell of warmth filled her at the sight of Claude. 'Good morning,' Madeleine said.

'Can we sew? Can we sew?' Natty said, bouncing around Claude and pulling on her hand.

'Natty, let Claude settle first, please,' Madeleine said.

'Do you have the bits ready?' Claude said, taking Natty into her arms and lifting her.

Natty clung on with her legs, wrapped her arms around Claude's neck and squeezed tightly.

Madeleine laughed at the tension in Claude's face and furrowed brow as she braced herself against Natty's fierce grip.

Claude released a choked chuckle and Natty freed her, wriggling in her arms. Claude lowered her to the floor. 'Something smells very good,' she said.

'Merde!' Madeleine shot into the kitchen. 'Pancakes!' she said.

Claude delved into her pocket and pulled out a paper bag. 'Here, I bought this for you,' she said, handing over the package.

Natty grabbed the bag, her small hand searching through its contents as she bounded around the room, squealing. 'Ribbon, hooks and eyes, lace! Chalk? Can we make the clothes now?'

'Yes.' Claude sat on the floor among the carefully laid out piles of sewing materials and the patterns they had traced earlier in the week, picked up the red cloth and started to mark up the pattern for the dress.

'Can I do that?' Natty said, taking the chalk and starting to draw random lines on the black cloth.

Claude's eyes widened, and she smiled at the piece of art in the making. The thumping of heavy feet on the stairs caught her attention, and she looked up. 'Good morning Albert.' His eyes looked brighter, the shading around them a hint of yellowish-green.

'Good morning Claude,' he said. He towered above them, watching, his hands deep in his pockets. 'That looks good Natty,' he said, his expression giving a different message.

Claude smiled at him. 'This is for you,' she said, presenting him with a small leather pouch.

'What is it?' he said, pausing before taking the gift. His eyes widened, and his jaw dropped as he unclipped the seal and pulled out the small pocketknife. 'Wow!'

Claude watched him studying the knife, turning it gently in his hand, flicking the blade and closing it again, turning it again. 'I thought you might like one,' she said.

His eyes held hers briefly, before fixing on the details of the knife. 'It's amazing,' he said. 'Thank you so much.'

'Breakfast.' Madeleine announced, placing a plate of ham and bowl of scrambled eggs on the table. She didn't wait for a response from the eyes that were focused on other things, instead, returning to the kitchen to collect the pancakes and bread.

She couldn't help but smile; comforted by Claude's easiness with the children and the excitement they showed in anticipation of her arrival. Natty had complained bitterly, the last two days, from the time school finished until she went to bed, that Claude hadn't visited. She too had noticed Claude's absence, but had at least seen her in the restaurant. More than that, she had observed her; the way she ate her food seeming to savour every mouthful. The way she talked easily with Xavier. Claude hadn't spoken to any other workers, but yesterday two men had approached her and said something, and they had all laughed together. Madeleine had been aware of Gustave's eyes on her, and then on Claude, and she had felt quite relieved he hadn't approached her. Though he had still dipped his hat as he left the restaurant, and bade her good day courteously, his gaze had seemed distant, and increasingly so as the week had passed.

She collected the pancakes and basket of bread and returned to the living room, surprised to find three faces smiling in her direction. She met Claude's gaze, cleared her throat, set down the food and returned to the kitchen, the rustling and clinking of heightened activity coming from the living room. Catching her breath, the fizzing sensation challenging her coordination, she picked up the pot of coffee and cups. As she approached the table, Claude's eyes following her, her stomach flipped. 'Coffee?' she said, placing the pot on the coaster.

'Breakfast is amazing, thank you,' Claude said.

A flash of light caught Madeleine's eye. 'What's that?' she said to Albert.

'Claude bought it for me,' he said. 'It's a pocketknife, maman.' He flicked the blade and shut it, flicked it again and shut it again.

'Gosh!' She looked from Claude, admiring the fine lines that framed the dark gaze and the smile that highlighted the elegant structure of her face, to Albert deeply engrossed in the knife, his food sitting untouched on his plate. 'That's a very generous gift,' she said, with an evasive glance at Claude, warmth infusing her cheeks.

'It's nothing,' Claude said.

The soft tone in Claude's voice drew her attention again, and the fluttering in her chest expanded, stealing her breath for a moment. Claude was staring at her, studying her. Heat building, a light film of moisture forming on her lip, she picked up the serviette and dabbed at her face. 'Well, it is rather a special gift,' she said.

'I thought Albert might like to learn to carve,' Claude said.

Albert's eyes flashed, and his grin widened. 'Can I maman?' he said.

'Yes, I think that would be a wonderful skill to learn.' She noticed the lightness in Claude's eyes, the gaze that softened as Claude admired her son. The honest smile, compassion, reflecting in her genuine desire to help — the sense of her own heart melting under the intoxicating spell that was Claudette Dupont.

'I thought we could go to the lake and find a piece of wood this afternoon,' Claude said.

Albert's nose scrunched a fraction with his frown. He wanted to run out now and start carving. Lunchtime was years away; they hadn't even finished breakfast. 'Can we carve our initials in a tree?' he said. He'd seen other letters cut out of the bark, sometimes with a heart around them.

'Yes, we can do that too.'

'Can you do mine?' Natty said. 'I'll be busy with Marie's clothes.' She tried to fit the whole pancake in her mouth, began chewing and started to speak. 'Can we…'

'Natty, please do not speak with food in your mouth,' Madeleine said, her tone gently persuasive, chin tilted down, looking through wide eyes.

Natty chewed while glaring at her mother, swallowed as if the food had got stuck in her throat, and then turned to face Claude, applying a wide smile before she spoke. 'Can we make the clothes now?' she said.

'Yes,' Claude said.

Madeleine found herself nodding, her eyes locking with Claude's in tacit approval. She stood, collected the plates from the table and started towards the kitchen. 'Would you like to help me with the wood?' she said to Albert, drawing a huff. 'You might find a piece to practice on,' she said. He leapt from the chair collected up the mugs and darted into the kitchen.

Claude chuckled, her attention on Madeleine until she left the room. She watched Natty as she delved, poking her hand into the sewing box and turning things on top of each other. Sitting on the floor, she frowned at the frantic, focused activity. 'Are you ready mademoiselle?' she said.

'I'm just looking for more better buttons,' Natty said.

'I thought you took them to bed the other night,' Claude said.

'I lost one, and I need more,' Natty said.

How could you lose a button in a bed? Claude continued to observe Natty with a warm smile. Leaning her back against the chair she drifted in thought to an image of Madeleine chopping wood.

*

'Can I chop, maman?' Albert said. He watched her wielding the axe, splitting the wood near its centre-point, and jumped sideways to avoid a flying splinter.

She stopped with the axe head resting on the ground, her instinct to refuse him, and then leaned the long handle towards him. 'You must follow my instructions,' she said. 'Don't try and hit the wood hard. Keep your eye on the top of the log, here, and feel like you are landing the axe on it,' she said.

He nodded with big head-movements. His eyes alight, his hands gripped firmly around the handle.

She set a small log onto the tree stump, stifled a laugh as he strained to lift the heavy object above his head, the implement wavering in the air then dropping with a thud on the wood. He was frowning, the blade having missed the log and lodged firmly in the tree-stump. She watched him struggle, trying to pull it free, stopping herself from stepping in and helping him. Within a few seconds, he had wriggled it sufficiently, the broadest grin and rosiest cheeks glowing at her. A wave filled her with warmth, and she watched him lever the axe into position again. 'Keep your eye on the middle of the log,' she said, the crack of splitting wood drowning out her words.

'Yes,' he said, tugging at the axe that lay buried in the stump. 'I did it.'

'You did,' she said, admiring his enthusiasm as he set another log on the stump. 'Don't rush; just be safe. You have all day, and there's plenty of logs to chop,' she said, watching as he wielded the axe again, missed then split the log the second time, lifted the tool again. She picked up the chopped wood, stacked it in the basket and set the next log for him. They very quickly got into a rhythm, taking a pause with the basket half-full. She had expected him to stop then, tired, but he continued, albeit slowing his pace until the job was done.

'That was fun,' he said, staring at the overflowing basket.

She gazed at him with a sense of wonder. He was growing up so quickly, and she should give him the opportunity to do more things; things that he would probably be doing if he had a father. His exuberance reached into her, and she melted, seeing the man in him clearly for the first time. He was becoming handsome, he was kind, and he was smart. Infused by warmth, she wrapped an arm around his shoulder and squeezed him to her. 'You did a great job, Albert. Look how much wood you chopped,' she said.

'Can we chop more,' he said.

'Tomorrow. We have no more space in the basket, and if we cut it and leave it here it will get too damp,' she said.

He nodded.

'Shall we take a drink?' she said, observing a trickle of sweat slide down his temple, his cheeks a shade darker and rosier.

He nodded and reached for the basket.

'I'll bring that,' she said, but he had already lifted the basket and was struggling with the weight of it. She smiled.

10.

'When did you get your first knife?' Albert said, matching his stride to Claude's.

'On my eighth birthday,' she said, recalling the moment with clarity, the memory eliciting a warm smile. 'I had wanted one since I was six.'

'How did you learn to carve?'

'My papa taught me,' she said. She glanced at him, expecting a reaction.

His eyes fixed on the path, and they continued in silence to the lake, the crunching of footsteps and whistling breeze, her eyes scanning the undergrowth for the right piece of wood.

She picked up a smallish log, turned it in her hand then threw it back, aware of his eyes questioning her. 'It was rotting,' she said. She picked up another piece, inspecting it in the same way, and then handed it to him. She continued her search. 'Perfect,' she said. She picked up another piece of wood and continued down to the lake. The boat caught her attention, images of rescuing Natty and the first time of meeting Madeleine. Time seemed to have stood still, and she had never felt more at home than she did with the Vietti family. Albert was staring at her, knife poised. 'Let's sit,' she said, moving to a point on the bank where they could lean against a tree. 'So, the first thing is, that you must always work the knife away from you. Never towards you! Like this,' she said, demonstrating, stripping a slice of bark with ease.

Albert nodded.

He looked like an old man; such was the intensity of his concentration, tension in his jaw from the effort of trying too hard, the creases deepening across his forehead. She ruffled his hair, 'Relax, or you'll cut yourself,' she said, her broad grin giving him permission to smile, softening his features and lightening his touch with the blade. 'That's better,' she said. 'Now, slide the blade, don't dig it into the wood, or it will go too deep and get stuck.' She observed his movement, nodding as he followed her instructions, a slither of bark falling to the ground. 'That's it. Now, same again and strip the bark off. It's not a race, so get comfortable,' she said, leaning against the tree and starting on her wood.

They worked in silence, and she was aware of his eyes drifting to her hands from time to time. He would watch the movement of her blade and then try to mirror it. She didn't instruct him, just slowed down the action so he could take it in. He slowed his pace, emulating hers, his knife skills improving. The car shape emerging, imprecise in its lack of fine-detail, was a long way from the original piece of wood covered in bark.

He studied the crude, rough shape, a beaming grin plastered to his face, his finger caressing every part of the uneven surface. He looked across at her carving, smooth, perfect, though still lacking in detail such that one loosely resembled the other. 'Yours looks like a car,' he said, his eyes flitting between the two objects.

'Yours does too. My first carving wasn't as good as that,' she said, pointing to the wood in his hand. There was a glint in his eyes as he held her gaze, and her heart blossomed, warmth spreading across her chest. 'Shall we leave our mark?' she said, standing and pressing her knife to the tree.

Albert stood and scratched away, the letters AV eventually appearing next to Claude and Natty's initials.

They stood back admiring their work, then grinned at each other. They ambled back up the path in silence, him walking taller, their steps lighter.

'Why did they beat you, at school?' he said.

'I was different,' she said.

'How?'

She paused. 'I always had short hair.'

He studied her. 'So!'

'I guess back then it was unusual for a girl. Still is.'

The lines appeared on his forehead again and his nose wrinkled. 'I don't understand,' he said.

She wouldn't tell him the truth, though she wished she could. She had worn a pinafore dress like all the other girls, but her short hair had made her look like a boy in girl's clothing. She would have preferred to climb trees rather than skip, and play-fight rather than squeal like the other girls, but the boys wouldn't include her in their games. She had watched both groups from the outside, filled with hollow emptiness. She had never once looked at a boy with doe-eyes, giggling and wanting them to kiss her like the other girls had talked about.

On the contrary, the thought of kissing a boy didn't stir her in any way. It never had. There had been a girl at school though, and the feelings that had tormented her days and occupied her dreams at night were of an entirely different quality. The children at school had sensed that she wasn't like them, and she had suffered for it.

'I guess some people get scared when others aren't like them, and so they fight or exclude them. It's a kind of natural instinct to defend oneself, like an animal that feels threatened,' she said.

'Oh!' He scratched his head, stuffed his hand in his pocket. Eventually, he said, 'I'm not like the others either.'

Her lips thinned a fraction, and she nodded her head. There was no tension in his voice, more a sense of inner strength, and at that point, she knew he would be fine. They continued the last few yards in silence, and she followed his lead towards the rear of the house, and the entrance to the kitchen. He stopped, just short of the door, his eyes fixed on hers.

'Thank you,' he said. 'I've had the best day ever.'

She nodded, smiling, aware of the strength of bond they shared. 'Me too.' she said.

A sense of foreboding rose within her suddenly and tightness wedged between her ribs. How would Madeleine respond when she found out about her? The feeling, the foreboding, had a name she decided. Rejection. It didn't sit well, and an image of her father came to her. She swallowed against the constriction in her throat. She had to tell Madeleine at some point; she couldn't run the risk of her finding out from others, and she didn't want Madeleine being labelled, either.

Albert opened the door to a wave of heat and the sweet smell of baking. Claude inhaled, the aroma distracting her from her concerns.

'Can I have some cake, maman?' Albert said.

Madeleine turned, her eyes meeting Claude's, hesitating before directing her gaze at her son. 'After dinner,' she said.

Claude felt Madeleine's lingering, warm smile and the softness in her light eyes soften the residual tension her thoughts had stirred. Turning her attention to Albert, she smiled.

'Would you both like a drink?' Madeleine said.

'Oui, maman.'

Claude sensed Madeleine's attention on her again, with such tenderness, and so enticing, and she met her gaze. In a hoarse voice, 'That would be lovely,' she said, and thought she noticed Madeleine's smile shift subtly.

'Coffee?' Madeleine said. Unsure as to whether she had heard the word as broken or just imagined it, she smiled, warmth filling her cheeks.

'Maman, look what we made,' Albert said, drawing Madeleine's focus from Claude. He held out the carved wood, watching his mother's response.

Madeleine crouched to his height, cupped his cheeks and kissed his forehead. She took the object and turned it delicately in her hands. 'That looks like a car,' she said.

'It is. I made it!'

Madeleine glanced briefly at Claude to see she was nodding in affirmation. 'Wow!' she said. 'That is very clever.'

He shrugged. 'Claude's is better,' he said.

Madeleine's eyes were looking up at her. 'He has a natural talent,' Claude said.

'I'm sure Claude has had lots of practice,' Madeleine said, staring at Claude. Turning back to her son, she traced a finger over the wood. 'You are very clever, Albert.'

'You can have it,' he said and ran into the living room.

Claude watched a film of moisture change the tone in Madeleine's eyes and her heart skipped. There was something deeply endearing about the display of vulnerability, the tenderness captivating her.

'Thank you for... helping Albert,' Madeleine said.

Claude noticed Madeleine's slender fingers, the tremble in her movement as she placed the carving on the kitchen surface. She resisted the urge to reach out, steady the hands and draw Madeleine into her arms. 'I had a fun time too,' she said, her breath tight in her chest.

Madeleine remained focused on the work surface. 'You will stay for dinner,' she said.

Claude hesitated. 'Yes,' she said in barely more than a whisper.

*

'Claude's going to read me a bedtime story,' Natty said. She shovelled the last of her food into her mouth, her fork clattering on the plate. 'But, I need to give Marie her tea first. Maman, can I get down please?'

'Yes, Natty, you may leave the table,' Madeleine said.

'May I leave the table, maman?' Albert said.

He had been sitting with an empty plate for a while, one hand firmly wedged into his trouser pocket. Claude imagined his knife, the handle hot, and smiled.

'Yes Albert, thank you for waiting patiently.' Madeleine stood and started to clear the plates.

Claude mirrored her movement, picked up Albert's plate and her own and walked into the kitchen. 'I don't mind reading to them,' she said, offloading the plates to the drainer, her eyes searching Madeleine's. The quiet intensity behind Madeleine's stare rooted her to the spot, her stomach fluttering so fiercely as to render her speechless. Relentless, the moment seemed to last for longer than a casual glance, and if it hadn't been for the sound of Natty's voice breaking the spell, she didn't know for how long she would have lasted before she weakened completely. 'I'll go and get them ready for bed,' she said, striding into the living room.

Madeleine stood for a while, her cheeks flushed, her eyes fixed on the door separating the two rooms, Claude's calm voice penetrating the peals of laughter emanating from her children. She turned to the sink, ran the water, added the suds and started to wash the dishes. By the time she had finished clearing the kitchen, the noises had stopped. She filled the kettle and put it on the stove, spooned the cocoa into the cups and waited. She tapped the kitchen surface, her fingers creating a rhythmical beat and released a deep sigh, her eyes narrowing and creasing her brows. She stopped, released a long breath then paced across the floor and back again. She ran her fingers through her hair then settled it back to where it started, and then straightened the front of the dark blue wrap-around dress, flattening the material over her stomach.

Claude stood in the doorway, the kettle whistling. She watched as Madeleine poured the water into the cups and stirred, all the while oblivious to her presence. A warm glow filled her as it occurred to her that she wouldn't be able to get

Madeleine's attention without causing her to jump. The thought brought with it a moment of daring, her conscience making the respectful choice, grounded by her commitment to speak openly and honestly to Madeleine.

She ducked back into the living room, moved towards the table, her heart racing. She rubbed her hands together, pressed thumbs into the palms, the twisting in her gut a reflection of her determination to do the right thing, the honourable thing. But, what if Madeleine wanted her to stay away from the children? The hollow feeling, low in her stomach expanded, her hands started shaking, and her thumbs left marks where they pressed.

Minded of Natty's affection towards her and Albert's comment about today being the best day of his life, it had been the best day of her life too. The sense of emptiness grew with the idea of not being able to see them, of not being able to see Madeleine, of not being there after this evening. She gazed around the room that had become so familiar, so comforting in the few times she had visited, and released a long breath. She had never experienced the concept of a home before, but she imagined that this must be what it was like. What made it special wasn't the vast array of possessions or the clutter she had seen in other homes. On the contrary, the space was simply decorated, ordered, and with basic furnishings. What made it was something far more profound; something that couldn't be traded, it just existed. It was called love.

'Claude!' Madeleine said.

Claude jumped, her thoughts instantly banished, and Madeleine juggled to not spill the drinks. Claude started to chuckle, holding her chest, Madeleine's smile slower to appear but expanding as she too broke into laughter.

Righting the drinks, the moment settling as their eyes locked onto each other, Madeleine held out the cup. 'Sorry, I didn't mean to startle you,' she said. 'I hadn't realised. I thought you were...'

'I finished reading a moment ago. I think they are asleep already.' Claude said. She took the drink, studied the pinkish-brown surface, and approached the table.

'I think they're exhausted. They've had such a good day,' Madeleine said, taking her regular seat.

Claude sat, leant back in the chair and widening the space between them, the slight tremble in her stomach starting to grip. It was now or never.

'Are you okay?' Madeleine said.

Claude could feel the wave rising, tingling down her spine, her gut twisting. This was going to end badly, but she couldn't hide the truth. It wouldn't be fair, and she couldn't accept any harm coming to the children or Madeleine as a result of her selfishness. People could be cruel and would surely judge by association. She tried to breathe before speaking, but the air wouldn't fill her lungs.

'Claude, is there something the matter?'

Claude sipped at the hot drink, barely wetting her dry mouth. She studied Madeleine, the wide eyes staring at her seeking an answer, the teeth pulling on her bottom lip, the fine lines running across her forehead. For the briefest moment, her insides melted with the thought of not saying anything and then her gut twisted again. She hesitated, allowing commitment to build and firm her resolve, her back straightening, her eyes closing. 'There's something I should tell you,' she said.

Madeleine stared intently, her brows creasing, a slight shrug of her shoulders, her head shaking. 'What is it?'

Claude observed her, a dull ache lingering in her stomach as the words formed and repeated themselves in her mind's eye. 'I' she paused, released a breath, her voice coming softly. 'I am a lesbian,' she said.

11.

Madeleine sat perfectly still, her mouth agape, her gaze distant.

Claude waited, suspended in expectation for what seemed like an eternity, her gut spiralling in anticipation, watching as Madeleine came to regard her again.

'What does that mean exactly?' Madeleine said.

Claude swallowed. She hadn't reckoned on explaining the term. The ache now heavy in her chest reminded her of her first and only conversation on the matter with her father, his adamant dismissal of her and claims that her admission was both preposterous and frivolous. She had fought to insist that her feelings were honest, genuine and not likely to change, but he had shunned her and been unwilling to engage with her on the matter since. Formality and respect, based on a relationship that centred on their mutual love of engineering, had connected them over the years, and even then he had only supported her to find the job in Génissiat to get her out of Paris. 'I umm... I like to be with women.' Claude said.

Madeleine sat taller in the seat, her head on a tilt, keen eyes seeming to toy with the information. She frowned, though her eyes sparkled. 'I too like...'

Madeleine stopped speaking, and Claude watched the colour flush her cheeks, her eyes skittish.

'Oh, you mean...'

Madeleine looked at her with an odd expression she couldn't define. It wasn't harsh, piercing features tight like her papa's had been. There was a sense of gentle curiosity. Fascination maybe? Calmness settled her, the instant rejection she had expected hadn't materialised. She nodded. 'Yes,' she said, her voice quiet, steady.

Madeleine opened her mouth, closed it again. Her lips twitched as if trying to smile, her focus on her innermost thoughts.

Claude waited, dropped her shoulders, her hands resting in her lap, hoping for Madeleine to say something. Anything. Silence becoming slowly more painful, Claude held her gaze. 'I thought you should know from me, rather than...' She stopped. Madeleine made a faint nodding movement, and she felt the dark eyes assessing her differently. She wondered whether Madeleine could see her pounding heart and whether she should say something else. She went to speak, her words clashing with Madeleine's.

'I appreciate you telling me.'

'If you want me to stay away from the children, I will understand.'

'No!'

The passion in the short word stunned Claude into silence, and when she held Madeleine's gaze again she felt struck by a spell so strong she struggled to breathe.

'No,' Madeleine said, her tone softer. 'That's not what I want.' She broke eye contact, sipped from her cup.

Claude wanted to reach across the table, take the trembling hands and hold them. She picked up her cup and sipped instead, noticing the slight shake in her own hands. 'That's not what I want either,' she said in a whisper.

Madeleine returned her cup to the table.

Claude motioned to speak. 'Are you...?' She hesitated. 'Are you okay?'

Madeleine cleared her throat. 'Would you like a Cognac?' she said, standing and walking into the kitchen before Claude could respond, returning with two short glasses and an unopened bottle.

'Don't open it just for me,' Claude said.

'I think I need a drink.' Madeleine said.

Claude watched Madeleine pull with increasing urgency at the seal, her hands unable to coordinate the simple task. She reached out and her fingers brushed against Madeleine's; Madeleine's remaining receptive to the brief touch. Their eyes locked for the shortest moment, before Claude eased the bottle away, carefully pulled off the seal and twisted the top. The familiar squeaking of cork against glass and then the pop released the sweet, spicy aroma into the room. She poured two small shots and held one out; noticed Madeleine studying her hands and with a sharp intake of breath Madeleine's eyes diverting to the dark liquid. She watched as Madeleine raised the glass to soft, rouged lips and tipped it back in one sudden movement, swallowed too quickly and started coughing, hand clasping at her throat. She smiled through a cloak of affection and tender amusement and sipped the drink.

Madeleine regained her composure, landed the glass on the table with a heavy tap, and poured another drink.

Claude could feel the mild sense of amusement growing, gripped by Madeleine's edgy, yet quietly fascinated, response to her revelation. She smiled. 'Are you okay?' she said as Madeleine swigged the drink.

Madeleine swallowed, and nodded.

Claude succumbed to the dark eyes and tempting lips, savoured the warmth that caressed her and the slight trembling that was starting to excite her. She finished her Cognac, turned the glass in her hand.

Madeleine placed her glass silently on the table. She cleared her throat, looked to Claude and smiled. 'I'm so sorry, I seem to have lost my voice,' she said.

'I'm sure it's a lot to take in,' Claude said.

'I don't really know what to think,' Madeleine said.

It didn't look like disgust, Claude thought, releasing a sigh. Definitely not rejection, or she would have been ushered out already. Her heart thumped. 'You can ask me questions,' she said, 'if you want?'

Madeleine filled her glass and cupped it in her hands, her eyes moving from Claude to the room and back again. 'When did you know?' she said.

Claude placed her hands in her lap. 'I was ten.'

'Ten!'

Claude jolted with the ferocity in Madeleine's tone.

'Sorry, I just didn't expect. Gosh, so young.'

Claude breathed deeply. 'I didn't know for sure, why I was different. I just knew I felt differently from other girls, about boys, and I had feelings for a girl.'

'Like a crush?' Madeleine said.

'A bit like a crush.'

'Oh.'

Madeleine seemed to drift in thought. 'Not all crushes are the same,' Claude said. She noticed Madeleine's appearance shift again.

'Oh.'

'My crushes on girls didn't go away,' Claude said, with gentle amusement.

'Of course.'

Madeleine remained lost in thought and silence filled the space between them. 'Have you kissed a woman?' she said, suddenly.

Claude chuckled and then felt overcome by a wave that pricked at her conscience. If Madeleine knew how many women she had kissed, and slept with, she would surely reject her. 'Yes, I have kissed a woman,' she said, her tone calm, noticing Madeleine's gaze shift to her mouth.

A log crackled, and Madeleine lifted her eyes. 'Oh,' she said. 'Have you always…'

'Yes,' Claude said. She had always liked women and only ever been with women. She could never see herself with a man, no matter how kind and gentle they might be. She wanted to ask if Madeleine had ever considered kissing a woman, but the words remained as thought, and she moved them to the back of her mind.

'Oh!' Madeleine said.

Claude stood. 'I had better go,' she said.

Madeleine stood. 'Yes, of course,' she said.

Slightly unsteady movements and eyes unfocused; she felt Madeleine's vulnerability as a burning sensation within her. She wanted to hold Madeleine, reassure her, but she couldn't.

Madeleine's attention returned to Claude. 'Sorry, I feel I've been quite rude,' she said.

Claude's lips twitched at the slightly slurred words. She would have probably drowned in Cognac had she been in Madeleine's position, and it was clear that Madeleine wasn't used to drinking. 'Not at all, and thank you!' she said. 'I was worried you might not want to see me again.' She allowed the smile to grow, Madeleine's gaze reaching her with tenderness.

Madeleine smiled and then shivered.

'I really should go,' Claude said.

'You'll come back tomorrow?' Madeleine said, wrapping her arms around her body, which was starting to tremble.

Claude lowered her gaze then lifted it, resisting the urge to pull Madeleine into her arms. 'I'd like that,' she said.

'Natty would be very disappointed if you didn't; Albert too.'

'Yes.' She studied Madeleine a little longer. 'Good night, Madeleine.'

Madeleine went to say something then hesitated, and when Madeleine spoke, Claude sensed a moment had been missed. 'Good night Claude.'

Claude turned and walked to the front door. One last glance over her shoulder and a nod of the head, the door clicked shut, and she stepped out into the dark night.

12.

Claude followed the trail of her breath, her pace upbeat, not least to combat the colder early mornings. At least her journey to work had shortened by three kilometres now, having laid new track almost as far as town. She shoved her hands deep into her pockets, her shoulders sitting higher to keep the chill from her neck, extended her gait virtually to the point of a run and passed other workers, some moving in her direction, others heading towards the dam. Rumour had it the *Barrage de Génissiat* would be ready before Christmas and excitement for both events seemed to be stimulating people's imagination.

The opening of the dam had been the topic of much speculation since she had arrived, and the recent influx of workers seemed to have settled the debate. It would be a spectacular affair, and some had even suggested that the Prime Minister, Vincent Auriol, had agreed to attend. The dam opening would be reported in the press across France they had said, which would be good for business, and the townsfolk were already planning a party for which they had set up a special organising committee. Whether the opening of the dam would be declared a public holiday was still a moot point with the local council vying for a day of celebration, and large businesses against. Madeleine had offered the restaurant to cater for the event, and since Gustave chaired the committee, the chances of that happening were high.

'Morning Claudette,' two men said synchronously as they passed her, dipping their hats, their collars high around their necks, a trail of cigarette smoke hanging in the air behind them.

'Morning Arthur, Phillipe,' she said, nodding her head to the dam-workers she had chatted to on occasion during meal times at the restaurant. They passed each other every day at about the same time.

'Morning Claudette,' Xavier said, moving alongside her and falling into her pace.

'Morning Xavier.' Her head moved enough for her to notice his collar was down and he gave the appearance of not feeling the weather. She smiled. 'Cold one,' she said.

'A little,' he said with a tilt of his head, his eyes scanning the dark, clear sky.

Her skin prickled at the idea of the cold steel rails, and shovelling stones that clung to each other. It would be a hard day. 'Beautiful sunrise,' she said, her eyes indicating towards the fire-like slithers of light stretching along the horizon, the only light in the pool of near blackness above them. 'At least it won't rain,' she said.

He nodded with a smile that appeared and disappeared in an instant, the sound of boots on gravel disturbing the silence between them as they turned towards the row of lanterns that lit up the entrance to the railway site.

She often wondered if he might ask her personal questions, but he never did. She had caught his gaze on her one time when she had turned from the hotplate after speaking to Madeleine. His soft smile had lingered, and she got the impression he understood. He was aware that she spent most of her evenings and weekends at the house, played with the children... and helped Madeleine. He never broached the subject though, and yet she never got the impression that he wasn't interested either. He exuded gentle energy that contradicted his build, and he used both to great effect. Though she didn't need him to protect or defend her with the workers anymore, he always stood by her side and especially when Gustave came around to inspect their work. At those times he stood taller, his chest inflated, his eyes narrow and focused. He seemed vigilant of the group of men to which Gustave deferred, on occasion resulting in what appeared to be a standoff with them. He always backed down first though, returning to his work alongside her with increased diligence.

She removed her hands from her pockets, rubbed them together and picked up a shovel. She and threw it to Xavier, picked up a second, and walked down the track. Within minutes the clanging of metal-on-metal filtered down the line, increasing in volume. The fast-rising mist had started to ease the chill that stung her fingers, and she watched Xavier, his shovel sliding through the stones as a hot knife gliding through butter. She would need her foot behind her spade until the sun generated some warmth to move the rocks with such effectiveness. Taking a deep breath, she planted the tool and set to work.

'Have you seen the dam?' she said, standing and leaning on the handle, stretching her back.

He nodded. 'It's impressive,' he said, his lips thinning. He drew down on his cigarette as he lit it and blew out the smoke. 'I wouldn't want to work on it though.'

'Why's that?' She tilted her head.

'I can't swim.' he said, his tone unflinching.

She held his gaze, looking for a sign that he might be joking with her, but his features didn't change. She could feel the bubbling in her chest and held it back. Lines appeared around eyes that glinted at her, and a second later they were both laughing.

'I do prefer the railways,' he said with a shrug, his eyes darkening again as he pondered.

'Me too,' she said. She tapped him on the arm and indicated with her eyes. Gustave was approaching them at a pace faster than his legs should be able to carry his oversized body. She held back the chuckle, thinking better of upsetting her boss. Xavier's snort reaching her ears; she coughed to release the pressure.

Gustave stood to face them, cleared his throat, his moustache twitching wildly and his eyes skittish. He pulled himself up, but it didn't make him look any taller. It must gall him to have to look up to most people, she thought, noticing how his eyebrows made his eyes look even smaller, giving him a deranged kind of appearance. The distraction amused her.

'Break's over, get to work,' he said.

They nodded in unison, Xavier discarding the butt of his cigarette to the ground at Gustave's feet. Both picked up their shovels, turned their backs and started to dig. She could hear the group of men close-by continuing to chat and laugh, their behaviour going unchecked; but that was always the case. It would be another five minutes or more before they resumed work.

Xavier placed a hand on her arm. 'Ignore them,' he said.

She softened under the appeal, released a breath, her eyes affirming his request. The desire to fight still reared its head from time to time. Maybe it always would. Should she feel a hypocrite talking to Albert about turning the other cheek, when she struggled to do the same? Her conscience pricked. She needed to try harder.

*

The condensation inside the windows made it impossible to see into the restaurant as Xavier and she approached, but it didn't stop Claude trying to catch a glimpse of Madeleine. The urge to quicken her pace, driven by the tingling warmth that filled her, was stifled by the long queue of men in front of her. Hopping from foot to foot, she inched forward, the smell of roasted meat emanating from the kitchen increasing her discomfort. Her stomach rumbling and jittery at the same time and her chest tight enough that she struggled to breathe, she waited in line, reminiscing about the afternoon she and Madeleine had spent walking in the woods with the children. Albert hunting down the right piece of wood to carve, Natty grumbling that her legs ached and needing to be carried, all of them collecting pinecones and other bits to make Christmas decorations.

The conversation had flowed smoothly, though Madeleine hadn't broached the topic of the previous evening and Claude hadn't felt the need to expand on her time in Paris either. They had talked about her life as an engineer instead, and working in the factory, and how the war had changed France, the hardship the restaurant had experienced and how thankfully that was all a thing of the past. She had noticed Madeleine gazing at her from time to time as they walked, smiling softly when their eyes met. Her beauty, the light of the sun catching her eyes, had left her breathless and wanting.

'When did you realise you weren't in love with Raoul,' she had said in a moment of unconscious bravery, as they sat watching the children throw stones of various sizes into the water. She had felt something shift inside her when Madeleine said that she had never loved him, or it seemed any man. That she hadn't realised how much she had never loved another man until their discussions recently and that she had been thinking about a lot of things since meeting Claude. Madeleine hadn't been explicit about feelings for another woman, but she had reached out and touched Claude's arm, thanking her, and Claude had sensed the fondness Madeleine held for her. They had laughed casually, walking unhurriedly back to the house, and she had set the fire and laid the cones out on the hearth to dry, and then helped Madeleine in the kitchen while the children played in the living room. She had put the children to bed and then returned to the kitchen and watched Madeleine.

'How much detail would you like?' she had said frivolously as Madeleine, hands immersed in the washing up bowl, had asked her what it was like to kiss another woman. She had smiled at the scene of domesticity, completely at odds with the mesmerising, elegant style of the dress that revealed the back of Madeleine's slender legs. The fact that her body seemed to be enticed and enthralled by both aspects of Madeleine entertained and alarmed her. When Madeleine had turned sharply at the question, eyes piercing through her and sweeping the breath from her, she had felt touched on another level. At that moment the description she had given was out of her hopes, the object of her dreams staring straight at her. 'Soft, tender, warm, yielding,' she had said, sensing the texture as she spoke. 'Skin as smooth as silk.' Madeleine had wetted her lower lip and stared, her gaze vacant. Claude had quite literally felt the essence of Madeleine's lips on hers at that moment, so exquisite as to render her speechless in the face of Madeleine's continued questions.

Xavier had nudged her through the doorway, and somehow she had made it to the hotplate. She stood facing Madeleine, the picture of the imagined kiss at the forefront of her mind, heat scolding her cheeks. Clearing her throat sounded more like a groan, and she could have sworn Madeleine's smile expressed the same conclusion. 'Lunch smells delicious,' she said.

'Why thank you, Claudette,' Madeleine said.

Claude studied the bright eyes and rosy cheeks for the short length of time before Madeleine broke eye contact and started serving the food. 'Thank you,' she said, taking the stacked plate. She stalled before moving away and finding a seat, aware of Madeleine's gaze on her back, tingling sparks following the line of her spine. Glancing around the room, the few available seats obscuring her view of the hotplate, she walked to the pair of empty seats at the table closest to the window.

'Do you mind if I join you?'

She recognised his voice, before her eyes located him, something in his tone making the hairs on her arms prickle and her heart thud. Her stomach turned as she rested her plate on the table and she was aware of an unfamiliar weakness taking over her legs. She sat as he pulled out the chair she had planned for Xavier, his plate hitting the table before she could give a response. She thought his smile gave away more than his eyes, stretching his skin, deep creases forming on his cheeks.

'Monsieur Blanc,' she said.

'Claudette,' he said, sitting opposite her.

Even the room silenced to her ears as she stared at him, her desire to eat, but a distant memory. She observed him, setting out his cutlery, folding his napkin and placing it at the side of his plate, contemplating his food, closing his eyes, his moustache wriggling as he spoke quietly to himself. When he eventually looked up at her, he still hadn't eaten, and neither had she. She forced herself to mirror his movements and as he picked up his knife and fork and cut into the sliced pork, so did she. The food resisted being swallowed and sat heavily in her stomach, but she continued to eat, trying to drive the tension from her body, unsuccessful in pursuit.

'The food is excellent, no?' he said.

'Yes,' she said.

'Are you enjoying your job here?' he said.

'Yes.' She paused, aware that her clipped responses may appear defensive, an impression she didn't want to give him. 'I enjoy it very much. I hope you find my work acceptable,' she said. Her eyelids closed slowly then opened again, wishing she hadn't sought his opinion. For some reason, he had that effect on her; caused her to feel the need to justify herself, seek approval. His vacant stare and tight-lipped smile twisted in her gut. The feeling wasn't unfamiliar; it simply alerted her. No matter what he may or may not say, she got the impression he didn't like her. Not one little bit.

'I find your work satisfactory,' he said, his tone irritated. Gravy spilt onto his chin, and she wondered how it was that he hadn't noticed. She curbed her instinct, to reach across the table, pick up his napkin and hand it to him, and continued to eat.

His eyes on his food, 'You seem to have flattered yourself with Madeleine,' he said. There was an edge to his voice.

'I have been helping with the children,' she said. The wave of heat bringing a strong sense of discomfort that lodged in her chest.

'Yes, your involvement has been noticed,' he said. 'The people of the town watch out for each other, Claudette. It's the right way,' he said.

She caught his emphasis on the word right, the implied message coming through loud and clear, any response escaping her. She swallowed the food she had chewed to within an inch of its life, picked up a glass of water and sipped. 'They are good children,' she said.

'Indeed! Madeleine has tried to be a good mother to them.'

A flame ignited, driving her blood to boiling point in an instant. Tried to be a good mother! How dare he! 'Madeleine is an excellent mother,' she said trying to control her anger. The look in his eyes told her he knew of her feelings towards Madeleine.

'Indeed!' he said. 'However, they still need a father, Claudette. The absence of Raoul, God rest his soul, has been clearly disturbing for their healthy development. A man is essential in such matters, as I am sure you will appreciate.'

She hoped the spasm in her chest wasn't a heart attack, the sharp, tight band constricting around her ribs and suppressing the burning intensity that had flared, lest she should rise to his words and lash out in a way that she would surely regret. Her knuckles white, her hands gripping her cutlery, the tension in her arms preventing any further movement, she glared at him. He didn't give any indication that he noticed the shift in her demeanour.

'I have asked to escort Madeleine to dinner this week,' he said.

His eyes held hers, his words sucking the air from her lungs and trapping her voice deep in her throat.

'She has agreed, naturally,' he said, impervious to the pain he was causing.

She watched him shovel the food into his mouth in the same way she would cast the stones onto the track. He has the manners of a pig, she thought. The idea of him with Madeleine, him with the children, him in their lives, brought acid to her mouth. 'If you will excuse me, Monsieur Blanc,' she said. She stood, not waiting for a response, stepped from the table and made her way out of the restaurant.

13.

Madeleine glared in Gustave's direction, though his eyes were fixed on the plate of food that Claude had deserted, his fork poised over the half-eaten sautéed potatoes.

She had watched his interaction, at first pleased that he had taken the time to speak with Claude, imagining he had taken on board her comments that he would do well to make an effort and get to know her. Unsure what had just passed between them, one thing was clear; Claude had walked out without finishing her food and without a glance in her direction, leaving her with an unfamiliar ache in her chest. The desire to run to Claude and find out what had happened had risen instantly, frustrated by her inability to move from the hotplate and the line of men still waiting for food. Gustave was looking up from his plate, his eyes tracking the room and settling on her, his moustache rising on his face. She didn't smile back, and when he stood and started walking towards her, she rested her hands on her hips and squeezed.

'Excellent food, Madeleine,' he said. He chuckled to no one in particular. 'I will get some work out of the men this afternoon,' he said.

'Is there something the matter with Claude?' she said.

'Claude!' His moustache twisted and his eyebrows shot up, the name crawling off his tongue with more than a hint of disdain.

Irritation burned inside her. 'Claudette,' she said, through the tightness in her jaw, her heart racing. Claude was the only name she had thought of Claudette by since Natty had first introduced her. Of course, he would question the term; Claude was a man's name.

'Indeed!' His eyes wandered to the door. 'She did seem... a little peculiar,' he said. 'Nothing to do with your food,

102

I'm sure. Maybe a little acid,' he said, twisting the tip of his moustache as he spoke.

She tried to hold his gaze, but his eyes shifted. 'Is there anything I can get you, Gustave?' she said, crossing her arms in front of her chest.

He cleared his throat, pumped up his chest and looked at her. 'I was hoping you would escort me to dinner tomorrow evening,' he said. 'I have a meeting with a potential investor for the opening of the barrage, and I thought your presence might add a little colour to the occasion.'

His smile didn't touch her, the burning sensation escalating. 'I have the children to look after. It's my one night off,' she said.

He pressed the back of his hand to his mouth and coughed before speaking. 'I already arranged for Antoinette to sit for the children. She was more than delighted to be able to assist, especially given the importance of this event to the restaurant,' he said.

A flame engulfed Madeleine, and her arms squeezed tightly around her tense frame. She motioned to speak but thought better of it. He was right about the event; it would bring a great deal of attention to the restaurant. She hadn't realised she was nodding.

'That's settled then, seven pm tomorrow,' he said. 'Good day to you, Madeleine.' He dipped his hat, turned and walked away.

Madeleine stared at the door that had long since closed behind him, her ability to focus challenged by the emotional turmoil spinning in her mind. The sound of a man clearing his throat drew her attention and she continued to serve, dazed from the assault that had just floored her.

*

'It will be good for business,' Antoinette said, scrubbing at the plate in her hand, her back to Madeleine.

'Well, why don't you go with him?' Madeleine said.

Antoinette turned her head, her hands continuing to work as she spoke. 'He specifically asked for you to go with him and begged me to look after the children. He said you needed a break and he's right. Mother thought it was a fine idea too. Anyway, he knows you run the restaurant. It's your job to speak on our behalf,' she said.

Madeleine stood, her hand pressed to her forehead. She raked her fingers through her hair and groaned. Antoinette stared at her, the softness in her eyes failing to penetrate the barrier she had erected. 'I'm going to chop wood,' she said.

Antoinette's gaze rested on her sister until the door shut, then turning slowly towards the sink she continued to wash the dishes.

Madeleine stepped into the cold air and leaned against the back door, unable to shift the tightness in her chest. Her eyes had started to burn, water readily coming to their surface. Damn the cold. Fixating on the woodshed, she strode toward the pile of logs, selected one without thought and placed it on the tree-stump. Wielding the axe, she hadn't been aware of screaming out loud. Consumed by the fierce flow of energy coursing through her, she devoured the logs effortlessly, the basket filling all too quickly. She stood back, quietly assessing the space around her, the trees that spanned the rear of the buildings, the path leading down to the lake. Only then did she become aware of the steady flow, warm wetness on her cheeks, blurred vision, and a heart beating with a heavy thud. She had been looking forward to spending the evening with Claude, more than she had realised.

Shaking her head, she returned to the kitchen, the image of Gustave causing her to feel quite giddy and sick. Damn her sister for agreeing to sit for her children without asking her of her wishes. Damn her mother for interfering. Damn Claude for coming into her life and turning her world upside down. Damn the world for the confusion that had occupied her waking hours for the past weeks. The scenes that filtered into her dreams and coloured her nights with shades of impossibility. Tempting, titillating, leaving her ragged and raw, for something - someone - that she must always deny.

Entering the kitchen, she caught Antoinette's eye. 'I'll ask Claude to sit the children,' she said.

Antoinette tilted her head to the side. 'The railway woman?' she said, faint lines appearing between her eyes.

'Yes, the railway woman, whose name is Claudette and who prefers to be called Claude,' she said with sharp movements, unloading the wood and stacking it next to the stove.

Antoinette's eyes widened, and her jaw dropped. 'Are you alright?' she said.

Madeleine continued stacking the wood. 'No, I am not. I had planned my one night off already, but that has been sabotaged and worse still I now need to spend time with a man I find most distasteful,' she said.

'I thought you liked Gustave,' Antoinette said, in a quiet voice.

Madeleine covered her face with her hands, her fingers smoothing around her eyes, before resting her hands on her hips. She took in a deep breath, Antoinette staring at her intently, and spoke with as much restraint as she could muster. 'No Netty, you like him. I, most certainly do not,' she said.

'But I thought...'

'Everyone seems intent on considering him my best suitor. Lord knows, I almost started believing he might be a good father to my children,' she said, her mind replaying the horror, her stomach turning.

'He's a good man,' Antoinette said.

Madeleine watched Antoinette fidgeting, curious as to the rose-tinted lens through which she imagined Gustave. 'Hmmm,' she said. After seeing Claude leave the restaurant in such haste, uneaten food on her plate, she wasn't so sure about the good Monsiour Blanc's real intent. 'I'll ask Claude to sit the children,' she said again.

'Are you sure?' Antoinette said. 'She does seem to spend a great deal of time with you and the children, and, well...' She stilled.

Madeleine reacted to the boiling blood pulsing through her. 'Well, what?' She maintained her glare, observing the shift in colour of her sister's cheeks and the quivering of her lip as she moved to speak.

In a tone as if sharing a dark secret, 'Well... people will talk,' she said.

Madeleine's mouth opened then closed, and then opened again. 'I am shocked at you,' she said. 'It is no business of anyone's who I spend my time with, and I would have thought my own sister would refrain from engaging in such unjust tittle-tattle.' She watched a tear trickle from Antoinette's closed eyes, and released a deep breath that sounded more like a huff.

'I'm sorry, you are right,' Antoinette said, opening her eyes and rubbing her finger across her wet cheek. 'It isn't anyone's business.'

Madeleine rested her hands on her hips, well aware that the pose might come across as defensive. That was precisely how she was feeling. She knew Antoinette was right, people would start talking sooner or later, but the hot surge that flooded her had nothing to do with those people and everything to do with the fact that she wanted to spend time with Claude. She couldn't spend enough time with Claude, and now she was forced into a position where she had to entertain Gustave and this business friend, rather than spend a delightful evening with Claude and the children. 'And, there is no *it*, Antoinette. There is nothing in my life that is anyone's business,' she said, unable to make sense of the strength of feeling behind the words. She rubbed at her eyes. 'I need to prep for tonight,' she said. 'Where's mother?'

'She's at the butcher's.'

'Of course, she is,' Madeleine said, rolling her eyes.

Their mother had been secretly courting the town butcher since the war broke out. Some said, it was such a well-kept secret that even he didn't know it, and even now the war had ended she continued to trade eggs for meat. Regina Moreau had a good grasp of her feminine power and her liaison with Jean-Jacques Florret had served them well during the war years. She always did well out of her negotiations, and it would seem that no man could resist the sparkle that radiated through her effervescent personality. She made men feel good about themselves; made them think they had a special place in her heart. The truth was, there had never been and never would be any man worthy of sharing her life, other than her late husband, Gaston Moreau.

'She'll be back before dinner,' Antoinette said.

'You can tell her from me, in fact tell all of them, to stop trying to set me up with Gustave Blanc. I'm not interested in him. Not now; not ever.'

'Don't say that, Madeleine. You're still young, and what about the children?' she said.

'What about the children?'

'They need a father figure.'

'Oh my God in heaven! Not you as well.' Madeleine tensed, aware that the same words had come from her own lips just a few weeks ago.

'What?'

Antoinette stood, palms open, her brow creased, apparently oblivious as to the implications of her beliefs. 'Why does a woman always need a man?' Madeleine said, heat flushing her cheeks.

'Perhaps Albert wouldn't get into such trouble,' Antoinette said, turning sharply and moving swiftly across the kitchen.

Madeleine sighed. 'He hasn't been in trouble since...' She paused, aware of how long it had been but unwilling to suggest that Albert's behaviour had shifted dramatically since spending time with Claude. 'For a long time, now,' she said.

'Well, mother thinks...'

Madeleine rolled her eyes. 'Of course, she does,' she said shaking her head. 'Well, I don't think,' she said, picking up a large pot and placing it on the work surface. She walked into the pantry, dragged a sack of potatoes back to the table, collecting a knife en route. 'I'm going to start on the vegetables,' she said.

Her hand coordinating in a smooth rhythm, she circled the potato with the knife, the skin dropping into a bin at the side of the workbench. The potato clattered as it landed in the empty pot and she selected another, the knife poised.

She knew now she couldn't be with a man just to provide a father for her children. She mulled over her shift in perspective, wondering how the conversations with Claude had influenced her. Of course, it had dawned on her that others might think her godless or immoral, but surely to be considered as such she would have to be doing something. She didn't feel godless, though discussions with Claude had certainly caused her to question her own beliefs. And, she wasn't the only war-widow in France now bringing up two young children on her own. And, more to the point, she was doing just fine as she was. Damn them all!

Heat flooded her body in a wave, reminded of the quiet, unassuming woman who laughed with Natty and studied with Albert. The way Claude gazed at her when they talked, a

108

penetrating, steady gaze that made her feel considered. An equal. Claude never imposed on her; the men in her life always imposed. Claude listened to her; men seemed to think of listening as an unnecessary inconvenience. Even Raoul was... had been, like that. There was transcendental ease with Claude that she found quite intoxicating, drawing her in even as Claude played with the children. She could gaze at Claude all day and not feel offended. She liked Claude a lot. And, she told herself, just because Claude was a lesbian, didn't mean anything. Others would gossip because they always did, but that didn't mean anything either. Both statements landed without sticking. Suddenly aware of the unpeeled potato in her hand, the knife poised and her sister watching her, she continued to peel.

14.

Claude noticed the movement of the curtain, struggling to find her amusement, a dull ache occupying her. The door burst open as it always did, big smiling eyes staring up at her, the tiny hand grabbing hers and pulling her into the living room.

'Claude's here!' Natty said.

Claude's lips fought against the muscles that kept the smile from forming. A tight, thin-lipped expression hovered for long enough to greet the children but when she turned to face Madeleine her lips parted. She hadn't thought it possible for her heart to sink any lower. It dropped with the weight of a boulder. Madeleine looked stunningly beautiful in the dark blue dress that accentuated every glorious part of her slender body. It wasn't that she hadn't noticed her figure before, she had, but it was as if she saw Madeleine through new eyes. Dressed in elegant clothes, the hang of the dress revealing, she looked younger, like in the photograph. Entranced, her senses consumed, a warm smile formed as she stared. 'You look very beautiful,' she said. She continued to observe the heat flushing Madeleine's cheeks, struck by the contrary appearance of fine lines and tightness in her jaw.

Madeleine picked her handbag from the peg. 'I'm so sorry,' she said.

'We'll be fine, maman,' Albert said.

Madeleine raised her brows. 'I know you will, sweetheart. Mummy's just sorry she has to go out. I'd rather stay here with you,' she said.

'Just stay then,' Natty said. She didn't look up from the wooden building blocks that held her attention.

'I can't stay,' Madeleine said, softly. Natty hadn't heard.

Claude studied the weary expression, the dullness in her dark eyes, realising for the first time since Madeleine had asked her to sit for the children the previous evening, that she really didn't want to go. The thought should have eased her discomfort, but it didn't. Her chest constricted. 'I'm sorry you need to go out too,' she said, holding Madeleine's eyes, a soft sheen coating their surface.

Madeleine nodded. 'I need to go, I won't be late.' She looked at Natty then across to Albert. 'Go to bed when Claude tells you,' she said.

Albert looked up from his book. 'Oui maman,' he said.

Natty squealed as the stack of bricks fell and started to construct the tower again.

'They will be good,' Claude said. She paused, holding Madeleine's gaze. 'I hope you have a pleasant evening.' She hoped Madeleine hadn't sensed the regret in her tone, though the eyes studying her seemed to suggest Madeleine's remorse weighed in equal measure.

Madeleine cleared her throat and when she spoke her voice was hoarse, quiet. 'Would you stay for a drink with me, when I return?' she said.

Claude's heart fluttered, and a blanket of warmth embraced her. The muscles in her face softened, allowing a smile to form and the fine lines to appear at the side of her eyes. Her mind rushed ahead, and she found herself wishing that time would pass quickly between now and then. 'I would like that, very much,' she said.

Madeleine turned the bag in her hand, her eyes searching the room, the beep of a horn grabbing her attention. She put on her coat and released a sigh. 'I had better go,' she said, her feet making no move to shift her towards the door.

'Yes,' Claude said. She smiled.

Madeleine's gaze lingered on Claude.

With a gentle click, the door closed and Claude turned to see Albert gazing at her, his head resting on a tilt.

*

Madeleine walked slowly towards the parked car, her heart aching, a vivid impression of Claude's dark, sensitive gaze.

'Good evening, Madeleine,' Gustave said.

The shiver that passed through her had nothing to do with the cold evening air and everything to do with the way Gustave's eyes assessed her. 'Gustave,' she said. He seemed to release a chuckle, apparently untouched by her clipped response.

'You look very delicious this evening,' he said.

She wondered how he could see what she looked like in the dark, and she was thankful for the long coat that concealed her. She had no desire to know of the images that played out in his mind, the mere sight of him the source of sufficient discomfort. 'I need to get back for the children by nine-thirty,' she said. Her eyes averting his as she spoke, taking the seat in the car.

He climbed into the driver's seat and revved the engine. 'It's such a pleasant evening, no need to rush,' he said.

She sat in silence, staring into the darkness, the churning in her stomach voicing itself increasingly with the constant chattering that spilt from his loose tongue. She hadn't heard a word, and yet, by the time they arrived at the hotel restaurant she had already heard enough.

'What do you think, Madeleine?' he said, as they walked into the hotel.

'Hmm?'

'Should I buy shares in the automobile company?' he said.

'Um, I don't know Gustave, if you feel it is a wise investment,' she said in a tone that reflected her lack of interest.

'You are so smart Madeleine, such a rare quality in a woman. I knew you would understand,' he said, puffing out his barrel chest.

If she cared what he thought, a frown would have appeared at his enthusiastic response to her indifference; instead she released a long sigh, slipped her hand into the crook of his arm and walked with him into the restaurant. She released him as they approached the maître d'.

'Your table Monsieur Blanc,' the waiter said, dipping his head, taking her coat, pulling out a chair for her to sit, and then a chair for him.

Two embossed, leather cased menus rested on starched white linen. Two sets of highly polished silver cutlery, crystal wine glasses and small bone china side plates made up the uniform place settings. She stared at the table for what must have appeared minutes, glanced around the quiet room, the well-spaced tables offering privacy to their occupants, and more, should the occasion desire. Eventually, her eyes settled on his. 'I thought we were meeting your friend,' she said, her heart thumping.

'Ah, yes, about that! I'm afraid he had to cancel at the last minute,' he said. Avoiding her gaze, he picked up the menu and opened it. 'I thought it a shame to cancel an excellent table at the finest restaurant in town,' he said, studying the options.

Consumed by a fire that touched every part of her, she glared at him, her hands clenched in her lap. She swallowed against the burning in her throat, the words at the tip of her tongue retreating.

'I can recommend the lamb,' he said, his eyes firmly fixed on the menu.

Her jaw wouldn't move, and she stopped trying. If his skin hadn't been so thick, he would have felt the hole she bored through him with her eyes.

'A bottle of Château Haut Brion would be a fine accompaniment,' he said.

The waiter approached, and he ordered for the both of them. The menus removed, she studied him. The exposed part of the top of her breasts seemed to draw his attention, his moustache twitched on one side more than the other, and his eye on the same side of his face had a slight twitch she hadn't noticed before.

He cleared his throat. 'I thought we might spend some time getting to know each other a little better,' he said.

The waiter returned and presented the bottle, momentarily occupying his focus as he tasted and accepted the wine. She remained silent, bristling inside. The waiter dipped his head again and departed.

'I care for you, Madeleine,' he said. 'And the children, of course.'

His reference to the children sounded every bit the afterthought that it was. She sat up in the chair, the movement freeing the tension that had locked her in a position since taking the seat. She couldn't bring herself to speak though, having no wish to be rude to him and the only words on her lips deeply offensive.

'I know things have been tough for you, what with Raoul's death, God rest his soul.' He drew a small cross on his chest then brought his fingers to his mouth, as he spoke.

She observed the ritual, her head adopting a slight angle, her eyes narrowing. He had never been friendly with Raoul when he was alive.

'And of course, Albert is a bit of a handful,' he said.

Fury flared through her. How dare he!

'He clearly needs a father figure to respect,' Gustave continued. 'A boy of his age needs to be taught a thing or two, and sometimes a firm hand that a mother doesn't have.'

She motioned to speak, but he interrupted her.

'And Natalie, of course, needs to behave more like a young lady. She's becoming wild, and that never bodes well as young women age,' he said.

Tension rising to a peak, she lifted a hand from the table. The waiter arrived at that moment with two plates of lamb, placing one in front of each of them, stalling her response.

'Mmm…' He inhaled the aroma emanating from the plate, picked up his cutlery and started to eat.

Staring across at him, her stomach twisting as she watched, she clenched her hands in her lap. He moved from his food to his wine, consuming both with ease, his movements gross, his mouth revealing his food as he ate.

'You're not eating,' he said.

'I feel unwell,' she said.

'Oh, how unfortunate. The lamb is excellent. Would you mind if I finished yours?'

She shook her head, which he took as an invitation, swapping her full plate for his empty one.

'I need to go home,' she said.

He looked up, picked up his glass and slurped, half-emptying the glass. 'Oh, yes, of course,' he said. 'I'll just finish this.'

She sat up, noticed the whites of the knuckles in her lap.

'So, I was thinking, Madeleine.'

She glared at the top of his head as he ate.

'I think I would make an excellent father to your children and I would take care of your every need,' he said. Another forkful of food stopping any further words.

Madeleine's jaw dropped. Her head shaking back and forth, an overwhelming sense of disbelief replacing the rage, she stood. Her hands trembling, 'Take me home, now,' she said, managing to maintain an even tone and avoid creating a scene.

'But you haven't eaten anything,' he said, stumbling to his feet. He reached for his glass and downed the last of his wine, dabbed the napkin to his lips.

'Is everything okay with your meal?' the waiter said, rushing to assist Madeleine with her coat.

'Yes, unfortunately, I have come over quite peculiar,' she said.

'I'm terribly sorry Madame, perhaps another time,' he said.

'Thank you,' she said, stepping towards the door.

'Shall I put the meal on your account Monsieur Blanc?' the waiter said.

'Yes, yes.' Gustave gave the waiter a cursory glance before following Madeleine to the car.

She sat the furthest point from him she could, her body stiff, pressed to the door, her lips forming a tight line, her eyes focused on the road.

'I'm sorry you didn't feel up to talking tonight,' he said. 'Maybe we can revisit the conversation another time, when you are feeling recovered.'

He parked the car against the curb, a short walk from her house. She stood on the path and slammed the door. He leaned across the passenger seat and unwound the stiff window, as if they hadn't finished talking.

Madeleine took in a deep breath, the fresh air clearing her head. Being so close to home was helping to dissipate the emotional turmoil that had raged for the past hour. 'We will never have this conversation again Gustave,' she said.

'Goodnight, Madeleine. I hope you feel brighter in the morning,' he said. He righted himself in the driver's seat, crunched the gear, and pulled away.

She stood at the curb, staring into the darkness, wondering whether the evening had been just a bad dream. The fire in her belly calmed, the tension in her shoulders eased, her hands steady, she walked up the path, turned the key and stepped across the threshold into virtual darkness.

15.

'Shhhh,' Claude whispered, drawing Madeleine's eyes deeper into the room. Natty lay, tucked between the back of the sofa and Claude's shoulder, her leg hooked over Claude, sound asleep. Claude repeatedly blinked then yawned. 'Sorry, she had a nightmare, and I couldn't console her in bed, so I brought her down here.'

Madeleine adjusted to the scene. The contrast with her evening couldn't be more noticeable, and the feeling of warmth that softened her now couldn't be more opposing either.

'I didn't expect you so soon,' Claude said, wriggling to ease out from Natty's clutches.

'It's a long story,' Madeleine said, weariness suddenly coming upon her. She hung her coat and stepped towards the sofa, pulled Natty up into her arms, freeing Claude who stood. Natty murmured, but her body remained limp, and her head fell onto Madeleine's shoulder. 'I'll take her up.'

'Would you like cocoa?' Claude said.

'I think I would prefer Cognac,' Madeleine said, climbing the stairs.

Claude took her at her word, searched the kitchen cupboards, pulled out the bottle and two small glasses and returned to the living room. Madeleine stood in the low light, her arms folded across her chest, her eyes darkened by the shadows shading her skin, her gaze distant. 'Did your evening not go well?' Claude said.

Madeleine continued to stare. 'Not at all well,' she said.

'I'm very sorry,' Claude said, placing the glasses and bottle on the table. The cork squeaked as it twisted and popped as it released, infiltrating the silence. 'Would you like to talk?' The liquid glugged, the glasses filled. She picked one up, handed it to Madeleine, leaving the bottle uncorked.

Madeleine took the glass, studied the drink as she turned the glass. 'He took me out to suggest he be a suitable father to my children,' she said.

There was calmness in her voice, her eyes fixed on the pattern forming as the Cognac moved in a gentle wave around the inside of the glass.

Claude clenched her teeth as the urge to seek out Gustave and give him a piece of her mind gripped her.

'He said they needed a father to provide appropriate discipline, keep them in line,' Madeleine said, looking up and holding her gaze. 'Can you believe that?'

Claude acknowledged the disbelief with a shake of her head, felt the pain in Madeleine's gaze that rendered her speechless. How dare he, she thought, with gritted teeth.

Madeleine sipped at the drink. 'It was a table for two, his business friend cancelled, apparently.'

Claude downed the Cognac in one slug, her eyes distant.

In a quiet voice, 'I don't really want to talk about it,' Madeleine said. She looked to Claude. 'Would you just hold me, please?'

Claude stood, paralysed by the defencelessness, the eyes weary from a life that had endured so much, and in need of comfort. Slowly she placed the empty glass on the table and took the two paces that separated them. Madeleine fell into the embrace and Claude felt the warmth of her, the sweet scent of her, and melted.

Madeleine rested her head against Claude's chest.

Claude tightened the embrace and Madeleine nuzzled closer, releasing a barely audible sound that vibrated through Claude's racing heart. Claude's skin prickling, tingling down the length of her spine, the soft, tenderness of their bodies moulding effortlessly, she closed her eyes and allowed the essence of Madeleine to fill her with softness.

The movement slight, swaying, the sense of time standing still; they bathed in the comfort of each other; comfort that extended beyond the physical contact that joined them. Madeleine lifted her head, and Claude opened her eyes. They held each other's gaze, their hands remaining in the small of the other's back for a long moment, soft synchronised breaths holding the space between them.

Claude studied the wet, dark eyes, the softness she saw there paralleling the tenderness she felt. She released a hand from the curve of Madeleine's back, wiped the tears gently from her cheek, and continued to trace a line, cupping her face, holding her gaze, asking, answering. She felt Madeleine's waiting lips burning low in her belly; the ache in her heart, the love that wanted to protect Madeleine, bringing the restraint she needed to maintain. Though she couldn't bring herself to move away, and she knew she should, she wouldn't act on the desire either. You are so beautiful, she thought. Her heart heavy, her hand trembling against the softness of Madeleine, she smiled.

Madeleine was staring at Claude, exploring her. The touch gentle, the fingers stroking and brushing across Claude's dry lips, intensified the heat that burned in her cheeks. Claude tried to swallow and couldn't. Her heart pounding in her ears, Madeleine's thumb moving across her lips again, resting there and causing them to twitch, Claude stopped breathing. Madeleine was studying the contact closely. The groan seemed loud to Claude's ears, but the expression on Madeleine's face didn't change. Madeleine's palm, hot against the arch of her back, pulling her closer, Claude closed her eyes.

For a brief moment, Claude couldn't tell whether she had imagined the brush of tender lips against her own. Hoped for it, willed it maybe. Her eyes bolted open, fixed on Madeleine's warm smile, the thumb still tracing her lips. Her broken voice didn't sound very convincing. 'I need to go,' she said.

Madeleine nodded, though her eyes seemed to linger on Claude's mouth as she withdrew her hand and created a space between them.

Claude felt a cold wave sweep through her, the arms that had been wrapped around her, now wrapped around their owner. Madeleine felt the absence too, she thought, sensing the air of vulnerability that surrounded them.

'Will I see you tomorrow?' Madeleine said.

Claude nodded. 'Yes.'

Madeleine smiled.

Claude remained transfixed by the fingers that gripped Madeleine's arms close to her body in a self-embrace; fingers that had touched her with such tenderness, arms that had held her willingly just a moment ago. The small of her back still burned as she turned slowly, picked up her coat and slipped out the door.

*

Claude drew the hammer back just as Gustave approached. The head landed on the steel pin with more force than she realised she possessed. She repeated the process, again and again, the harsh sound ringing in her ears and failing to numb her thoughts. She averted his gaze, turned her back and attacked a second pin.

Xavier appeared by her side and started to knock in another pin.

Gustave changed direction and walked towards the group of men who stood chattering, their words a muffled baritone.

Xavier stopped. 'There's something about that man.' he said.

She studied the back of Gustave, the men laughing. 'Yes.' she said. She turned back to the rail, aware that Xavier continued to watch the group.

She worked in silence, as she had done most of the day, her thoughts oscillating between Gustave and Madeleine. The words he had spoken at lunch made sense to her now, the posturing and the veiled threat. Had he guessed about her? Her stomach churned. She swung the hammer with all her weight, each ring as it connected with the metal pin an outpouring of the frustration locked into her muscles. Silent tears slipped onto cold cheeks, her movements becoming more urgent as concern bubbled.

Then there was Madeleine. Oh God, Madeleine. The memory of Madeleine caressing her lips, the soft warmth of her pressed to her chest, and then the fierce heat that had risen within her. She recalled the depth in Madeleine's dark eyes that had caught her by surprise and left her wanting, in a way that she had never experienced with any other woman. The desire to bring Madeleine's lips to hers had been intense, to taste her, to succumb to the softness of her. She had sensed Madeleine's yearning too; the way Madeleine's hand had moved across her lower back; the way Madeleine's thumb had brushed across her lips; the way Madeleine had stared, keen eyes observing the fingers that explored. In vivid recollection, weakness overcoming her, she stopped working.

'Everything okay?' Xavier said. He stood the hammer at his feet, stretching his back.

She met his eyes and nodded, conscious of flushed cheeks and the trembling low in her belly. 'Yes, everything's fine,' she said.

In unison, their eyes lifted, as the command to break passed in a Chinese whisper along the line of the track. Xavier picked up his hammer, and they walked back up the track in silence, deposited the tools and ambled up the road.

'Want a drink?' he said.

She paused. 'No, thanks.'

'I'll see you tomorrow then,' he said.

'Are you not eating?'

'No, I'm going into town.'

She nodded. 'Have a good weekend.'

'Take care, Claude.'

He had crossed the road before it dawned on her he had used her shortened name. He must have overheard Madeleine at the restaurant. There was no edge to his tone. If anything, he had spoken with compassionate concern.

She pulled up her collar, thrust her hands into her pockets and started to walk. The cold already settling into the early evening, the sky darkened by the absence of a moon, there had been truth in rumours that winter was fast approaching and this night would be the coldest of the year yet.

The fluttering in her belly increased as she approached the restaurant, determined to eat quickly and then return to her room. Her heart racing, she opened the door and stepped up to the hotplate, making every effort to avoid being drawn into the dark eyes on the other side of the counter. The thrill pulsing through her told her she had failed. She had no protection where Madeleine was concerned. Madeleine's warm smile, the light reflecting in her eyes, the faint lines shaping her face, and the memory of her touch, cloaked her in emotion. Claude struggled for breath, the tiny hairs on her neck rising and releasing a flow; a rush, that settled low, stealing the power from her legs.

'Good evening, Claudette,' Madeleine said.

Claude warmed at the colour in Madeleine's cheeks and the shine in her eyes as she spoke. In a soft tone, 'Good evening, Madeleine, the food smells wonderful,' she said, though she couldn't bring her eyes from the beautifully entrancing smile to look at the hotplate.

'I hope you enjoy it.' Madeleine said, serving the chicken and vegetables. She held out the plate.

Claude took it, careful to avoid contact. 'Thank you,' she said, taking a pace to the side. She shifted her gaze to the plate in her hand. Missing the connection she looked back towards Madeleine and watched her as she served the next man in line. She looks different, she thought. Turning from the hotplate, she chose a table and sat, her back providing a natural barrier, her attention on the plate of food.

Aware of the slight tremor in her hand as she raised the fork to her mouth, she smiled in amusement. No one had ever disarmed her in this way. The light feeling, warmth flowing softly and causing her heart to flutter, the essence of Madeleine lingered. She glanced towards her again, observed the ease with which she worked, the welcoming smile with which she greeted the hungry men. She acknowledged others as they joined the table, their chatter elevating the noise in the room until a low hum filled the restaurant, plates landing on the wooden surface and the clatter of cutlery going some way to distract her thoughts. She could feel Madeleine's eyes on her as she stood. Turning, she met the dark gaze with her own, the moment extending in the absence of a queue at the hotplate. Suddenly, Madeleine broke eye contact, and her expression shifted. Claude noticed the movements become jittery, Madeleine's focus directed to the man heading towards the hotplate.

She could feel the food compress with the weight that dropped from her throat. Gustave's stare had landed on her, and remained there as he approached Madeleine. To an onlooker, his expression might appear neutral, but his eyes, unblinking, carried a slight squint and his brows sat a fraction lower than usual. One side of his moustache twitched repeatedly. She could feel the tension build around her eyes, carry down her neck and into her shoulders. Determined not to be the one to break the standoff, Madeleine's eyes shifted from him to her. He relented immediately before reaching the hotplate, his lips twisting into a smile as he addressed Madeleine. He took the offered plate and turned to the other side of the restaurant, away from Claude. Madeleine looked up, the residual effect of his presence clearly visible in her gaze. Claude breathed deeply, aware of the density of the thumping beat in her chest. She walked to the counter next to the hotplate and studied the desserts, though they were virtually identical. 'Is everything alright?' she said, her eyes on the éclairs, set out with military precision on the tray.

'Not really,' Madeleine said.

The honesty struck her, and she looked up, observed Madeleine's eyes water, helplessness gripping her. A tear spilt onto Madeleine's cheek, and she watched her swipe it away, paralysed by the distance that would remain between them. Madeleine looked to the ceiling. This is my fault, Claude thought. 'I'm so sorry,' she said in a quiet voice.

Madeleine shook her head, regained her composure.

Claude called to her in a silent plea, drawing her gaze and holding her with tenderness. 'When do you finish work?' she said. She watched the faint smile appear and then disappear.

'In an hour.' Madeleine said.

'Shall I come round?'

Madeleine nodded. 'Would you?'

'Yes.' Claude said. Sensing relief, in the softness that returned to Madeleine's expression, 'I can wait here, if you would like,' she said. The faint smile appeared again, and Claude became distracted, admiring the shape of Madeleine's lips, again.

Madeleine shifted her attention to the approaching man. 'Enjoy your éclair,' she said to Claude.

Claude glanced down and selected a plate. 'I'm sure I will,' she said.

She went to the table and ate slowly, occasionally looking towards Madeleine, one eye on Gustave. Xavier was right, there was something about the man that was deeply distasteful. It wasn't just that he was crude and held low regard for others. On the surface, he might display a strong sense of propriety, but that veneer was thin, beneath which lay a controlling, insecure man, with too much power and influence. She had seen his type before and was under no illusion that he was both a cad, and dangerous. She didn't trust that he wouldn't wield his power in whatever way necessary to get what he wanted, and that included Madeleine. The éclair lost its appeal, and she rested the fork on the plate, stood and walked to the coffee pot.

Sipping at the drink, she mulled over her thoughts. Through the corner of her eye, she noticed Gustave leaving the restaurant and her shoulders relaxed, her breath deepening effortlessly with each inhalation. She continued to take in the remaining diners, settling her gaze on Madeleine. The warm smile, directed at her, seemed to dissolve the residual tension she had felt in the presence of her boss and she eased back in the chair, watching Madeleine as she cleared the hotplate. When Madeleine returned from the kitchen and walked towards her, her heart raced.

'I can finish now,' Madeleine said.

Claude stood, her gaze unwavering. 'You look...' She sunk her hands deep into her trouser pockets, moved her tongue around a dry mouth to try to free up her words, and spoke in a soft tone. 'You look tired,' she said.

'Would you like cocoa?' Madeleine said.

Claude nodded. She followed Madeleine through the restaurant kitchen. Stepping into the house, her ears alerted to an unfamiliar voice.

'They are both asleep, though Natty didn't stop telling me that Claude tells a better story than I do,' the woman said, entering the kitchen from the living room, and eyeing Claude.

'Maman this is Claudette,' Madeleine said, looking from Claude to Regina.

Claude noticed a familiarity about Madeleine's mother that she couldn't place. She tried to dismiss the thought that their paths had crossed, though the way the woman was assessing her, Claude wondered if Madeleine's mother had a similar recollection. The niggling feeling persisted.

'Ah! Good evening Claudette. I've heard a lot about you this evening,' Regina said, her features softening.

Claude 'Good evening, Madame...' she hesitated, without a name.

'Regina. Please, call me Regina.'

'Regina, delighted to meet you,' Claude said, registering that the name wasn't familiar.

'I feel I know you very well already,' Regina said. 'Albert showed me his carvings, quite the collection. And a fine set of clothes for Marie. You are clearly very talented,' she said.

It wasn't the words that coloured Claude's cheeks, it was the way Regina eyed her up, trying to place her in a distant memory, maybe? The wave of heat spiked, and she felt sure both women would think her guilty of something sinister. Neither seemed to respond to her discomfort though, and she cleared her throat. 'Thank you,' she said.

'Right! Anyway, I need to get to work before they start complaining,' Regina said, her eyes indicating the restaurant as she picked up her handbag.

'Thank you, maman,' Madeleine said. She placed a kiss to her mother's cheek. 'I'll see you in the morning.'

'Don't stay up too late,' Regina said, her gaze shifting to Claude. 'Good night, Claudette.'

'Good night.' Claude watched the door close, the soft click, and felt able to breathe again. She caught Madeleine watching her, the warm smile holding her with tenderness, and the chuckle on Madeleine's lips. 'What is it?' she said.

'You look stunned.'

'Um! I wasn't expecting...' She glanced at the door then back to Madeleine. Fixating on the broad smile, she too grinned.

Madeleine went to the sink, filled the kettle, and set it on the stove.

Claude couldn't prevent her eyes drifting, taking in every part of her. The line of her shoulders, the narrow waist and hips that curved perfectly. The way she moved around the kitchen, it was as if she caressed everything she touched with love, and when Madeleine turned to face her, she felt that caress on her.

'Would you like a Cognac?' Madeleine said.

Claude swallowed, shaking her head back and forth. 'No. Thank you. Cocoa will be lovely.'

Madeleine smiled, her head tilting as she studied Claude. 'You don't really drink, do you?'

Claude smiled. 'No. Not really. Do you mind?'

'No. I find it quite refreshing, actually,' she said, mindful of Raoul's excessive consumption habits and Gustave's ability to drink the best part of a bottle of wine without apparent effect.

Claude mumbled, 'Hmm,' and the whistling kettle pulled her from her reverie. Madeleine turned to finish the drinks. Claude watched, heart racing.

'I'm so sorry about yesterday,' Madeleine said, stirring the cocoa. She glanced at Claude. 'I was in a bit of a state.'

'Please, don't apologise. I think I would have reacted the same way. Men can be very determined.' Her ex-lover's husband came to mind, and then her own father.

'Yes.' Madeleine continued to stir. 'Do you think all men are the same?'

Claude reflected, and Xavier came into her thoughts. 'I think most men have a strong will, and there is the expectation that they should be decisive.'

'Hmmm.'

'I think women are more often repressed by them,' Claude said and observed Madeleine's back straighten then worried that she might have offended.

In a soft voice, still stirring the drink, 'Yes, I think you are right,' Madeleine said.

When Madeleine turned to face Claude again, her eyes seemed locked in consideration.

Claude took the offered cup, and they went into the living room.

16.

Claude walked taller, her hands stuffed deep into her coat pockets, her breath hanging in the frosty air, radiant heat keeping the chill from penetrating her skin. The grin on her face turned to a silent chuckle, bubbling in her chest, absorbing her attention. Even the sound of her feet didn't reach her ears; blinded by the image of Madeleine, her heart light as she made her way home.

The route, though familiar, was pitch-black with the absence of the moon, the array of sparkling stars scattered across the sky too high to throw any significant light onto the path. Her eyes tracked her feet. Voices came and went drawing her attention briefly; two men walking in the opposite direction on the other side of the road, neither seeming to notice her as they continued their conversation, their voices loud, their words slurred.

The approaching car slowed, and she stopped walking for a moment, closed her eyes to avoid the lights that would otherwise blind her night-vision. She turned to catch a glimpse of the back of the two men occupying the front seats as the car passed. The rear lights weren't disappearing into the distance as they should though, and with a squeaking sound, the car stopped suddenly. The clicking noise alerted her, and she squinted into the darkness. She didn't see the shadow rushing towards her until the last second, crouched instinctively, too late to avoid the blow.

The crack to her head didn't register in her brain, her legs instantly crumbling beneath her, her head bouncing on the path as she fell. The man kicked several times at the unresponsive body then ran back to the car. The door slammed shut, and the vehicle sped into the night.

'Claude! Claude!'

The low tone, her name, faintly familiar, the sharp pain, everywhere, as she moved, her eyes trying to open, the searing pain through her head, eyes squinting into the darkness; seeking, trying to locate the familiar voice, eyes closing. Darkness.

'Claude! Claude!'

The voice again... drifting, the hand on her arm, the pressure on her back, fingers pressed against the side of her throat, cupping under her neck, lifting, lifting, and then the warmth.

'Speak to me, Claude!'

Me? Groaning silently, head thumping too loudly, can't think, chest hurts, head hurts, stop bouncing. Darkness.

'Who did this to you, Claude?'

Me? Who did this to me? The familiar tone, safe, floating, pain going. Darkness.

Two voices broke into her awareness. The higher pitched one, at first the words streaming too quickly for her to make them out, slowed down.

'Claude! What on earth happened? Who did this to her?'

'I didn't know where else to take her. You were the closest.'

'Bring her inside.'

Claude tried to move her eyelids, but they were too heavy. Her body pressed against something soft, her head also. The warmth that held her withdrew.

Tender touch, soothing. Burning, sweet, woody smell, comforting. Safe. Chest hurts; breathing hurts. Madeleine?

'You are safe, Claude.'

The tender touch on her cheek again, and in her hair. Pain. The hand now resting in hers, soft, warm, fingers caressing and squeezing. Better. The words registering, awareness returning, sore lips tried to move, and she heard a groan.

'Claude, can you open your eyes?'

She tried to follow the instructions, her mind saying yes. Another groan registered in her ears and she felt a mild sense of satisfaction. 'Sorry!' she mumbled.

'I'm going to get a cloth and some water, Claude. I will be back.'

She groaned again as the warm hand slipped from hers. Her arms wouldn't follow the instructions from her mind, to reach out and stop Madeleine moving away from her, her body remaining listless.

'I'll get the water.'

The man's voice again. Xavier. Footsteps fading.

'There's a cloth under the sink, and the kettle is still hot,' Madeleine said.

Crackling wood. The fire. Warmer.

'Thank you,' Madeleine said.

Madeleine. I love that voice. Warm face. Nice. 'Ow!'

'Sorry, Claude, I'm trying not to hurt you, but this might sting a bit.'

'Ouch!' Claude's eyes flickered, squinted in the dull light, closed again.

'Is she okay?' Xavier said.

'I'll be fine,' Claude mumbled, trying to raise her head. She groaned, stopped trying to move, and slumped back into the cushion.

'Don't move, you need to rest.' Madeleine said.

Claude's eyes opened and she tried to smile, wincing as her lips moved. Madeleine's wide eyes stared back at her, and then the stern expression softened, but the smile on Madeleine's lips remained strained.

'What happened?' Madeleine said.

'I don't know.' Claude searched her memory. 'There was a car, bright lights, and then it stopped.'

'Shall I get the doctor?' Xavier said.

Claude lifted her hand. 'No, I'll be fine,' she said.

'Police?' he said.

She shook her head. 'No.'

'I'll leave you with Madeleine,' he said. 'If that's alright?' he said, addressing Madeleine.

'Yes. I'll keep an eye on her,' Madeleine said. 'Thank you so much for bringing her here.'

He made his way to the front door. 'Please look after her,' he said, the gentle click of the front door leaving the room quiet, but for the crackling fire.

Madeleine broke the silence. 'Who did this to you?' she whispered, her gaze searching Claude's face. She placed the damp cloth to Claude's temple, holding it firmly in place. Her heart responded with a dull ache, to the pained expression and groaning that her actions elicited. 'I'm sorry, I don't mean to hurt you,' she said.

Claude studied Madeleine, her complexion paler than when Claude had left the house earlier, and her eyes darker, intense. 'You didn't do this to me,' she said, reaching up slowly, the movement sending a sharp, burning, sensation through her ribs. She wiped the tear trickling down Madeleine's cheek.

Madeleine washed Claude with the damp cloth, gently removing the dried blood and dust from tender skin, her other hand resting in Claude's.

'Thank you,' Claude said. She tried to shift up the sofa, tensed, the sharp pain coming again and spearing her in the chest.

'Don't try to move,' Madeleine said softly, placing the cloth in the bowl. 'I just need to check your ribs,' she said.

Claude tensed.

133

Madeleine undid the buttons on the heavy coat and slowly eased up the shirt beneath. A silent gasp jolted her, and she froze. Then her fingers moved lightly over the swelling.

Claude tried to swallow, her throat constricted, the delicate touch igniting a flash of goosebumps that spread across her skin, faster than a forest fire in the dry heat of summer. Her voice broken, 'Is it bad?' she said.

Madeleine withdrew her hand and picked up the cloth. 'It's quite swollen already,' she said. 'You may have a broken rib.'

Claude shivered when the cool cloth touched her skin and her eyes closed. The soft groan she released had more to do with the dark piercing gaze and the prickling sensation riding in waves down her spine, than the pain that gripped her body.

*

Claude opened her eyes, closed them again, opened them and moved her head, the throbbing sensation reminding her of the incident that had brought her here. A faint glow from the fireplace directed her eyes to the shadow on the floor, and she lifted herself up in the sofa, the groan on her lips remaining silent, her eyes squinting, her hand reaching to her protect her ribs.

Madeleine stirred. 'Claude!'

Claude watched her rub tired eyes as she rose from the floor. She looked beautiful.

'How are you feeling?' Madeleine said.

'Sore,' she said.

Madeleine knelt and took Claude's hand. 'You scared me,' she said.

Claude cleared her throat. 'I'm okay,' she said.

'No, you are not.' Madeleine said, moving backwards, her head rising, her hands squeezing. 'Someone beat you up last night. You have a lump on your head the size of an egg, and you may have broken ribs, as far as I can tell.'

Claude released Madeleine's hand and inspected her head. 'Ouch!'

'Exactly!' Madeleine said, watching the scrunched expression deepen. 'Someone tried to kill you, Claude.'

She coughed. 'I don't think so,' she said, knowing full well that if that had been the intention, she wouldn't be here now. 'Scare me, maybe.'

Madeleine had cupped her face and was staring into her eyes, her thumb moving lightly under her eye. The fingers trembled against her skin, and she reached up, pressed Madeleine's hand to her cheek, moved the palm over her lips. Inhaling the scent of Madeleine, she closed her eyes.

Madeleine stilled.

Claude opened her eyes and released Madeleine's hand. She reached up with a smile at Madeleine's dishevelled hair, and swept it behind her ear. 'Thank you for being here,' she whispered.

Madeleine started to tremble. 'I was so afraid,' she said, and a tear slipped onto her cheek. 'Who would do such a thing?'

Claude held Madeleine's gaze. 'I don't know,' she said.

Madeleine looked at Claude.

'It's alright,' Claude said, settling back into the chair, wincing as she moved.

'Would you like a drink?' Madeleine said.

Claude's tongue moved around the inside of her mouth. 'Yes, please.' she said. Madeleine stood and went to the kitchen. The deep breath pulled at her ribs, and her eyes closed again.

'Claude! Claude!'

The squeals of delight thrust Claude's eyes wide open, immediately before the impact that sent a bolt of lightning through her. Suppressing the yelp, she tensed and groaned, her hands keeping Natty from pressing too firmly against her chest, as her eager arms swept around her neck and squeezed. The sharp pain easing, her breathing resumed, 'Good morning, Natty,' she said.

Natty released her, studied her intently. 'Did you fall over?' she said.

Claude's mouth twitched. 'Yes, I did.'

Natty sat back in the chair, lifted her nightdress. 'Look at my graze. I did it at school, in the playground,' she said, pointing.

Claude shifted, grimaced with the pain, and squinted at a healthy-looking knee. 'Did it hurt?' she asked.

Natty leapt up and ran into the kitchen. 'Maman, Claude fell over, she's got a bruise like mine,' she said.

Madeleine returned with the coffee and an apologetic smile.

Albert descended the stairs, studied her with narrow eyes, his lips tight. He swallowed. 'Are you alright?' he said.

She nodded. 'A bit sore, but I'll be fine. I tripped on my way home and banged my head on the curb,' she said.

He knew she was lying, and she knew he knew.

He turned his gaze from her. 'Morning, maman,' he said.

'Morning Albert, did you sleep well?' Madeleine said.

Claude sipped the hot drink, the events of the previous night fading in the homely atmosphere, comforted by the sense of belonging that cloaked her in love and kindness. She lay back in the seat, watched Madeleine stoking the fire, Natty playing on the floor, Albert laying the table for breakfast, and fought the urge to jump up and help.

Madeleine turned from the fire and stepped closer, looked down at her, hands resting on her hips. 'I assume you will stay with us today?' she said.

Claude tilted her head, entranced by the moisture coating Madeleine's lips and the gentle tone in her voice. She returned a smile, suspended in an air of mutual vulnerability.

Madeleine cleared her throat. 'Good,' she said and went to the kitchen.

*

Madeleine placed a plate stacked with pancakes on the table much to the delight of Natty and Albert. Claude eased out of the chair, her arm clamped around her ribs, groaning as she tried to move. Eventually standing, she went with leaden legs to the table and sat slowly, a shiver passing through her, her face paling with the effort.

Madeleine watched the unsteady movements, through a narrow gaze. 'Would you like more coffee?' she said.

Claude managed a half-smile. 'Please.'

Madeleine studied her. 'Would you like a bath, after breakfast?' she said.

Claude nodded.

Madeleine returned to the kitchen and Claude watched the children dive into the breakfast feast. Slowly she explored her head, delicately pressing across her scalp. Her mouth twitched as she located another tender spot. She glanced at the bruising that had already started to appear around the ballooned flesh on the back of her right hand. She must have tried to protect herself. She slowly clenched and stretched stiff fingers, her thoughts drifting to the car with the headlights, the shadow before the darkness came, Xavier finding her, and then Madeleine tending to her. She had been lucky.

*

Madeleine watched through the corner of her eye, Claude grimacing as she moved, trousers dropping to the floor, trying to unbutton the shirt, failing and then getting frustrated.

'Do you need a hand?' she said, turning the taps, the water eventually stopping but for a slow drip.

Claude swallowed, her hands stalling. 'I... I think...I.'

Madeleine smiled. 'I was brought up with three sisters,' she said. She reached towards the shirt and undid the top button, and then the next.

Claude froze, her stomach fizzing with the feel of Madeleine's fingers brushing her skin, twisting the buttons to release them, each movement revealing her. Goosebumps accumulated in a rash, tingling as they spread across her.

Madeleine's adept movements suddenly faltered, the button refusing to budge from the thick cotton material and her eyes met Claude's. 'Sorry,' she said.

Claude studied the dark intensity in Madeleine's lingering gaze, the heat that suffused her cheeks, her teeth pulling gently on her lip, and the fingers that trembled against her skin.

Madeleine fumbled. Coordination seemingly a challenge, she undid another button then stopped. The words flew out, unchecked, on the back of a gasp. 'You have no bra on,' she said.

Claude blurted out a laugh, reached for her ribs. 'Aww!' she groaned, chuckling. 'No.' she said. 'I was trying to explain before. I don't wear one.'

Aware of the sensitivity of her nipples pressing against the loose material and Madeleine's gaze on her partly exposed chest and the pounding behind her ribs, a wave of goosebumps flooded her again. With the realisation that Madeleine was reaching towards her to undo the last button, she stopped the hand. 'I should be able to manage,' she said softly.

Madeleine studied Claude's hand covering hers for a moment, her lips parting then closing. She looked up, fixed her gaze on Claude, and with small movements continued to release the shirt. As she twisted the fabric, Claude removed her hand and allowed her arms to hang by her side.

Immobilised, her heart pounding harder against tender ribs, her breathing coming in short, shallow gasps, Claude stood. The heat flaming through her scolded her cheeks. She could feel it. Madeleine must be able to see it too. Oh God, did Madeleine know the effect this situation was having on her? Could Madeleine know how much she wanted the feel of her against her skin, caressing her, kissing her, holding her, and how much she wanted to touch her the same way too? The tingling low in her core seemed to sap the last remaining strength in her legs with every second that passed, the pressure building and pulsing. There was a question in Madeleine's eyes, her awkward persistence with the buttons and then that dark intensity, again. Her stomach trembling, her breathing laboured, she remained paralysed.

Did Madeleine feel it too?

She should stop her now before it was too late. It was already too late, Claude countered, in defence. She had already reached the point of not trusting herself. But Madeleine was her own woman too, and free to make her own choices. The scent of her seemed stronger, the closeness overwhelming and weakening her resolve. Madeleine was pulling at the shirt, separating it down her length, her eyes fixed on hers. She tried to swallow, but her mouth was dry.

Madeleine stared. The shirt hung open, and her eyes moved slowly down Claude's body to the smooth, soft ridges that defined Claude's stomach, and then the slender hips. She followed the same line back up, to meet Claude's eyes. 'You are beautiful,' she said.

Claude smiled a tight smile that tried to maintain a distance between them. Madeleine was tracing the line of the shirt to the collar, with her fingers, reaching beneath the fabric and slipping it from her shoulders. Claude released a soft gasp, and noticed Madeleine's lips twitch into a brief smile. She looked away suddenly.

'I hope I didn't hurt you?' Madeleine said.

'Hmm, no,' Claude said, her voice hoarse. Madeleine was staring at her breasts, reaching out, fingers gently caressing without touching.

'They really hurt you,' Madeleine said, tracing the bruised swelling on Claude's ribs.

Suddenly spurred by a need so intense she couldn't contain it, Claude took Madeleine's hand and held it gently to the injury. 'It's not too bad,' she said, her voice barely a whisper. The warmth of the hand instantly drowned out the pain, and Madeleine's dark eyes rose to meet her. The space between them seemed to close, their hands remaining steady, drawing them into each other. Madeleine was moving, or was she? She closed her eyes, tried to focus on breathing deeply, every part of her aching; opened her eyes. 'Madeleine,' she whispered, before her lips stung with the softness of the touch, the effect igniting every cell in her body simultaneously. The soft lips lingered with gentleness, barely touching, caressing. Falling, drowning in softness, she succumbed to the kiss.

Madeleine eased back, her cheeks inflamed. She moved as if to speak but no words came. She explored her lips briefly with her finger then dropped her hand to her heart. 'I'm so sorry, I don't know what came over me,' she said, her eyes lively and evading Claude.

'Madeleine.' Claude spoke softly and reached for Madeleine's hands. 'Are you okay?' she said, aware of the trembling that still shook her in waves.

Madeleine nodded, struggled to hold Claude's gaze, and released a long breath. 'I think so,' she said.

Claude squeezed the hands in hers.

'I'll let you bathe,' Madeleine said, pulling her hands free and leaving the bathroom without a second glance.

Claude stood, allowing her heart to calm, and the moment to fully register, savouring the brief touch. Madeleine had just kissed her. She wasn't dreaming. Her lips tingled and she touched them, reacquainting with the feel of Madeleine's soft, delicious mouth. Aware that she had started to shiver, she inched her underclothes to the floor and stepped into the bath, the pain in her ribs seeming to disappear, the sensation in other parts assuming a pleasant ache.

17.

Madeleine eased the spoon around the large pot, her regular rhythmical movements made erratic by her thoughts, her gaze unfocused, and seemingly unfazed by her mother observing from across the kitchen.

She had kissed Claude! A wave of exhilaration passed through her and instantly flushed her cheeks. She could still feel the tenderness etched on her lips, the heat that suffused her then, as now, the softness and thrill combining to form an overwhelming sensation, the like of which she had never experienced before. A gentle hum still vibrated through her.

She had left the bathroom in a flurry, consumed with emotion, and stood in the kitchen, her hands trembling against the work surface, her heart pounding for some time. She had tried to occupy herself by preparing the meal, but the knife shook in her hand with the image of Claude's pert breasts, the smooth muscular stomach and lean hips, and then there was the unique scent of her that had lingered even in her absence. She had never been drawn to another in this way. She had felt giddy over a boy when she had been very young, but it was nothing like this. This was deep, enduring, and so desperately compelling.

Aware that her musings had brought her work to a halt, she started to stir the pot again, but thoughts of Claude came to her through the rhythmical movement of the spoon and she drifted too easily.

Claude had stood in the kitchen after the bath, her hair damp, her face fresh, the bruising around her eye and cheek raw. Madeleine had felt her deeply then, in the pressure in her heart, and the urge to take Claude into her arms and kiss her again had been all consuming. Claude had stared at her and asked if she was okay, and she had lied unconvincingly.

Madeleine had continued to cook, served the food, and entertained the children, and after Claude had left the house, she felt her again in the hollow emptiness that remained. Even the children's voices hadn't filled the space.

Madeleine could feel Regina still studying her from across the kitchen, drawing her awareness to the present, the pot and the spoon in her hand, and pricking her conscience. She released a deep breath, looked down at the bubbling beef, and stirred with vigour. She tapped the ladle on the side of the pot and rested it on the stove. Turning, she caught her mother's eye, cleared her throat, picked up the knife, and started to chop.

'Gosh it's cold out there,' Beatrice said, easing through the door with a crate of supplies.

'I'll give you a hand,' Madeleine said, thankful for the chance to move from her mother's intense stare.

'The snow is heavy already. They think it will block the main road,' Beatrice said.

Regina's eyebrows lifted a fraction as she nodded.

Trays stacked, Beatrice stood, chest rising and falling with a wheeze. 'They say the dam's finished,' she said. 'And the Prime Minister is coming. It's confirmed.'

'That will be good for business,' Regina said.

Madeleine looked between her mother and sister, the conversation passing her by. 'Yes,' she said, her tone betraying her.

Regina walked to the sink, filled the kettle and placed it on the stove. 'You seem distracted, Madeleine,' she said.

'Hmm. Sorry, I was just thinking about the dam,' she said.

Lines formed across Regina's lips as she studied her daughter. She had been made aware of Madeleine's liaison with Claude. The butcher had passed on the information that had been given to him from a reliable source in the town. In fact, it seemed the whole town was talking about Madeleine Vietti, and the railway woman. The railway woman had stayed overnight and hadn't left the house until the following evening, in the dark of night, they had said. What on earth was Madeleine thinking? And what about the children?

She had seen the look in her daughter's eyes when she had introduced Claudette for the first time. The intensity between them had been palpable; she had known it then, that this situation was going to cause a problem. Someone, it seemed, had already tried to take care of things, according to the rumours. Madeleine could get hurt too. The lines across her lips formed deep crevasses. The whistle interrupting her thoughts, she made coffee.

'Oh! Did you hear, some chap from the railway got beaten up on Friday?' Beatrice said. She sipped at her tea, brimming with excitement at the local gossip.

Madeleine stopped, the cup poised, her heart suddenly racing. The contents starting to sway, she placed the cup on the table.

'He was on the way home from the bar, apparently,' Beatrice said.

Madeleine looked across the table, her mother's searching eyes staring back at her. 'Gosh,' she said.

'Got ruffled up quite badly,' Beatrice continued.

Madeleine stood. 'Biscuits anyone?' she said, heading to the pantry. She waited for a moment in front of the shelves, looking with unseeing eyes, breathing slowly, Beatrice's voice fading into incoherence. Taking a deep breath and blowing out hard, she focused on the biscuit tin, collected it up and walked back to the table.

'Apparently, it was another railway chap who did it,' Beatrice said. 'Can you imagine if we beat each other up every time we had a disagreement?' She laughed, dived into the biscuits, dipped one into her coffee and slipped it into her mouth. She continued talking around the food. 'Cl...' Coughing violently, the words stalled.

Madeleine froze. Everyone knew Claude had been attacked?

Beatrice continued to cough, patting at her chest. 'Wrong way,' she said, eventually coming out of the fit. 'Clement,' she said. 'Never liked him particularly. Something about his eyes being too close together. Mind, he had it rough; no father and his mother always drinking,' she said.

Madeleine suppressed a groan as realisation dawned. The sudden absence of tension causing her to muscles to soften, her shoulders dropped, and she took a deep breath. 'Gosh!' she said again. She knew of Clement; everyone did. The instant sense of relief passed, replaced by an altogether different feeling, concern turning over in her mind. Who attacked Clement? It all seemed too much of a coincidence. Did Clement attack Claude?

'Are you okay?'

Beatrice was speaking to her, wide-eyed, her mouth moving with another biscuit.

'Madeleine's fine, just a little distracted today,' Regina said. She reached across the table and squeezed her daughter's hand, drawing dark eyes towards her, a tight-lipped smile and head nodding.

'I'm fine,' Madeleine said, the sound of the door suddenly distracting her.

'Snow's thick on the road already,' Maude said, stamping her feet on the mat, snow-sprinkled lightly on top of the logs in the basket she carried.

'Yes,' the three women said in unison.

Beatrice poked another biscuit in her mouth. 'Did you hear about the beating?' she said excitedly to Maude.

Madeleine's eyes lowered as she stood. 'Honestly, Bea. You're such a gossip!' she said, her tone sharper than usual.

Maude's gaze moved from her mother to Beatrice, who shrugged, and then to the back of Madeleine as she marched to the other side of the kitchen. Maude's expression shifting from a frown to wide-eyed confusion, she went to the stove shaking her head, and started stacking the wood.

*

The day had passed quickly until lunchtime when Claude hadn't shown up, and worry had swiftly turned to panic even with Xavier's words of reassurance. Madeleine had stared at the graze across his swollen knuckles, and a sense of knowing had passing between them. Claude isn't in work today, he had said, the glint of revenge lighting up his eyes as he spoke. He had taken food for Claude, and she had made sure the portion was a large one. It had occurred to her more than once during the afternoon to go to Claude's room, to check for herself and provide any necessary help she was sure Claude would need. She had even stopped at the kitchen door, coat in hand and no rational reason for leaving, her mother's quizzical gaze bringing her to her senses.

Now, the snow two feet deep in places and glistening under the light of dusk, she watched through the steamy kitchen window; Albert and Natty pushing the growing ball of snow up and down the backyard, wondering, hoping, that Claude would come to the restaurant for dinner. The thought of not seeing Claude sat uneasily, aching emptiness expanding within her.

The door opening drew Madeleine's eyes fleetingly. 'Hey Antoinette,' she said, in an air of disappointment.

'Gosh it's thick out there,' Antoinette said, unwrapping from her coat. She walked to the kitchen window and smiled. 'They don't seem to feel the cold,' she said. She looked at Madeleine. 'How are you?'

They had obviously been talking, she thought. 'I'm fine,' she said, continuing to gaze out the window.

'I'll take over from here,' Antoinette said, taking the knife from Madeleine's hand and pointing her to the door.

'Of course.' Madeleine stared at the entrance to the restaurant, the weight of the evening shift releasing in a sigh. 'Thank you,' she said. She hesitated at the door then turned to Antoinette. 'Would you mind staying later? There's something I need to do after work.'

Antoinette nodded. 'Be careful, Madeleine,' she said.

'If I'm really late, can you stay over?' Madeleine said.

Antoinette nodded again. 'Of course.'

Tight-lipped and with a brief nod, Madeleine stepped through to the restaurant, picked up the basket of clean cutlery and began to file the items into their appropriate drawers. Returning systematically for napkins, salt, pepper, and mustard, she replenished the condiments. The evening wouldn't pass quickly enough, no matter how diligently she worked.

*

Madeleine counted the two hundredth man through the hotplate, a sense of urgency overtaking her. There may be a few stragglers to come through, but Beatrice and her mother could handle the rest. She placed the serving utensils on the tray, collected the food parcel and stepped through to the kitchen. Removing her apron, 'I need to go out,' she said. Avoiding eye contact with her mother and Beatrice, she picked up her coat. 'Antoinette will stay with the children until I get back,' she said. She stuffed the package into her handbag, walked back through the restaurant, out the front door and into the cold blast.

'Gosh, Madeleine! Is the kitchen on fire?' Gustave said, as she almost tumbled into him.

He held her shoulders, peaked through the window and then looked at her with amusement, his twitching moustache causing her skin to crawl. She twisted out of his grip and glanced at her shoulder. 'Good evening to you, Gustave,' she said, in a tone laced with irritation.

'I was just coming in for dinner,' he said.

'Beatrice will serve you,' she said.

'But it's rather late to be going out, Madeleine. I wouldn't want any harm to come to you,' he said.

She held his gaze; the corner of his eye twitching and he cleared his throat. 'I think I will be safe, don't you?' she said.

'Take care, the snow is quite treacherous,' he said, glancing down the road. 'Good evening to you, Madeleine.' He dipped his hat, stepped around her and into the restaurant.

She closed her eyes and gathered her breath allowing her heart to settle, opened them and focused on the road leading into town.

The snow had stopped falling, and the path was brighter for the glistening white on its surface. A silent hush hung in the space around her. Eventually, her feet moved. The rhythmical crunching gathered speed, and her breath frosted in air that burned her throat and lungs. Her heart thumping, she couldn't help but look around her as she walked.

Passing the entrance to the railway site, she looked into the darkness and goose bumps shot up her spine and worried the back of her neck. She looked over her shoulder, realising the only sound was coming from her feet on the snow.

The town lights coming into view, her pace slowed, and her heart quieted. The guesthouse was only a hundred metres into town, before the main high street and shops. She had passed it many times heading into town, only recently noticing its rundown appearance. The other evening, the night of the meeting, she had seen two women entering the place, ladies of the night in brightly coloured dresses inappropriately short for the time of year. Gustave's eyes had strayed past her at the time, and he had released a snorting-groaning sound.

She stared up at the three-storey building, and it occurred to her she didn't know which was Claude's room. A sinking feeling landed. She would go to every room if she needed to, she determined, opening the front door and stepping into the hallway. She poked her head into the first room, the sweet smell of pipe-tobacco, recently smoked she guessed, and logs almost spent, glowing in the fireplace. The room had a cosy feel, heady with a robust male perfume. She walked down the short corridor and into the dining room. Dishes neatly stacked on the sideboard, the tablecloths wiped clean; suds merged with bleach in a familiar taste at the back of her throat. The place was spotless. Laughter stole her awareness from the room suddenly, and she rushed into the corridor and followed the footsteps up the stairs. 'Excuse me,' she said.

The man closest to her stopped and looked down, his bright eyes, curious, before he spoke. 'Hello,' he said. He smiled, and his demeanour seemed soft and welcoming.

'I'm looking for Claude.' Her mind faltered with the pace of her heart. 'Claudette,' she said.

'Second floor, room on the right,' he said, indicating with his head. He raised his hand in salute. 'Good evening, Madame.'

'Thank you.' She waited, watching, his feet heavy on the stairs as he climbed, chatting merrily with the man in front of him until the closing of the door muffled their voices. She started up the stairs with a rising sense of anticipation.

Standing outside Claude's bedroom, her heart thumping, trying to settle her breathing, she imagined what the inside must look like. Did it have the same dark, patterned décor as the hallway? How big was it? Did the curtains close properly? Did sound travel into the room, as it seemed to, from the rooms she had passed? She admonished her thoughts, looked around

149

her and tapped lightly on the door. She hadn't expected the rush of energy that overwhelmed her, and instantly wished Claude hadn't heard the knock, or better still wasn't in. Her concerns streaming incoherently, the door opened, and all thought evaded her. The shadow under Claude's eyes as darker than Madeleine remembered, the colour of her cheeks paler, and she looked as if she had lost weight, though that seemed an impossibility given she had none to lose.

'Madeleine!'

Claude looked surprised. Of course, she would be. Finding her tongue, 'I hope I'm not disturbing you,' Madeleine said.

'No, I was just resting.'

Claude seemed to hesitate to invite her into the room. 'I brought you something to eat,' she said, reaching into her handbag and handing out the parcel.

'Sorry, come in.' Claude said, taking the gift and stepping back. She closed the door behind Madeleine.

Madeleine stood in the centre of the room, clutching her handbag in front of her, taking in the space in the subdued light. The room, sparsely decorated, held the essence of Claude, she thought, the spirit of her, and she could feel the bag trembling in her hands.

'It's not much,' Claude said, following Madeleine's eyes from the walls to the bed, and the small bedside table.

Biting on the inside of her lip, trying to stem the burning desire that had her captivated, Madeleine stared at Claude; studied her in the most exquisite detail. The short hair precisely trimmed, perfectly clipped over her ears, her pulse visible through the smooth skin leading to the base of her neck, and the rise and fall of her chest. One hand rested lightly on her ribs, the fingers gently caressing the shirt that covered her beautiful body. The urge to see that body again peaked and triggered a new sensation in the pit of her stomach. Her hands dropped to her side, and she released the bag to the floor.

Claude's gaze disarming her, Madeleine inched forward, closing the space between them. Her hand met Claude's at her ribs, and Claude's dark eyes shifted there. She looked to their hands, the warmth of Claude's shirt against her palm, Claude's palm locking them together. When she looked up, her breath stopped, her lips parted, and she closed her eyes, the image of Claude's lips on hers becoming a reality. The gentleness she discovered, more exquisite than she had imagined, and the intensity that burned with hunger so fierce. She fell into the kiss, and in the heat of passion, a desire to explore and experience Claude rose quickly within her. Claude's strength and confidence around her, drawing her closer, Claude's lips kissing her with increasing urgency, cheeks hot against hers, her lips parted, and Claude's tongue met hers. Intoxicated by emotion, her fingers eased naturally beneath Claude's shirt. She murmured at the sense of the hot skin to her cold fingers, and Claude jolting in response. She sensed the tiny prickles dancing across Claude's skin, her fingertips tracing the shape of her, the muscular form that had held her fascination since seeing her for the first time. Claude's mouth so soft, so sweet, unhurried kisses to her cheeks, her eyes; fingers sweeping through her hair, hot-breath against her ear; the tiny hairs responding to the tenderness of Claude's mouth against her neck. 'Claude!' she moaned.

The gravel-like tone in Madeleine's voice seemed to charge the energy between them.

Claude pulled back and looked at her with fierce intensity. 'You are so beautiful,' she said.

Claude was undoing the buttons on her coat, slowly, deliberately, and slipping it from her shoulders, and she shuddered as if suddenly vulnerable.

Claude came to her again with soft lingering kisses to the top of her exposed breasts, and she held her there, immersed in the softness of her. Claude's tongue aroused her and then came to her mouth again with increased firmness, quashing the groan that hovered on her lips.

Claude eased out of the kiss and gently lifted Madeleine's hair from her face. She traced the line of Madeleine's jaw, brushing across swollen lips, and parting them with a small downward movement of her thumb.

Claude took Madeleine's mouth again, with sensitivity, and at that moment she experienced Claude as if she were making love to her soul.

18.

Claude looked out from the window of the breakfast room, a light smattering of snow falling onto the white landscape, throwing light into the early morning. She sipped at the coffee, tepid and too coarse for her taste, swallowed, and bit into the pastry. She continued to watch, sparkling flakes dancing and growing heavier. Releasing a sigh, awareness of the stiffness that remained locked into her ribs, she massaged the spot. By the time she walked into town the sun would be up. She could at least get a decent coffee before heading to the bookstore to collect the Christmas present she had ordered for Albert. She had already bought Natty another doll and a dress set, hat and boots. She finished the pastry and walked out of the room.

Rows of bunting lined the streets in blue, white and red; flags pinned to railings and protruding from windows flapped with vigour. With the opening of the dam fast approaching, and Christmas just around the corner, there was a bustling excitement about the place. Cheery smiles greeted her as she passed by storefronts, vendors cheerily sweeping snow into piles at the side of the road.

Arms wrapped tightly around her, body hunched, she dived into Café Noir, the tinkling bell announcing her arrival and a wall of steam stinging her face. 'Bonjour Pierre.'

'Bonjour, Mademoiselle Dupont, how are you today?'

'I'm good, thank you.'

'Your ribs are healing, I hope,' he said, keen eyes on the tight grip with which she held herself.

She released her arms and smiled. 'Yes, much better thank you! It's freezing today,' she said, shaking her arms then blowing into clasped hands. 'Bitterly cold.'

Rumour had soon spread about Clement assaulting her, and his actions hadn't gone down well. In spite of his protestations that he had been put up to it, by a stranger who paid him handsomely, he had been forced to leave town under instruction never to return. She hadn't welcomed the attention, and the *railway woman* had become a title she would have to live with. Some folks looked at her oddly, but most welcomed her with open arms. Pierre was one of the latter. She approached the bar and greeted him with a kiss to each cheek.

'Coffee?' he said.

She nodded, taking a seat at the empty bar. The door chimed and a man she didn't recognise entered, ordered a coffee and sat at a table by the window.

'All ready for the grand opening?' she said.

Pierre chuckled. 'I will be here,' he said, with a shrug of his shoulders. He picked up his cigarette, took a long drag, the smoke finding its way out as he spoke. 'Are you going to join the celebrations at the restaurant?'

'Yes, I offered to help Madame Vietti with the catering.' Heat spread through her at the thought of Madeleine.

A week had passed since Madeleine had visited her room and the imprint of her hadn't faded. The soft kisses that had lingered between them until the early hours, fingertips that had barely touched her skin yet affected her so profoundly as to leave her weak and wanting.

She hadn't been able to work since the incident, but had walked to the restaurant for lunch the last couple of days. Her appetite suppressed by the fluttering in her stomach, she had picked at her food and Xavier had nagged her to eat. The daily routine, even the nagging, had provided a bizarre sense of purpose. Gustave had kept his distance, extending common courtesy and wishing her a speedy recovery in front of the others, and always seating himself at a table other than hers, but that didn't ease the discomfort she experienced in his

154

presence. Madeleine's expression dulled too, whenever he appeared, and it had occurred to her that Madeleine had grown to dislike him.

'Of course,' Pierre said.

'Natty has been unwell this week,' Claude said, enjoying the cordial nature of the conversation. She rubbed at her ribs. Natty hadn't quite understood the pain she was in as she had snuggled into her, snuffling with a blocked nose. Every time Natty had wriggled she had tensed, her breath refusing to release, and Natty fidgeted a lot she had decided.

'Not too bad, I hope,' he said, placing the coffee in front of her.

'Just a cold, but she's an impatient patient,' she said.

He chuckled.

She sipped at the hot liquid, the bitter sensation tickling her throat. 'It's good,' she said.

The door clicked, the bell rang, and another man entered and took a seat. She glanced at him fleetingly then finished her coffee, put two coins on the bar and stood. 'Have a good day, Pierre,' she said, bracing before she stepped out the door.

She walked up the street and into the bookstore, and the heady aroma of leather and paper, and the palpable silence that filled the small space. She walked through to the rear of the shop, up two narrow steps and to the right, where a round coffee table and set of three armchairs defined an intimate reading area. She picked the well-thumbed book from her pocket before removing her coat, relaxed into the chair, and started to read.

She turned the pages, lost in the passing of time, footsteps coming and going outside of her awareness, her eyes soaking up the words on the page.

'Claude!'

Her eyes shot up, and she snapped the book shut, standing abruptly before focusing on the face behind the voice. 'Madeleine!' she said, raking her fingers through her hair. 'I didn't expect to see...'

Madeleine smiled. 'Me neither,' she said. She looked to the front of the shop, and then to Claude.

Claude felt nourished by the sparkling eyes and responded with an encouraging smile. 'Will you join me?' she said, pointing to the seat next to hers, overcome with light-headedness.

Madeleine inched past her.

Claude mumbled incoherently as Madeleine's fingers trailed across her abdomen, and warm breath caressed her cheek. The impulse to pull her into an impassioned kiss didn't pass as Madeleine took the seat next to hers.

'What are you reading?' Madeleine said, glancing at the book.

'Umm, it's called The Well of Loneliness, by Radclyffe Hall.'

'Is it any good?'

Claude flushed, minded of the lesbian content. 'I think so,' she said. 'How's Natty?'

'At school, thankfully.'

Claude smiled, watched Madeleine ease back in the chair and rest her head, and wondered how beautiful she looked. They had never met outside of the restaurant, or the house and most often the children were present when their paths crossed. Madeleine's eyelashes fluttered, and her irises seemed lighter, brighter; her skin smooth, but for the fine lines accentuating the shape of her eyes; she looked... different, younger. 'You look beautiful,' she whispered. When Madeleine smiled the lines deepened, and she looked radiant.

Madeleine lifted her head, held Claude's gaze. 'I've missed being with you,' she said.

The intensity like lightning, struck her, fuelling her desire to pull Madeleine into her arms and kiss her, restrained by circumstances alone. 'Come back with me,' Claude said.

Madeleine nodded and stood.

'I just need to collect something,' Claude said, rising from the seat.

'I'll meet you outside,' she said.

Madeleine set off towards the front of the shop, Claude's eyes on the slight sway of her hips.

Claude approached the counter, her heart racing. 'I've come to collect a book,' she said. 'The name is Dupont.'

The woman studied her, checked through paperwork and then stepped into a small back office, reappearing with a book wrapped in brown paper and tied with string. 'It's already paid,' she said.

'Yes, thank you.' Claude hastily tucked the package under her arm and stepped out the door.

'Hello, Claudette!'

Claudette stopped and her jaw tightened. 'Monsieur Blanc,' she said, forcing the words through a tight smile.

'I was just saying to Madame Vietti how spectacular the town looks, with all the preparations coming along,' he said.

His twitching moustache and eyes scanning the decorations with a sense of self-satisfaction riled Claude, leaving her speechless.

'Of course, it needed influence of the right kind,' he said. Without pause, he continued. 'I take it you will be back to work on Monday, Claudette?'

'Yes.' she said.

'Very good.' He looked to Madeleine. 'Perhaps I could offer you a lift home,' he said, holding out his arm.

'No, thank you Gustave, I have business to attend to in town,' she said, her tone clipped.

'Hmm,' he mumbled looking at Claude and then at Madeleine. 'The paths are thick with snow, and icy, Madeleine. Do you think it wise to walk all that way on your own?'

I walked here, Madeleine thought.

'I can walk with Madeleine if she would prefer the fresh air,' Claude said.

'Thank you, that would be most kind, Claudette,' Madeleine said before he could respond.

'Harrumph!' he grumbled.

Claude watched Gustave's moustache take on a life of its own and swallowed the laughter bubbling in her chest. She smiled politely, the muscles in her face remaining taut.

Gustave pumped up his chest, preened his facial hair to a fine point on either side of his face, and looked to Madeleine. 'I hope you make the right choice for the sake of your children, Madeleine. Good day to you both,' he said. He turned away, climbed into his car, and drove off.

Claude released a long slow breath. 'Are you okay?' she said a tremor building inside her as her muscles relaxed. Madeleine was shaking too, her face pale, her eyes heavy, fatigued.

'Gustave unnerves me,' she said.

'Yes,' Claude said.

'Are you okay?' she said.

Acutely aware of the distance the man's presence had created between her and Madeleine, 'I have some concerns,' Claude said.

'About us?' she said, lowering her eyes.

'I don't want any harm to come to you or the children,' Claude said. 'Shall I walk you home?'

'There really is no need.'

Claude stepped closer, Madeleine's perfume catching her awareness. 'I would very much like to escort you home, Madame Vietti,' she said.

Madeleine looked up at the warm smile. 'In that case, I shall accept your kind offer, Mademoiselle Dupont,' she said.

Claude held out her arm, and Madeleine hooked hers through it without hesitation. They set off in silence, the snow crunching under their feet.

'How long has your family lived here?' Claude said as they walked.

Madeleine squeezed her arm. 'Forever, I think. My great-grandfather had a brasserie of the same name, before the restaurant. It was much smaller then of course, and when they built the railway, he decided to open the place we have now. The workers came to eat because it was close, and cheap. He didn't have the contracts we have now, but word got around, and the business grew quickly. He was lucky, I guess.'

'The harder you work, the luckier you get,' Claude said.

Madeleine turned to face Claude with a smile. 'How did you get to be so wise, so young?' she said.

Claude's cheeks flushed, mindful of her life in Paris. She dismissed the thought that Madeleine might look at her in a different light if she knew the truth about the time she had spent there. Paris was a long way from Génissiat, and she had changed since then too.

Yvette had been a long time ago, her first experience of being with a woman. The older woman had been right that their relationship was just an intense affair. Wild nights had followed discrete daytime liaisons, and although Yvette was not the love of her life, the pain when they parted had been excruciating. The twenty years in age that had separated them had shown in many ways; Yvette's children being older than her; Yvette controlling her, dictating when they would meet and often leaving her waiting; and then there was Yvette's husband. The upside was that she had learned how to delight woman. Yvette had been a very attentive and experienced lover, and she a very keen student. 'My father,' she said, her attention back to the question. It wasn't a complete untruth.

'He sounds like an interesting man,' Madeleine said, her tone thoughtful. 'My father was distant, detached. I think he and maman loved each other, there has never been anyone else for her, but he was never that involved with us. He used to work long hours at the restaurant, and we would hardly ever see him,' she said, her tone indifferent.

'Do you miss him?'

'Sometimes I think I might, but it's not with any sadness. It's as if his opinion matters in some way. Do you think me strange?'

'Not at all! You respected him so it would be perfectly natural to want to seek his counsel.' She shrugged and felt the pressure of Madeleine's hand increase against her arm.

'I missed you this week,' Madeleine said, her tone shifting. 'I enjoy talking with you more than I should.'

I've missed you since the first day I set eyes on you she wanted to say. 'Yes, me too,' she said, drifting in reflection, to the week passed.

People had been murmuring about their acquaintance, she had noticed it more in the last week, the looks and the whispers as she had walked past people in the street. The titillation of her liaison with Madeleine appealed to some, and whether as a topic for gossip or a reflection of their own hidden desires, their smiles had conveyed wishful thinking or bashful regard. There had only been a small number who hadn't smiled at all, those whose eyes never met hers.

Paris had been an entirely different, even after Yvette, she reflected, and she had found comfort in the isolation she experienced there. She could be herself in Paris and fade into obscurity. Paris had felt more like home to her than anywhere she had lived at that time.

Now though, nothing could compare with the feeling of acceptance she felt in Madeleine's company and with the children. Could she forego a vibrant life in Paris? Yes. Would it be possible to be with Madeleine in this insular town? The emptiness she had felt pondering the question, alone in her room, had given her the answer.

And then, she had considered the moment Madeleine had come to her room and kissed her, fallen asleep in her arms and awakened in her bed. She had watched Madeleine sleeping; the gentle rise and fall of her chest; the flickering of her eyelashes, and she had wondered as to the nature of her dreams.

Claude had missed Madeleine, even though she had seen her in the restaurant during the week and visited the house to help with the children while Madeleine worked. It hadn't been enough though, and she wondered whether it ever would be?

And then, seeing Madeleine in the bookshop, walking her home now, she felt the answer in her heart.

'Will you stay with us tonight?' Madeleine said. Her eyes fixed on the path of snow, and she casually swayed into Claude as she walked.

Claude hesitated, coming to her senses. 'Do you not worry what others are saying?'

Madeleine stopped instantly and turned, fierce determination and the stiffness in her posture causing Claude to tense.

'No, I do not!' She took a deep breath, stared into the sky for a moment then focused her attention on Claude. 'I have recently come to change my thinking on a lot of matters I once thought important, Claude. Do I need a father for my children or a man to tell me what I should or should not be doing, for example? Is there a God?' She shrugged. 'Does my son need disciplining or guiding?' Her voice softened. 'Is it wrong to feel…

161

to have feelings for another woman? You have brought answers to questions I didn't even consider before I met you. I feel as if I have stirred from a dreadful dream that kept trying to pull me back in. People will talk Claude; they are talking. I am well aware, and so is maman, and Antoinette too!' Her voice was starting to vibrate. 'But, I have never felt about anyone as I do about you.' Wetness glistened in her eyes and spilt onto her cheek, and she wiped it away, the passing car diverting her attention momentarily.

Claude resisted the urge to reach out until the car had passed and moved out of sight. 'Life together would be difficult,' she said.

'I know,' Madeleine said. She sighed. 'But not impossible, Claude.' A pleading smile replaced the fierce gaze.

Claude smiled with tenderness. 'Your passion is enthralling,' she said softly. She offered up her arm, and Madeleine took it, her thoughts drifting to Madeleine's mother and sister as they walked together in silence.

'So, will you stay?' Madeleine said.

'Yes, just for a while though,' Claude said.

Madeleine didn't respond.

Sensing the subtle shift in Madeleine's demeanour, she pulled the tucked arm into her body. 'And perhaps we could take the children to the fair tomorrow?' Claude said.

'They will enjoy that,' Madeleine said.

'Me too,' Claude said.

Madeleine chuckled.

19.

Claude descended the stairs, leaving Natty in bed still chatting to Albert, Albert doing his best to ignore his sister. She wandered into the kitchen and watched Madeleine glide around the room effortlessly, returning plates to cupboards, wiping down the surfaces, rinsing her hands, drying them, unwrapping her apron and tidying it away. 'Can I help?' she said. She hoped the giddy feeling would never go away, and as Madeleine approached her, she sensed the nervous tension in her stomach transform into a flurry of joy that filled her. 'You...' Tender lips scalded her cheek; stole her breath, and her words.

'You.' Madeleine said, her voice hoarse.

Madeleine's lips felt supple, warm on her cheek.

'Are.'

Again, the soft lips came, teeth nipping gently at her mouth.

'Beautiful.'

Claude froze, Natty's voice carrying down the stairs.

Madeleine met Claude's alert gaze with a warm smile. 'It's okay, they will be asleep soon,' Madeleine said.

Claude moved without hesitation into Madeleine's arms and became enveloped by the warmth of her, the soft exploring kisses and fingers that gently stroked her flushed cheeks. Claude's lips met Madeleine's, guided by the scent and softness of her, and she felt the racing pulse with her tongue as she trailed a line to her collarbone and then to the top of her breasts. Eliciting a shudder from Madeleine, she felt hands clasp her shoulders and tug her closer. She retraced the path, her mouth finding soft full-lips, silky, warm, open to her. Madeleine's touch, delicate against her cheek again, down her neck, and then fingers running through her hair, gave her cause to still. The moan, inaudible she thought, reached Madeleine and she felt her fingers move beneath her shirt. This time, she groaned loudly, and Madeleine pulled back and studied her with dark eyes that lightened as she smiled.

'Hmm.' The word lingered on Madeleine's lips as she continued to explore Claude's taut muscular body beneath the shirt, her eyes silently assessing. 'You feel so soft.' She hesitated, drawing her lip between her teeth. 'And strong, and smooth; so smooth! I love the feel of your skin,' she said.

Claude felt the ripple across her abdomen set off a wave of vibration that trembled in her hands and inflamed her cheeks. She enjoyed Madeleine too. Yvette's image came to her then disappeared in the same instant. That hadn't been like this. Maybe it was the depth of the ache in her heart that made Madeleine so very different from her other liaisons. Or the sense of completeness that came to her whenever Madeleine was close, and the emptiness in Madeleine's absence that overwhelmed her. 'You feel exquisite to me,' she whispered, the burning sensation from Madeleine's gentle strokes becoming almost unbearable.

Madeleine closed her eyes and moved her hand slowly upwards, stopped at the recovering ribs for a moment, then touched Claude without reservation.

Claude gasped at the tender brush of thumb to the fleshy underside of her breast.

Madeleine moaned as she claimed Claude's mouth.

Whispered satisfaction ignited a fuse that burned quickly to a spot below Claude's hips, the sensation expanding, pulsing, and a sense of urgency returning to her. She pulled back to discover Madeleine's dark eyes fixed on her. 'You are driving me wild with desire, Madeleine,' she said. Madeleine's thumb lingered on her nipple, her gaze unwavering as if carefully considering the impact of her touch. She could see the corners of Madeleine's mouth lift when she shook with lust and she covered Madeleine's hand with hers to stop the movement and gather her breath. Lines formed between Madeleine's eyes and she tilted her head. 'Can we go to your room?' Claude whispered.

Madeleine's smile grew, and she slipped her hand from Claude's breast with a deliberate movement, fingertips running a trail back across her abdomen then taking her hand. 'Yes,' she said, leading her to the stairs.

The bedside lamp threw dim light into the room, sufficient for Claude to see the large four-poster bed on the rug on the wooden floor; a picture hung on the wall, and a dressing table held a framed-photograph and hairbrush on top. Settling her gaze, Madeleine standing by the bed staring at her, she became aware of her heart beating, racing, in her throat, in all of her. Moving closer, she reached to Madeleine, gently stroked her face and touched her hair, as she studied her. A sense of trepidation and want struck her, Madeleine's short, shallow breaths through parched, trembling lips. 'Is this what you want?' she said softly. Madeleine's mouth came to hers with tenderness, and Madeleine's fingers resumed their exploration of her hot skin.

Madeleine eased away, undid the buttons on Claude's shirt and looked at her, the garment falling to her feet. Her hands followed her eyes, and she cupped Claude's breasts, her thumbs tracing the firm nipples. 'I've never seen anything so beautiful,' she said, her tone quiet, considered. She leaned in, her lips delicately pressing to the soft flesh of Claude's breast, her tongue tracing its ever-changing surface. She discovered the contours of Claude's body, languid movements becoming insistent, Claude arching against her.

Claude's breathing laboured, she lifted Madeleine's head from her breast to feel soft, pliant lips against hers. She eased off clothing that fell slowly to their feet. Exposed, the warmth of Madeleine reaching her, the soft breast came to rest in her palm, and she caressed the nipple with her mouth before pulling back the covers and sliding into the bed. The chill of the sheets stung her hot skin, and she pulled Madeleine into her arms, desperate for the warmth of her again; the feel of her; the scent of her.

Lifting Madeleine to her again, she held her gaze, unspoken words conveying her deepest thoughts, her wildest desires. Her eyes closed as she claimed Madeleine's mouth with tenderness. Salt burned beneath her closed lids and water gathered at the corner of her eyes. Silently exploring with the whisper of a touch, she melted into the warmth and softness of Madeleine and felt her breath hot against her ear.

Madeleine moaned, and Claude covered her. Madeleine moved her legs, drawing Claude's firm thigh into her and moaned again as Claude met her warm, wetness.

Adoring the feel of Madeleine against her, she moved lower, fingers finding the fine hair, the soft silky heat, and firm swell of arousal. Madeleine moved with her, her hands tightening around Claude with every stroke; every spasm; every groan.

'Oh, God!'

Observing Madeleine, she felt her yearning in a timeless, all-consuming and unifying moment. With simple rhythm, Madeleine moved in tune with the sensations passing through Claude. Madeleine's murmurs of pleasure vibrating softly on Claude's lips, exciting the electric pulses that consumed her, and she felt Madeleine's rapturous response with a sense of wonder.

'Claude!'

She noticed the quiver on Madeleine's lips and then the lines appearing between closed eyes deepen with the rising intensity. Madeleine's head lifted, and her back arched with the play of Claude's fingertips. Shuddering, slowly at first, intermittent, building, suddenly becoming fiercely intense, she held Madeleine to her, savouring the pulse beneath her fingers.

Hot breath on her chest, Madeleine's arms closed around her, the blanket of satisfaction covering her with new warmth. There was strength in the tenderness, resilience in the softness and both settled deep inside her. She pressed her lips to the top of Madeleine's head and breathed her in.

Madeleine brushed her cheek against the soft, warm flesh and nipple then took the firmness of it into her mouth, her tongue forming circles around the puckering skin with increasing confidence.

Claude moaned.

Madeleine found the other breast with her mouth, abandoning the first to her palm, her thumb and fingertips following a similar pattern on the cool, wet surface she had left behind.

Heat shot through Claude, her head lifting from the pillow in spasm, and her hands clasped Madeleine's head, pulling her into a fierce, frantic kiss. 'Madeleine,' she whispered. Madeleine was kissing her back with equal force; equal passion; equal desire, the deep ache in her centre peaked. Easing from the kiss, Madeleine's head in her hands, she looked into dark, focused eyes. Her tone reflecting her need, 'I need you inside me,' she said. Madeleine's thumb, brushed across her lips, the warm palm, gentle on her cheek. Madeleine moved closer, kissed her with tenderness, slowly, the ache building to a peak.

Out of the kiss, 'You are so beautiful,' Madeleine whispered. Claude moved into Madeleine as she captured the firm flesh of her buttock. Her hand trailed down the outside of Claude's thigh and caused the muscles to tense, hard against her fingertips. Finding the softer flesh on the inside of Claude's leg, a soft moan fell from her lips.

Claude tensed again, consumed by the burning sensation as the fingers discovered her through languid movements, and then slipped inside her and moved within her. Tremors erupted quickly, and orgasm took hold. Waves of warmth rippled through Claude, stilling her. She drew Madeleine's mouth to hers, finding tenderness in unhurried kisses that came to a natural pause, and when she opened her eyes Madeleine looked flushed. 'Oh, Madeleine,' she whispered, her eyes stinging.

They lay together in stillness for some time, the scent and warmth of each other drawing them closer, dreaming the same dream of each other. And when they touched each other again, they rediscovered each other with less hesitation, and a renewed sense of liberation.

When Claude lifted her head Madeleine smiled with the same indefinable quality filtering through her eyes she had seen earlier, and Claude felt the dull ache of awareness hit her. 'I should leave,' she said.

Madeleine traced the line of her jaw. 'I don't want you to go,' she said.

Claude nodded with a smile then kissed the palm at her cheek. 'I think it would be wise,' she said. 'For now.'

Madeleine sighed. 'It won't always be this way,' she said.

Claude shook her head, though she couldn't bring herself to think what the future might look like. She dressed and made her way down the stairs, tensing as the floorboards creaked. The door clicked quietly behind her, and the cold air hit her harder.

Her footsteps crunching the snow, echoing in the silence of the night, seemed oppressive under the thick blanket of low cloud. She breathed shallow breaths through her nose to keep the bitter air from burning her throat, the memory of Madeleine in her arms, glowing warmth, preventing the cold from penetrating as she walked, the sound of feet on snow fading. Madeleine! How hard it had been to leave her bed. The touch of her lingered in her awareness, Madeleine pressed against her beneath the covers, wrapped tightly around her. The raw hunger she had perceived in Madeleine had been thrilling, the feel of her moving inside her, bringing her to ecstasy, more exhilarating than she could have imagined. Madeleine! She smiled for no one to see, her cheeks burning as heat and cold fused.

The taillight didn't capture her attention at first, its angle and proximity to the road confusing. As awareness registered, adrenaline surged, and she broke into a run. The engine was quiet, the car sitting at an angle down the ditch and resting awkwardly against a tree, its front end crumpled and the bonnet bent upwards. She approached the front of the vehicle, spotted the body laying over the steering wheel and a wave of anxiety hit her. She pulled at the door until it gave way, reached into the driver's seat and pressed her fingers to his neck. Finding a pulse, she carefully eased him back in the seat. Blood from his head had spilt down his temple, dried, and stuck to his moustache, his breathing faint, eyelids unmoving. 'Gustave,' she said, quietly at first, squeezing his shoulder lightly, repeating his name as she checked his body for injuries. His cheeks were cold and he remained unresponsive. She stepped back, scanned the empty road, and sighed. 'Gustave!' she said, trying to alert him, 'I need to move you.' She dragged him from the seat, his weight drawing her down. Her head close to his as she tried to lift him, the strong smell of stale alcohol caught her by surprise, and she drew back. Coming to him again, she avoided his breath and shifted him into a sitting position. Heavens, you're heavy, she thought. Finding some purchase on his coat, she heaved him into a fireman's lift, tensed with the pressure in her ribs, and set off on a slow walk back to Madeleine's house.

She stopped momentarily and leaned against a tree for support, thought about letting him drop to the floor and dragging him and dismissed the idea as even more challenging. She gathered her breath, fixed her gaze on the restaurant a ahead and continued with a stride shortened by the lead weight that sapped her legs. Going through the yard, past the woodshed she entered the back of the house. She made her way through to the living room and eased him onto the sofa, threw a log on the dying embers, and went back into the kitchen. Returning with a cloth and bowl of water, she started to clean the blood from his face, aware of the sunken dark appearance of his eyes, the pale skin around the unkempt moustache; the time she had sat in the same seat, having a cloth applied to the injuries she had sustained. She pondered his vulnerability and almost felt sorry for him. 'Gustave,' she whispered, gently wiping his face. He mumbled incoherently. 'It's all right; you're going to be okay. You're at Madeleine's house,' she said. The tips of his facial hair flickered and his eyes remained closed. She removed her coat, placed it over him and went to make a drink.

When she returned, she noticed a hint of colour had returned to his cheeks. She sat watching his cheeks darken further, sipping at the hot cocoa, wondering about Madeleine, alone upstairs in the bed she had not long abandoned. She had toyed with the idea of waking her, but something had stopped her. He was stirring, his eyes blinking, the darkness she felt towards him returning. 'Gustave,' she whispered, and he mumbled again. 'You are at Madeleine's house. You had an accident in your car,' she said. The thought suddenly dawned on her. Had he been watching the house? He had most certainly had a lot to drink.

He moved, opened his eyes, and stared blankly. Holding her gaze, he lifted his hand to his head.

'You have a cut,' she said. She sipped from the cup, and noticed his hand tremble at his temple. 'I don't know how long ago it happened, but you got very cold,' she said. He continued to stare at her with wide expressionless eyes.

'Claudette?' he said.

The vulnerability in his tone brought no comfort. 'Yes,' she said. 'I carried you here.' He moved his head slowly, his eyes swaying, taking in the room. She noticed his hand shaking on his thigh. 'I'll get you a hot drink,' she said rising from the chair.

He mumbled.

Claude returned with the drink, and he received the cup with unsteady movements, his face creased in tension. 'You have other injuries?' she said.

'My shoulder,' he said, the hair on his face contorting as he lifted the cup with one hand, the other hand remaining flaccid in his lap. He sipped, groaning as he swallowed. 'My neck,' he mumbled.

'Yes,' she said. Undoubtedly, he would have pain in places he had yet to discover. She released a long breath, watching him as he became aware of his discomfort. 'The car must have been taken by the ice,' she said.

'Yes,' he said.

'You hit a tree and ended up in the ditch, just down the road. You will need some help retrieving the car,' she said. He didn't respond, and she remained silent.

He finished the drink, and she returned their cups to the kitchen, clearing away the evidence of their brief visit. When she returned to the living room, he was trying to stand, his weight and the wounds hindering his mobility. She went to him and supported him to his feet. He stood, adjusting to the situation, and swayed as he started to move. He made his way tentatively to the front door, and she followed him.

'I'll walk with you,' she said.

'There is no need,' he said. He tried to stand taller and groaned.

'You're in pain, Gustave. I can see that. I can walk into town with you,' she said. She would leave him once they reached the guesthouse; his house just a short walk beyond that point.

He made a movement of agreement with his eyes, and she closed the door quietly behind them.

20.

'Albert, can you hold the seat up while I tie the rope?' Claude said, lifting the wooden slat into position. He took it from her, and she reached up, slung the rope over the branch and tied a knot.

'Will you teach me to tie knots?' Albert said.

Claude smiled. 'Yes, of course,' she said.

Madeleine watched Claude at work; deft hands making light work even in the chilled air. Heat rushed to her cheeks, the memory of those same attentive hands caressing her, triggering a ripple of fire that spread quickly through her. She had been surprised at her own energetic response; recklessness that had had a most invigorating effect. She had surprised herself at her sexual appetite too, driven by a desire so powerful she had later wondered as to its source. Being with a woman had never occurred to her before, and yet being with Claude had obsessed her since the day she stepped into their lives. She had considered whether she should feel guilty, but the truth was, she didn't. Something about the illicitness of their liaison felt exciting, but Claude was more than that to her. She didn't want a veiled relationship, their love concealed behind closed doors, and yet there was no other option. She noticed Claude with a dull feeling and turned her gaze to Natty.

'There, you can let go now.' Claude said to Albert. She pressed down on the seat before sitting on it and swinging.

Natty laughed. 'You're too big. Can I have a go?'

Claude jumped from the swing. 'I was just testing to make sure it won't break,' she said, ruffling Natty's hair as she climbed onto the swing.

Madeleine met Claude's bright eyes and tiny bubbles fizzed in her stomach. The sensation stayed with her as she continued to observe, Claude's smile broadening and, as she pushed Natty on the swing, Claude's gaze repeatedly returned to her. The axe suddenly felt heavy, and she rested it on the ground, picked up the wood pieces and threw them into the basket. By the time she stood, Claude had turned her attention to Albert and she couldn't help but study her again.

Albert stood next to the swing flicking the blade of his knife open and closed.

'Albert, would you like to learn about car engines?' Claude said, drawing his attention from the knife. She had mentioned to Madeleine about showing Albert how to service a car before, but they hadn't got around to it, and she hesitated, realising she hadn't asked specifically about the black Fiat Simca in the open fronted barn adjoining the yard. She had noticed the old-looking vehicle and assumed it belonged to them, although she hadn't seen Madeleine, or anyone else, driving it. She glanced to Madeleine and smiled.

'Yes please,' Albert said. He looked at Claude with a grin that spanned his face.

'Would we be able to work on that car?' Claude said, pointing to the barn.

Albert's mouth opened, and his eyes grew wider. 'Can we, maman?' he said. 'Can we fix our car, maman?'

Madeleine looked from Claude to Albert.

'Our car's always broken,' Natty said, kicking her legs forward as she swung.

Claude looked to Madeleine again.

Madeleine cleared her throat. 'I forgot to mention that,' she said. 'It stopped working a while back, but I never thought it important to get it repaired,' she said. 'I don't like driving.'

Claude smiled at her. 'Can we take a look at it?'

'I'm not sure what's wrong with it,' Madeleine said.

'Perhaps Albert and I can find out,' Claude said, turning to face Albert. 'What do you think, Albert?'

Albert nodded.

'The keys are on the hook in the barn,' Madeleine said.

Claude smiled at Albert. 'Best we get to work,' she said.

Albert was still nodding, the broad grin across his rosy cheeks lighting up his face.

Madeleine watched Claude wrap her arm around his shoulders as they walked towards the barn. She looked completely at ease, and so did he. As she studied them talking animatedly together a dull feeling descended on her, and it occurred to her that Claude might leave once her work on the railway line was complete. It was a thought she hadn't given attention to before now. Claude hadn't said as much, hadn't even hinted at the idea, but what if life became too difficult for her? What if there was another beating or an inexplicable accident at the railway site? If someone like Clement could do such a thing to her, there would surely be others out there willing to pick up where he left off. She glanced around the yard, suddenly gripped by irrational concern.

'Come in if you get cold,' Madeleine said to Natty, picking up the basket of wood and entering the kitchen. She stocked the stove, rinsed her hands and picked up the knife, noting the tremble had reached her fingers.

'Is everything alright, Madeleine?'

She turned sharply at the unexpected voice. 'Antoinette! I didn't hear the door open,' she said.

'Are you okay?' Antoinette said, studying Madeleine intently.

Madeleine swept a tear from her cheek, turned to the knife and started chopping. 'I'm fine,' she said, trying to control the wave of desperation that had just struck her, seemly out of the blue.

'Shall I make coffee?' Antoinette paused, waiting for a response. 'I brought biscuits for the children,' she said, and placed the plate of freshly baked cookies on the surface.

'Thank you,' Madeleine said. She took her eye off the blade as she chopped. 'Damn!' she cursed, dropping the knife. Blood started to ooze from the tiny cut to her finger, and she watched the red wet slowly expand.

'Goodness, Madeleine!' Antoinette searched the kitchen drawers, removed a linen napkin and pressed it to the wound. 'What were you doing?' she said.

Madeleine gazed at her sister blankly. 'Gosh, how silly of me,' she said, taking hold of the cloth. 'I must have been lost in thought.'

Antoinette searched Madeleine's face. 'What has happened?' she said.

Madeleine, compelled to look up from the cloth, held her sister's concerned gaze. 'I'm fine honestly, it was only a nick,' she said. 'Look, it's stopped bleeding already.' Antoinette stared at her. 'See, all fine. They smell good,' she said, turning her attention to the biscuits.

Antoinette stared for a moment longer. 'I tried a new recipe,' she said. 'Are the children playing in the snow?' She glanced out the kitchen window.

Sobs answered the question as Natty thumped through the door. 'Oww, oww!' she said, shaking her hands, running directly at Madeleine, tears bursting onto her cheeks.

'What is it?' Madeleine said, bending to eye level, cupping her daughter's face.

'My hands, my hands! Hurting, hurting!' she said. 'Oww, oww, oww!' Hands shaking, she jumped up and down.

Madeleine took the cold hands and squeezed them gently, 'Sshhh, it's all right Natty, you just got too cold.' She rubbed gently, blowing on the small frozen fingers until Natty calmed, Natty's chest jolting intermittently with the last of the silent sobs. She tugged Natty into her arms and rubbed her back.

Natty pulled away. 'I'm going to play with Marie,' she said, and ran into the living room.

Antoinette craned her neck again, looking through the window into the yard. 'Where's Albert?' she said.

Madeleine felt the fire exploding inside her and hoped she hadn't flushed too obviously. Antoinette's quizzical gaze made the heat hotter. 'He's with Claude, they're fixing the car,' she said. The words tumbled out, and she could see through the corner of her eye, Antoinette studying her with a frown. 'What?' she said. She turned from the window and reached for the kettle as it started to hiss. When she looked up, fine lines were taking shape on Antoinette's cheeks, and she noticed a sparkle in her eyes. She could feel the smile take hold of her and started to chuckle.

'Madeleine!' Antoinette said.

Antoinette's wide eyes peered at her from above the hand clamped to open lips. Madeleine held her gaze, sensing Antoinette's awareness of her situation, not knowing how to respond. 'You can't say anything,' she said.

Antoinette studied her. 'Are you, and Claude?' She stopped speaking and looked out the window, the barn at the other side of the yard, and back to Madeleine. She motioned to speak further, but could only muster stunned silence, locked in thought.

Madeleine tensed and waited. Knowing the gravity of the revelation, her eyes lowering in response to Antoinette's question, the smile slid from her lips.

'Really? How? When?' Antoinette said.

Madeleine looked at her and released a sigh. Questions felt better than rejection, and Antoinette's interest gave her the sense of being supported.

Antoinette closed the space between them and took Madeleine's hands. Studying her intently, 'Is *that* what you want, Madeleine?' she said.

Madeleine considered her sister's tone. Surprised, concerned? The faint amusement she thought she had seen in

Antoinette's eyes was no longer apparent, replaced by seriousness, and she suddenly questioned her earlier interpretation. Did she have her support? Should she feel troubled by what was to come? Antoinette was staring at her, her appearance shifting. 'I...' She had intended to deny the truth, but it was already too late for that, and then the grin slowly forming on her sister's lips halted any defence she might have put up.

'I knew it.' Antoinette said.

Madeleine breathed deeply and released a sound unfamiliar to her ears. Relief flooded her, and she could feel the trembling inside, and moving through her in waves.

'You've been acting so strangely these past weeks. Claudette. Claude has been here a lot too, and the way she looks at you, even in the restaurant, I've noticed,' she said. 'I wish someone looked at me like that.' She drifted with her imagination.

Madeleine noticed the dreamy look and shifted her attention to the barn across the yard. It was true, she had felt distinctly out of sorts since Claude first arrived, with Natty wearing her jacket, sleeves down to the floor. The image drew a half-smile, and she wondered at her feelings back then. Her pulse had raced at the sight of Claude with Natty, and she had put that down to anxiety. But if she were honest, she had noticed Claude with more than gratitude and not just simple fascination either. And, very quickly, she had found herself wanting Claude to visit, wanting to feel her presence, and even back then the very first time Claude left the house, she had felt strangely alone in the absence of her.

She had told herself it was the shock, but now she knew the truth. She had felt an attraction towards Claude from their first meeting, and then she had come to know her, and then her heart had screamed out such that she imagined it ripped from her, the sight of Claude beaten and bruised. It had taken all her strength to nurse Claude with confidence, all the while feeling raw and shaken. She contrasted the feeling with when Raoul left for the war, and knowing he might not return, finding them very different.

'There is something quite engaging about her,' Antoinette said, her tone contemplative.

There is, she thought. She had kissed Claude, and she had gone to Claude's room intending to nurse her, and instead, she had lain with her. She had been captivated by the softness of her, the tenderness of the touch that had aroused her, and then the way Claude had reacted to her. Images of the nights they had spent making love together since, discovering the depths of each other, in this house, upstairs in her bed. Claude leaving before the children woke, the empty feeling that resonated beyond the sense of the space growing cold in the bed next to her. Seeing Claude with Albert, teaching him to carve; making clothes with Natty; chopping wood together and the conversations they had shared. 'Yes,' she said, in a hushed voice. Claude is very engaging, she thought.

'What will you do?' Antoinette said.

Madeleine lowered her gaze. Had she been so consumed by an overwhelming sense of affection that blinded her to the realities of a relationship such as theirs? The only thing that scared her though, was losing the most precious things in her life, her children, and now Claude. She hadn't considered the practical details. She had told herself she didn't care what others thought, and now wondered if she had been deceiving herself all along. Assuming that no one knew how she felt had made denial easy. Now, she had admitted her feelings though, and it occurred to her that others' had guessed. People had been talking. Xavier? She had suspected Gustave had his suspicions, and maybe that was why he had become so possessive of her. But, that had changed recently, inexplicably; the palpable tension around Gustave had shifted. He hadn't made reference to his potential as a father for her children; on the contrary, he had maintained a respectful distance, mostly engaging with her on the catering plans for the opening of the dam. She had put this change of heart down to the bump on his head just knocking some sense into him. He had been fortunate apparently. One hour longer and he would most likely have died in the cold, had a stranger not been passing and helped him home, so the rumours had said. Suddenly struck by history, she shuddered. If Gustave still suspected, he wouldn't back off that easily, would he? She chased the dull feeling away again.

Antoinette pulled her into her arms. 'Well goodness me,' she said.

Madeleine released herself. 'Please don't say anything to the others,' she said. There would never be a good time to talk to her family, especially her mother, but now was definitely not the right time.

The door opened, and both women turned their attention to it with conspiratorial swiftness.

'Hello, Antoinette.'

Claude's voice sent a jolt through Madeleine, exciting her heart, and filling her with warmth.

Antoinette flushed. 'Hello Claudette,' she said.

'Would you like a hot drink?' Madeleine said, averting Claude's dark eyes.

'Yes, please. I think we both would,' she said, moving from the doorway as Albert bounded through.

'It's freezing,' he grumbled, hands tucked under his armpits, heading straight through to the living room.

'Why don't you go and sit by the fire?' Madeleine said softly. 'I'll bring the drinks.'

'Right, I'll be off then.' Antoinette said. She smiled at Madeleine with a squint, directed a broad grin at Claude, and went into the restaurant kitchen.

'Sorry, did I disturb you?' Claude said, glancing over her shoulder at the closed door.

Madeleine felt the heat settle in her cheeks. 'No,' she said. 'We were just chatting, she made biscuits.' Feeling the depth of Claude's gaze, the flush deepened. 'Go and warm up and then we can hear about the car,' she said, lifting the kettle from the stove. She could feel Claude's eyes on her back for a moment then the footsteps fading. Giggles, emanating from the living room, encouraged the smile to linger as she stirred the drinks. The children's bedtime couldn't come quickly enough, she thought.

'Maman, can we paint the cones?' Albert and Natty said in unison as she entered the living room.

Claude took the cups from Madeleine. 'I said they needed to ask you first,' she said.

Madeleine looked at the spread on the floor in front of the fire, paper strips and the cones, sticks and leaves they had gathered from their walk in the woods. 'That's a wonderful idea,' she said. 'Shall I make us some glue and we can make the Christmas decorations?'

Albert nodded. 'I'll get the paint,' he said.

Madeleine met Claude's eyes with hers, and her stomach flipped. She went to the kitchen, her heart racing, blinded by a strong sense of hope for a future they might share.

*

Madeleine stared at the flicking red flames, the new log taking hold, the fire spitting and crackling. Bathing in the heat, the painted cones drying quickly on the hearth, paper ring-chains hanging from the ceiling and randomly affixed around the room, she sipped at the glass, enjoying the relaxing effect of the Cognac. Oblivious to Claude's voice quieting upstairs, the story-telling coming to an end, she jolted at the sudden contact,

Claude's hands slipping around her waist and pulling her close. She leaned back into an altogether different experience of warmth and closed her eyes, the feel of Claude's chest pressing into her, Claude's breath on her neck.

'I love the smell of you,' Claude said.

Madeleine opened her eyes, turned slowly and caressed Claude's face with tenderness; held the intensity between them with her own sense of longing. She moved her fingers delicately through the short hair, noticing Claude's eyelids flutter and her breath shorten as she traced the spiky hair at the base of her neck. Claude moaned as she placed a tender kiss to her mouth, and she enjoyed the vibration of her on her lips.

Claude stopped kissing, looked at Madeleine and swept the hair from her face. 'I missed you today,' she said. 'I find myself wanting to touch you, and I know that I can't. You take my breath away, Madeleine.'

Madeleine gasped, the softness of the youthful skin beneath her trembling fingertips as she traced the line of Claude's cheek and jaw, down her neck to the top of her chest. She moved lower, seeking and finding the evidence of arousal that even the rough cloth couldn't hide. The coarse material and the tight nub pressing into her palm, intensifying the low ache that had distracted her all afternoon, she too groaned. 'You know, you do things to me I wouldn't have believed possible,' she said, studying her hand on Claude.

Claude lifted Madeleine's chin, her thumb brushing full lips that became pliant to her touch. 'I've never felt this way, Madeleine. I know we haven't known each other for very long, but...' The words continued inside her mind. From the moment I set eyes on you, my heart hasn't been the same. You captured it. You hold it. It is yours to break. I am yours for as long as you live.

Madeleine closed the short distance between them, silenced the conversation with a kiss so fierce that Claude stumbled backwards. Releasing Claude, and with a sharp intake of breath, 'I love you,' she said.

Claude cupped Madeleine's cheek in her hand and placed a tender kiss to her lips. 'You don't know me, Madeleine,' she said.

Madeleine's stomach dropped, and she jolted backwards. 'You don't know me either,' she said, creating a distance between them and closing her arms around her chest.

'I'm sorry, I didn't mean it that way,' Claude said, and reached out to Madeleine.

Madeleine ducked away from the hand, glaring eyes searching for an acknowledgement of the pain the thoughtless words had caused. None came.

Claude tensed. She looked to her feet and murmured something inaudible. When she lifted her head, water had filled her eyes. 'I'm sorry, I didn't mean to imply that you don't have feelings for me.' She paused, lips thinning, eyes searching, and then released a sigh. 'There are things you don't know about me, Madeleine. You may not feel the same way.' Her voice faded and a tear slipped onto her cheek.

Madeleine addressed her with a stern gaze. 'I know you saved the life of my daughter. You are the kindest person I know, and you get the best out of my son. You have won favour with the hard-nosed men you work with.' Her voice started to break. 'You are smart, tender, considerate, loving, warm. I've never known such sensitivity and intelligence in one person,' she said.

'You don't know… about my past, Madeleine.' She watched the words land, Madeleine's confusion apparent by the fact that her lips moved to speak and then closed.

Madeleine broke eye contact and silently massaged her temples. 'What could be so dreadful, Claude?' She pinched the bridge of her nose, eyes closed, slow deep breaths carrying across the silence.

Claude stood, arms resting at her side, eyes searching. 'I had an affair with an older woman when I was sixteen.'

Madeleine lowered her hand and stared straight at Claude.

Claude swallowed. 'It was a very intense relationship that lasted some years. She, her name was Yvette. She, and her husband Charles, had moved to Lyon from Paris to escape the war. Her husband was well connected and knew my father through his business, and they started to come to dinner regularly. One evening she seduced me while my father drank with her husband.'

Madeleine waited. Claude sighed.

'She was twenty years older than me, and I fell for her. I thought she cared about me, but it turned out I was just a game to her.'

Madeleine could feel the burning behind her eyes, determined not to release the tears. 'You're not a game to me,' she whispered.

Claude held her gaze, a faint smile crossing her lips. 'He knew that I had feelings for Yvette, and that became a source of power to him. He used to make me watch him with her, listen to her as he pleasured her, and then he insisted on watching her with me while he pleasured himself. I refused to let him near me, though he tried to.' Her eyes lowered. 'That's when it ended. Yvette said we couldn't carry on being lovers. I thought I had suffered a broken heart until I realised I had been taken for a fool. I really thought she and I had a chance together; she had promised to leave Charles and be with me.' Claude released a short breath through her nose. 'Of course, I was too naïve to realise the difficulties of living with another woman, let alone one already married.'

Madeleine stared, lines appearing between her eyes. 'You think I'm like her?' she said.

184

Claude flushed. 'No,' she whispered. She held Madeleine's gaze with tenderness. 'You're nothing like her.'

Madeleine felt something she couldn't define, a spike of betrayal, and she tried to dismiss it as irrational. She pondered the fact that she hadn't had a sexual relationship with a man until twenty-one; and sixteen seemed so young, and with a woman. She felt the information in tormenting thoughts that kept repeating. 'We all have a past we can't change,' she said, fleeting thoughts of Raoul and the debts and drunkenness. It didn't compare, but it was at least tangible to her.

Claude tried to smile, but her lips just formed a thin line.

Madeleine continued. 'You were very young. You have wisdom and an inner strength greater than people I know who have long passed fifty,' she said. 'You challenge the status quo, even the idea of God. Heavens, I don't know anyone who has that sort of courage. And, I find your arguments convincing, compelling. My mind has changed since knowing you; I have changed. I am not going to hurt you, Claude, and I am not going to let your past get in the way of us.'

Claude's eyes narrowed. 'Not being able to be with you hurts me, Madeleine, every day. I have lived this life for seven years. Been aware of my desires since a young child. Had to keep a distance from people I cared for, because of how others might perceive my relationship with them.'

Madeleine's heart dropped. 'What are you trying to say?' she said.

'It's just not that easy.'

Madeleine stepped closer.

'How will you explain to your family; the children?' Claude said.

'We,' Madeleine said. 'We will explain, not me. I want to be with you, Claude. I am old enough to know how I feel and I am not going to deny myself. I love you. It's a feeling so deep, God knows it pains me too.'

Claude took a step backwards.

Madeleine closed the gap; watching as Claude retreated further. She tilted her head. 'Are you afraid?' she said. Claude's edgy response told her all she needed to know. 'Is it love that scares you, Claude?'

Claude swallowed, tried to hold Madeleine's gaze and then her eyes closed and tears ran a line down her cheek.

Madeleine moved to Claude and wrapped firm arms around her, held her tightly, and kissed the top of her head. 'I won't reject you, Claude. Never!' She cupped her face, placed tender kisses to her forehead, her eyes and then her cheeks, lingered on Claude's soft lips and savoured the salty, sweet taste of her. She eased away and reached for Claude's hand, placing it on her own heart. 'You have my heart, Claude. You and you alone can break it.' Her lips curled into a warm smile, and she thought tenderness appeared in Claude's eyes.

'I don't know how...' Claude said.

Madeleine was nodding, and Claude stopped speaking. 'I don't know how either,' Madeleine said. 'But, we can find a way, if we want to.'

Claude met Madeleine with a gentle kiss. Releasing her, 'I'd like to try if that's what you want?' she said.

Madeleine held Claude's gaze with new awareness. The initial sense of betrayal diminished by the uncharacteristic vulnerability Claude displayed and their commitment to each other. 'It is what I want,' she said. She noticed the tremor in her own voice, a reflection of the susceptibility of her heart. She took Claude's hand and led them up the stairs.

21.

'Who on earth decides to open a dam in the middle of winter?' Madeleine said. She scurried, picked up a large pot and placed it on the stove. Tipping in oil and a pat of butter, she stirred. Onions sizzled as they hit the hot fat then large chunks of chopped beef quieted the process for a moment, the strong aroma filling the restaurant kitchen.

Claude chuckled, peeling potatoes for another large pot. Having agreed to help with food preparation for the dam opening, Madeleine had insisted she got some practice. It was a lot warmer than shovelling stones and shifting steels on the railway, and potatoes were softer than carving wood.

'At least it makes menu selection easy,' Antoinette said.

'Menu is always easy, take it or leave it,' Maude said, whisking frantically. She smiled to herself.

Beatrice chopped apples and Regina rolled out pastry. Between them on the work surface, a tray of pies awaited their turn for the oven.

Water trickling down the inside of the only window in the kitchen marked the difference in temperature, with snow still heavy on the ground outside. Virtually everyone in town had been out with shovels clearing the route for the procession that would come from the town past the restaurant and down the road to the dam, creating a buzz and enthusiastic anticipation. No conversation had taken place in the last ten days without making reference to the opening of the *Barrage de Génissiat*. Any talk of Christmas had fallen on deaf ears, except for Natty and Albert, for whom the dam opening held little meaning or interest.

'I'll go and get more wood,' Claude said.

'Thank you,' Madeleine said, pouring a large jug of stock into the pot on the stove.

Sensing soft eyes resting on her as she collected the basket from next to the oven, goosebumps riding a wave down her neck, 'I'll check on the children while I'm out,' Claude said.

Madeleine nodded, a warm smile forming.

The air wasn't as cold as in previous days, Claude thought, gathering the logs into the basket. The bright sun, set in the clear blue sky, didn't deliver any heat, but the snow sparkled like a thousand flickering stars. Something was heartening about the appearance of snow, something cleansing. Squeals drew her attention, Natty running straight at her, preceded by a snowball catching her squarely in the chest.

Albert stopped in his tracks, stared with a look of apology, and picked up another handful of snow. 'Sorry,' he said. 'Natty, you can't hide behind Claude.' He pulled his arm back, threatening to launch another snowball and Natty squealed again, tucking her head into Claude's leg.

Claude abandoned the log, grabbed a fistful of snow from the woodshed roof and threw it at Albert. 'Come on let's run,' she said to Natty, encouraging her to let go of her leg. She gathered more snow as she ran and launched it in his direction, but not before Albert had targeted Natty.

'Aww!' Natty said, brushing her coat. She bent down to pick up snow, and another snowball caught her on the back of the neck. 'Aww! That's not fair, it's my turn to hit you,' she said, rubbing frantically to get the snow off her.

Claude threw two balls at Albert in quick succession, giving time for Natty to scrunch a small fistful of snow. She watched Natty's ball disintegrate in the air, Albert laughing as the effort failed to reach him. 'Here throw this one,' Claude said, handing over a tight wad of snow. Natty swung, and the ball launched skywards, again landing a long way short of her target. Claude laughed, her attention on Natty, and failed to see the incoming snowball. 'Aww,' she said, the iced water sliding down her neck. She flapped at the snow, picked up another handful and launched it at Albert who dived out the way.

Natty squealed. 'Can we play something else now, my hands are cold.'

Albert, with a beaming grin, threw one more ball at Claude. 'Sure,' he said.

'How about I make cocoa?' Claude said.

'That would be most welcome.' The man's voice turned Claude's head. He stood, the other side of the low gate, his eyes moving from Natty to Albert. The shudder that passed down her spine and into her gut caused her to tense. Albert and Natty had also been silenced by his presence. Natty clung to her, hiding behind her legs; Albert felt exposed to her, and she wanted him closer. She wanted to say something, but the sight of the stranger had caused her brain to slow, and a feeling of madness overwhelmed her.

'You've grown, Albert,' he said.

He leaned his weight on the cane in his right hand, his face heavily scarred. His smile, tentative at first, broadened to reveal white teeth, his eyes remaining in shadow. There was cold detachment in them of the kind she had never seen before. Yvette's husband had looked at her oddly at times, but the chill in her spine with this man was of a different quality.

'Is everything...?' Madeleine stopped. Gasped. Her hand pressed to her mouth, eyes wide, her face turning ashen. 'Oh, my good God!'

She looked to Claude as if her legs were about to give way. Claude darted towards her, catching her before she collapsed. She could feel Madeleine trembling, her eyes fixed on him with a look she couldn't identify.

'Madeleine.' he said.

Albert looked from the man to his mother and back again, edging towards Natty.

The man's tone seemed apologetic, Claude thought, though his gaze remained distant.

'Raoul?' Madeleine said.

Claude felt the jolt sweep through every cell of her body, the force of destruction, annihilation. She tried to tell herself she had misheard the whispered name. It couldn't be right; Madeleine's husband had died in the war. There was a grave; everyone knew that. She could feel her mind shutting down, sucking her in, everything happening on the outside grinding to a halt, and a wave of nausea rising within her. Madeleine had moved away and was standing, staring, hands clasped across the front of her body. Albert and Natty stood behind her, their small hands gripping her coat.

'Father?' Albert whispered, poking his head around Claude, studying the man further.

'Yes,' he said, re-aligning his weight on the cane.

'Good God, Raoul, is it really you?' Madeleine said, her eyes still wide, her feet fixed to the spot.

'May I come in?' he said.

Claude could see Madeleine hesitate, sensed it was her obligation to the past driving her to open the gate to him.

'Of course,' Madeleine said, the words perfunctory in the absence of any connection with him.

He made no move to embrace Madeleine, she noticed. Albert had taken a small step to her side; Natty remained like a limpet attached to her leg. The instinct to comfort Madeleine, thwarted by the distance that separated them, reduced her to a feeling of utter helplessness. She reached down and squeezed Natty's hand, watching as Raoul limped his way to the door.

Raoul said, 'I'm sure this has come as a big shock to you.'

Madeleine said, 'Yes.'

Claude felt sick.

'You look well, Madeleine,' he said, entering the house.

Madeleine didn't respond.

Claude bent down, held Natty's wide eyes and brushed the hair from her eyes. 'Are you okay?' she said.

Natty shook her head from side to side, threw her arms around Claude and squeezed. 'I don't like him,' she whispered.

Claude fought the burning in her eyes, the clamped sensation in her throat. 'It's all right Natty, he won't harm you,' she said, but her voice sounded odd. She reached out to Albert's hand, and he took it. 'You can speak to him, Albert,' she said

Albert shook his head, lowered his eyes. Claude entered the house, Natty in her arms clinging around her neck, Albert tucked behind her.

'Raoul, this is Claude,' Madeleine said.

His dark eyes fixed on her, and he nodded. She tried to respond, but her movement was frozen by her own distaste for the man. She cleared her throat. 'Hello,' she said, forcing her hand towards him. He shook it with a warm, soft grip; the type she would associate with an office worker.

'I have a lot to explain,' he said, turning his attention to Madeleine.

'Yes, you do.' Madeleine said.

Claude noticed the trembling in Madeleine's hands as she poured hot water from the kettle, sensed her confusion, the brevity in her responses to him. He, on the other hand, held a calm demeanour, but then he was in control. He had planned this moment, probably rehearsed it thoroughly, she thought. 'I can make the drinks if you would like?' Claude said.

Madeleine dropped the kettle to the stove, the clang drawing pairs of eyes to her. 'Thank you,' she said, avoiding Claude's gaze. She walked into the living room, and he followed her.

'Right, who wants cocoa?' Claude said. She did her best to smile and sound enthusiastic, drawing the children's attention away from the man who had just turned their lives upside down.

'Me, me!' Natty said, wriggling in Claude's arms.

Claude lowered Natty to the floor, pulled both children into a bear hug and kissed them on the head. 'It will be alright,' she said. At least she thought she had said that. Thinking the comfort of being around their grandmother and aunts might help, 'Let's go and make cocoa in the big kitchen,' she said.

Natty ran for the door, Albert followed sluggishly. She closed the door behind them, unable to stop the devastation burrowing its way into her heart.

*

'I don't understand,' Madeleine said. She stood, hands on hips, her contempt for him feeding the strength she had summoned.

'I was in the hospital for three and a half years, Madeleine. Three and a half years. It was only in the last few months I started to recall my past. Us. Albert. The girl, is she mine?' he said.

Madeleine pushed away the sudden urge to lie. 'Yes,' she said, her voice a whisper.

Madeleine tensed and her lips pinched. Shouldn't she feel more warmly towards him? In truth, he couldn't feel more unfamiliar to her. He made a move to grab her arm, and she sidestepped him.

'Sorry, I have no right.'

'No. You don't.' She released clenched fists, her arms wrapping tightly around her chest.

'News about the dam opening is everywhere in France. Génissiat is being talked about even in Paris, and it brought back snippets of memories that I've pieced together in the past weeks. Even then, coming here, I wasn't too sure, until I saw the house, Albert... and then you,' he said. He gazed at Madeleine. 'You look beautiful. I can't believe I haven't remembered you all this time,' he said. 'I'm not the man I was, Madeleine. The war has changed me.'

'I'm sorry,' she said then questioned why she had lied to him. She didn't feel an ounce of sympathy. 'You can't just come back into our lives like this, Raoul.'

'I don't expect things to be easy at the start,' he said.

Madeleine could feel her stomach twist at his words, and her throat constrict around her objection. The idea of him in her life again, in the house, no! She could feel the tears burning at the back of her eyes, pressing hard. She squeezed her arms more tightly around her chest to block him out, but she could feel his energy coming at her. He was still her husband. She was no longer a widow. The thought turned her stomach. 'I can't...'

'Give me time, Madeleine, please. Give us time. We need to rebuild our lives; I understand that. I've learned a lot about myself these last years. I've had to re-discover myself in so many ways. The war does strange things to a man, Madeleine,' he said.

His words passed her ears, the pounding in her head blinding her thoughts, emotion surging through her in a tidal wave, crushing and sweeping away anything that was ever good in her life. Aware that Claude had taken the children out of earshot, the feeling of isolation hit her.

'I was living in Paris,' he said, as if Madeleine knowing that information would make a difference. 'My rehabilitation involved working in administration for a catering company. Apparently, I had talked about owning a restaurant when in hospital, with the drugs and stuff, and so the nurses thought it might help.'

You never owned the restaurant, she thought. You never even worked in the restaurant, she thought. You were a drunk and a gambler. The pressure in her head mounting, she turned towards the kitchen. 'I'm going to make coffee,' she said.

He sat.

She returned to the living room and handed him a hot drink, having had a moment to gather her thoughts. 'I don't understand,' she said. 'Why couldn't they trace you to here after the accident?'

He sipped at the drink. 'There was a mix-up. It happens a lot in wartime. Dog tags getting lost when...' He paused, and his eye twitched slightly. I wasn't wearing any when I was taken to the hospital, and by the time I recovered from the head injuries enough to speak, I couldn't answer their questions. I didn't know who I was any more than they did. My physical rehabilitation was easy by comparison, though obviously, I have this.' He lifted the cane in a demonstration.

'Couldn't they have found out, somehow?' she said, pacing across the living room. She stopped, waiting for him to respond.

'Apparently not,' he said.

His tone was irritatingly calm to her, and she resumed pacing the room.

'It's taken me a long time to recover, mentally, Madeleine. Physically, I'll never be fully right again either,' he said, glancing down at himself and then back at Madeleine as if she would know what he meant. His tight-lipped smile didn't touch her. 'But at least I have some good memories now.' He paused again. 'And, I hope you will help me fill the gaps.' He didn't smile. 'The doctors said I should remember more being here.'

No, she wanted to scream. No, no, no! She stopped pacing, studied his scarred face, searching for a feeling of empathy. Resentment came, and she pushed it back down again.

'How is your mother?' he said. 'Sorry, I don't remember her name. And you have other family?'

'Fine,' she said. 'They're all fine.' She sighed, stared at him, 'Where are you staying?' she said.

'I checked into the hotel in town.'

Lines formed between her eyes. 'I would have thought they had been booked up months ago.' She questioned whether his eye seemed to twitch in the pause and whether she had seen it move in the same way earlier too.

'I guess I got lucky,' he said. A faint smile appeared though his eyes remained vacant.

'I need to think about...'

'Of course.' He stood unsteadily, the cane taking his weight as he adjusted his balance. 'I'll leave you. Perhaps we can talk again later, after the parade?'

She looked at him, but no words of encouragement came.

'Maybe tomorrow?' he said.

'I need to think,' she said.

He nodded and turned towards the front door, stopping with his fingers wrapped around the door-handle. 'You look good, Madeleine,' he said. 'I'm glad you have been keeping well. I've missed you.' He dipped his head, stepped through the door and closed it behind him.

Madeleine wiped at the stream flooding from her eyes, her body shaking. She looked around the room, the pictures on the fireplace, the decoration, the furniture, and the rug. Everything she had brought into their lives, not him. Her heart trying to break out of her chest, she fell to her knees and pulled at her hair, silently crying out for no one to hear. Any pain would be better than this pain. She leaned forward and cradled her knees, rocking, whimpering, 'No, no, no!'

Strong arms wrapped around her shoulders and pulled her into the warm, familiar embrace. Eyes remaining closed she allowed herself to be held, continued to rock, cloaked in the comfort of Claude.

'Sshhh,' Claude whispered. She pressed her cheek to Madeleine's head drawing her closer, holding her tighter. 'I'm here. I'm here.'

Madeleine sobbed, her arms gripping tightly around Claude. A sense so overpowering; so devastating, cycled through her, with no route to escape. The trapped feeling building, the madness of it all taking a hold of her, she screamed and started to thrash wildly. 'No, no, no!' she said, the word becoming a mantra.

Claude tightened her grip until the thrashing ceased. She cupped Madeleine's face, and Madeleine's eyes remained shut, her lips uttering the word no, her head moving from side to side rhythmically. 'Madeleine,' Claude said, trying to wake her from the nightmare. 'Madeleine.' She pressed a tender kiss to her mouth, tasted the salt from her tears, Madeleine's lips unresponsive to the touch.

The warm swell of desire started to rise slowly, and then, alerted to Claude's caress, a sense of urgency came to Madeleine. She pulled Claude deeper into the kiss then released her suddenly, her eyes flicking open with a query. She studied the tenderness she had come to know, the deep pain, buried behind Claude's moist eyes, the absence of the warm smile that had become so familiar; and a sinister feeling caused goose bumps to prickle and a shiver to pass through her.

Claude stood, held out her hand.

Madeleine took it and rose to meet her. She could feel the hot breath on her face, Claude drawing her into her strong arms. Words escaped her, and she knew they evaded Claude too. She leaned into Claude's chest, listening to the thud of her heart. 'Are the children alright?' she said.

Claude cleared her throat, but when she spoke the words were fractured. 'Yes, they are baking with your mother.'

'Did mother say anything?'

'No.'

'The others?'

'No. They were all shocked. It will take time for everyone to adjust.'

Madeleine eased away from the warmth and stared at Claude. 'I don't know what to do,' she said.

'He is your husband, Madeleine.' Her words started to fade. 'You have no choice,' she said.

'Don't say that,' Madeleine said, shaking her head. 'I can't accept that. I won't accept that.'

Claude pressed a thumb to Madeleine's lips. 'I know,' she said in a soft tone. 'We all need time to think.'

Madeleine nodded. 'Yes, I need to think,' she said. 'Need time to think.' She had the sense of her mind swallowing her words but having nowhere for them to digest, no way of processing them, chaos spinning around with no possible solution. Feeling imprisoned by an enforced reality, she slumped into Claude's arms, the love and the loss of her merging in the tears that slid down her cheeks.

22.

Raoul is back from the dead! The news would be all around town before the procession reached the restaurant, Madeleine thought, the life draining from her. There would be cause for a double celebration; the war hero Raoul had returned.

Madeleine will be so happy, they would say, and she felt as if her heart had been ripped from her. She could hear their voices singing his praise, laughing dancing, rejoicing in him. And the children will have their father back, they will say to her, assessing her, and she felt the acid rise and burn her throat. The drums moved closer, and she watched through the restaurant window, the brass band leading the parade, approaching the restaurant. He would be among them, she knew, her thoughts drowning out the music, and she shuddered.

Albert bounded towards her. 'Maman, the band is coming, can we go?' he said.

She sensed the excitement in his tone, though he hadn't mentioned Raoul; no one had. Her sisters had looked at her with pained quizzical expressions; Antoinette, in particular, had clung to her as if trying to comfort herself. These things happen in war, her mother had said, her tone subdued. Something in the way Regina had looked at Madeleine had reached inside her, in a way she hadn't known before, a sense of deep empathy, and it had enticed her to want to confide. She hadn't though, not yet at least. Maude had said grumpily, she thought it all a bizarre affair. Madeleine didn't know what to believe, too consumed by emotion and a dull ache that just seemed to become more painful as the day progressed.

'Maman!' Albert said.

'Yes, Albert, when the band comes past, we'll join in,' she said. The excitement she had felt at the start of the day, before he had shown up, seemed distant and unreachable. She didn't have the will to try to find it either. Albert had her hand in his and was pulling her.

'Come on, maman, quickly or we'll miss it.'

As she lifted her head, she caught sight of Claude closing the space between them and her eyes started to sting again. She fought the sensation, forcing a smile, which must have appeared as tight as the one on Claude's face. Claude was wearing the same coat as the day she had turned up with Natty dragging the arms along the ground, and Madeleine had to look away to stop the tears before they spilt from her eyes. She brushed her finger across wet cheeks. 'Shall we go?' she said softly.

Claude nodded; Natty jumped up and down with a big grin on her face and a firm grip on Claude's hand.

I hope Natty isn't affected, Madeleine thought, gazing at her daughter. You could never really tell with children. She glanced at Claude who was looking at her with tenderness, softly caressing her. It didn't help, and the sadness formed an abyss within her. 'Let's go,' she said, shifting her attention and moving towards the door.

Trumpets blasting, drums rumbling, people moving enthusiastically, she joined the parade with a firm grasp on Albert's hand, one eye on Claude and Natty to her side. Madeleine, you must be so happy, she could hear them saying. People were grinning, their eyes fixed on her, their heads nodding emphatically. The sounds formed incoherence, and she could feel her mind closing down. Locked in an inner world, she merely nodded at anyone who spoke to her, maintaining awareness of Claude and Natty at her side.

Claude leaned towards her, and she felt safety in the briefest contact, their arms touching.

'I'm here,' Claude said.

Madeleine fell into step with the parade, the band intruding and becoming loud.

Gathering by the dam, the vast concrete structure looked impressive. The coloured bunting lining the office building looked out of place, the perspective was wrong, Madeleine thought. She watched the water seep through holes at the bottom of the concrete wall. 'It is spectacular,' she said.

'It's an amazing feat,' Claude said.

I love that look in your eyes, Madeleine thought, watching Claude assessing the dam.

'Bonjour, Madeleine, Claude,' Xavier said.

'Bonjour, Xavier, it's beautiful, no?' Claude said. She glanced at him and back to the dam.

'It is magnificent,' he said.

He seemed to want to talk to Claude, Madeleine thought. His lips tight, his eyes unsettled. Maybe it was the volume of people, milling and bumping that disconcerted him. She had always thought of him as a private man.

The band stopped playing suddenly, and the voice of the mayor drew their attention. Claude had lifted Natty to sit on her shoulders, and Madeleine scanned heads looking for Raoul.

The speeches, applause, cameras flashing, all passed in a blur; and Albert tugged on her arm.

'Maman, can we go home now,' he said.

The words boomed from the microphone, '...and, what a wonderful day it is that our dear friend, one of our very own family, Raoul Vietti returns from the war. A man we all thought dead, our hero, is back.' She felt the trembling start in her stomach, churning, her legs weakening, Albert pulling on her arm, apparently oblivious to the mention of his father's name.

'Maman, can we go home now,' he said.

She caught Claude staring at her, the hand reaching across and squeezing her arm briefly. It was enough to steady her, as cheers of joy filled the air around her. She tried to smile, those close to her, nodding in affirmation, expressing their wonder at the news. She glanced at Albert. 'Let's go home,' she said. She held Claude's gaze again. 'There will be a lot of hungry people coming our way soon,' she said.

Claude nodded.

'Balloons!' Natty said, pointing.

Xavier frowned. Sure he had recognised the distinctive colour of the man's hair; cropped as it had been when their paths had crossed. The burn marks marring his face caused him to question his instinct, but there was something in the emptiness in those dark eyes. Coldness seeped into the man's gaze with effortless ease, undetected by those drawn to his bright white smile. A cane supporting his feeble state, his movements seemed hindered by a leg that didn't function well. Raoul Vietti? The name wasn't familiar either. He looked more closely; camera's flashed in the face of the disfigured man shaking hands with the Prime Minister of France. Vietti's demeanour shifted, too subtle for many to detect, but noticeable to one who knew the signs. There was something insincere about him of that he was sure. Xavier turned his head and followed Madeleine and Claude with his gaze for a while then settled again on the man they all called a hero.

*

'What are you going to do, Madeleine?' Antoinette said. She scrubbed at the dish in her hand then placed it on the kitchen-drainer.

'I don't know.'

'He is going to want to live with you.'

Oh, God, please don't say that Madeleine wanted to say. She looked up, eyelids closing, tears close to the surface.

Antoinette looked across the kitchen, their mother busying herself. Beatrice and Maude were still tidying in the restaurant. 'What about Claude?' she whispered.

Head shaking, Madeleine wiped at her cheek, the image of Claude sitting in front of the fire on the floor playing games with Albert and Natty right now. 'I can't,' she said then stopped, unable to finish the sentence. He can't live with us, she thought with certainty, but without a solution.

'Maybe there are rules or something,' Antoinette said. 'A way of annulling your marriage because he has been away for so long.'

How she wished that were true. She wondered how many other women had struggled with the return of their husbands after the war. How had they dealt with the situation? This was years later. Is there a God? The question she had discussed at length with Claude sprang to mind. God wouldn't do this to anyone, she thought. 'I don't think so,' she mumbled.

Antoinette placed another dish in the sink. 'Did he say anything?'

'No, he's being quite respectful. He knows I need time.' She considered the fact that he hadn't approached her at the event, just a brief, polite conversation as she had served the food. He had been occupied of course; in high demand by those who wanted to know about his heroic endeavours. She had watched him entertaining the crowd, memories of a past she would rather forget returning vividly to her.

'I never liked him much,' Antoinette said.

It didn't help.

'I'm going to check on the children,' Madeleine said.

'Yes, of course, we can manage the rest,' Antoinette said.

Madeleine stepped out of the kitchen, aware of her mother's gaze on her back. Shutting the door, leaning against it, she breathed deeply, a light feeling coming over her. This was her space, her home, and the children's home. He didn't belong here. No matter what, he couldn't come back. Laughter trickled into her awareness, softening the tension that had blocked her smile, and her lips twitched. She moved the kettle onto the hot stove, made cocoa, and went into the living room.

Claude jumped up from the floor. 'Hey!' she said, taking the two drinks. 'Look, we have cocoa,' she said to the back of the children's heads as they continued to play.

'Come and play with us, maman,' Albert said.

Madeleine felt refusal in her initial resistance then crouched to the carpet and sat on the floor next to him. Claude sat next to Natty. 'What do I need to do?' she said.

'You need to pick up the stick and not move the other sticks and if they move it's my go,' Natty said.

Madeleine, aware that Albert and Natty had their eyes glued to her hand and the stick she was trying to move from the pile, smiled then started to chuckle. Her hand jiggled, and one stick knocked another one. Both children squealed and jumped around.

'My go, my go,' Natty said, picking the stick Madeleine had just failed to retrieve with ease and placing it in her pile.

'Is it my turn? Claude said.

'No, no! I get another go,' Natty said, studying the sticks carefully.

The game finished with a big pile of sticks in front of Natty, a smaller pile next to Albert, three in front of Claude and two in front of her. That was fun, she thought, and rustled Albert's hair. He smiled.

'Can we play again?' Natty said.

'Not tonight, Natty, it's time for bed now,' she said.

Natty grabbed the sticks, 'Can mine come to bed with me?' she said.

Claude chuckled.

'You might spike yourself in the night,' Madeleine said, holding out her hand.

Natty clung to the sticks, pressing them to her chest.

'What about Marie?' Madeleine said. 'You wouldn't want to hurt her.'

'Marie wants the sticks too,' Natty said.

Madeleine looked at her, 'Alright,' she said. 'But how about we tie a band around them?'

Natty nodded, ran to the sewing box and pulled out a piece of ribbon. 'Can you tie a knot?' she said, handing over the fabric and tumbling the sticks onto Claude.

Claude took the ribbon and started gathering the sticks, lined them up, and tied a bow around them. 'There!'

Natty took the bundle and shook them. Two fell out of the middle, and she picked them up and poked them back into the pile.

'Up you go,' Madeleine said.

'Claude's reading a story,' Natty said. Wide eyes pleaded to Claude.

Claude stood, 'Come on then,' she said, taking the small hand in hers.

'Night, maman,' Albert said, clambering up the stairs.

'Night Albert, Night Natty,' Madeleine said.

'You can sleep in my bed,' Natty said to Claude.

'Maybe if I get really tired,' Claude said as they climbed the stairs.

Madeleine sighed.

When Claude returned, Madeleine's eyes were damp. Claude opened her arms, and Madeleine fell into them, eyes closed. She felt the consistent beat of Claude's heart against her cheek and released a long breath, experiencing the soothing effect in the numbing of her thoughts. The delicate caress to her eyelids as Claude placed the lightest of kisses there, easing away the tension that had pained her eyes. She felt the groan play on her lips, the hunger flaming deep inside. The light kisses came again to her lips, and then Madeleine's eyes opened in the cool air that filled the space between them. Claude was staring at her with a dark gaze, full of something she hadn't seen before, and with a sinking feeling she released her, barely able to swallow.

'I need to go,' Claude said softly.

She wanted to scream, no. She shook her head back and forth. 'Please don't go, I couldn't bear it if you left now,' she said. She reached out and cupped Claude's face.

Claude captured her hand, kissed the palm and rested it against her chest. 'You have this, remember.'

Madeleine wasn't sure if she could feel the heartbeat with her hand, or the desire that vibrated through her hand. She held Claude's eyes with intensity, and moved to cover Claude's breast.

Claude gasped. In a hoarse voice, 'This is what you do to me,' she said.

The trance drawing her in, her hand caressing with a will of its own, Madeleine pulled Claude's lips to meet hers, groaning as waves of pleasure moved through her. If this would be the last night they shared together, then she wasn't going to let it pass that quickly.

23.

Claude slammed the shovel into the snow and heaved. She repeated the movement without looking up. The tears had stopped stinging her eyes now, but the weight in her heart wouldn't budge.

It hadn't taken long for Raoul to claim his place in the Vietti home; she felt sick. Standing for a brief moment, she inhaled deeply. Returning to the snow, she shovelled with increasing speed.

She had stopped going to lunch at the restaurant, walking instead to Café Noir for the inadequate snacks they offered. Pierre hadn't asked questions, and she didn't know if she felt grateful for that or not. Xavier had given her a food parcel Madeleine had sent, but she hadn't been able to eat it. It had stayed on the bedside table in her room for the best part of a week before she had thrown it away. It was as if another part of her had died then too.

She kicked down on the shovel, digging deeper, working harder, her frustration abating a fraction with the effort needed to work. She missed Natty and Albert more than she could have conceived. The raw hot pressure trying to escape her body wouldn't leave, no matter what she did, and the sense of loss moved with her, haunting her.

'What are you going to do?' Xavier had said. He had gone to the Café with her that evening, and she had taken pastis with him. After three drinks, her thoughts swimming in confusion, 'Leave,' she had said. The drink had been harsh against her throat, adding pain to bruised eyes, jaw clamped. She had stood from the table, carried by a false determination to leave town... to leave Madeleine.

Xavier had looked at her, placed his arm on her shoulder and told her not to give up. How could he have such faith? She had played the words don't give up Claude through her mind repeatedly on the short walk to her room. Sat on her bed, her hand had strayed to the space where Madeleine had slept, the essence of her imprinted deeply, and she had sobbed.

She still felt like sobbing, but had promised herself she wouldn't. Not at work. She couldn't show that kind of weakness and fortunately it was easy to blame the weather for her swollen, red-rimmed eyes. She looked to the white sky. With snow falling heavily, the battle to keep the track clear so they could continue to lay the steel tracks was fast becoming a futile one. Word travelled down the line for them to stop work, and she rested her shovel with the others, pulled up her coat collar and headed to the site exit.

'Coming for a drink?' Xavier said. 'A few of us are going.'

She watched the snow sticking to his hair; he swept his hand at it, throwing it off. 'No, thanks, I need to walk,' she said. She noticed the lines appear on his forehead, his lips thinning. 'I'll be fine,' she said.

'If you're sure?' he said.

She nodded.

She wandered down to the lake; to the rock where she had first sat, now exposed by the absence of the green canopy that had once provided shade from the sun. She brushed the snow off it and leant against the hard, cold surface, staring up at pregnant clouds and the strips of white steadily expanding on top of the bare branches. The lake was motionless, its blackness set in stark contrast with the surrounding snow, flakes landing softly, disappearing, becoming one with the water, muted silence filling the air. She could hear her heart beating, a dull, heavy thud, and wondered at its persistence given her lack of desire to live. This place had once held such joy, such promise. The times she had played with the children, and carved wood with Albert on the opposite bank. The time they had taken a picnic and rowed the boat to the farthest end of the lake, and picked berries together. Madeleine had made a pie with the fruit, and it had been sour. Caught by a wave of emotion she swallowed, diverting her attention from her thoughts to the movement coming into view from across the water. Albert! She jumped up and set off on the path around the lake.

'Albert.' She called his name as she approached and wide eyes gazed at her momentarily before he threw himself at her. She held him to her chest, sensing the vibration in his body. 'Hey, what's up?' she whispered, kissing the top of his head. He didn't speak, and his arms wrapped more tightly around her. She ran her hands through his hair, stroked his cheek then crouched to meet his damp eyes. They had the same look in them as they had when she first met him, duller even. She rubbed the tears from his cheek. 'What is it?' she said.

His eyes averted hers. His voice barely a whisper he stuttered through sobs. 'I don't like him,' he said.

She cupped his cheek, opened her mouth to speak then closed it again, realising she had no response. She didn't like Raoul either, but the man was his father, and that was that. She had been fortunate to have a supportive father as a young child, but not everyone was as lucky. 'How's your mother?' she said.

He shook his head. 'Natty cries a lot too,' he said.

Claude felt the constriction in her throat work its way to her stomach, twisting into a ball of fire then a wave of helplessness consuming her with crushing weight. She pulled Albert into her arms, wishing it were Madeleine. She cleared her throat before speaking. 'I'm sorry,' she said. The words didn't even begin to express how she felt. He was leaning into her, his body jerking from time to time, recovering from the sobs.

'Claude!'

She looked up. Her heart burst then continued to race as she stood. 'Madeleine!' Albert remained, clinging to her waist, his head buried in her coat. God, how beautiful you are, she thought, in a wave of sadness. 'How are you, Madeleine?' she said. You look stunning, she thought. God help me, please.

Madeleine hesitated, her eyes fixed on Claude. 'I'm.' She stopped.

Claude studied the glassy appearance in Madeleine's eyes, the slight quiver of her lips, the urgency to run into her arms building. 'You look well,' she lied. She watched a tear slip onto Madeleine's cheek, the snow settling in her hair and onto her cardigan, and it dawned on her. 'You must be freezing, where's your coat?' she said.

Madeleine didn't respond with words. She stepped closer to Claude.

Claude held out her arm and Madeleine came to her. She pulled her close, the snow cold against her cheek, Albert still clinging to her waist.

'I'm so sorry,' Madeleine mumbled repeatedly.

'Sshhh!' Claude tightened her grip. 'Where's Natty?' she said.

Madeleine eased away, her bottom lip trembling, her gaze withdrawn. 'She's at the house. I thought Albert was in the yard.'

'Is she alone?' Claude said. She couldn't bring herself to mention his name.

Madeleine nodded. 'He's out,' she said.

'Come on.' Claude removed her coat and placed it around Madeleine's shoulders. Taking Albert's hand, she walked with them to the house.

'Claude!' Natty jumped up from the floor and ran to her as she entered the living room.

'Hello there, how have you been?' Claude said, lifting her up.

Natty threw her arms around Claude's neck. 'I missed you,' she said.

Claude hugged the small frame, and melted. I've missed you too, she thought. 'It's nearly Christmas!' she said.

Natty stared into her eyes. 'Did you write your list for Father Christmas yet?' she said.

Claude chuckled. 'No I haven't.' Natty wriggled, and Claude lowered her to the floor.

'Will you help me write a list?' Natty said, running and gathering paper and pencils.

As she looked up, Madeleine was watching her. She wasn't smiling, and her eyes looked heavy with sadness, and longing.

'Can I get you a drink?' Madeleine said.

She glanced over her shoulder towards the front door. 'If that isn't going to cause a problem.'

Madeleine shook her head. 'He will be out until late,' she said. She turned away, and Claude's eyes remained fixed on the place she had occupied.

'Come on,' Natty said, grabbing Claude's attention.

'Ah, yes, sorry. I was just thinking about Christmas presents,' she said.

Natty giggled. 'What are you going to ask Father Christmas for?'

Claude paused, drew in a deep breath and released it slowly. 'I really don't know,' she said. 'What about you?'

'How do you spell clothes,' Natty said, holding the pencil over the paper.

Albert smiled from the chair. 'I want an electric train set,' he said, the flicker of a sparkle crossing his eyes.

Claude sensed the desire behind his muted excitement. Natty's obvious enthusiasm drew a smile, and a wave of joy welled in the pressure behind her eyes. Her throat tightened, Natty waiting on her words, and she rubbed at burning eyes. She released the tension in her neck and started to spell the letters.

Natty's tiny hand moved across the page with steadiness, her tongue poking from her mouth and when she had finished, she thrust the paper into Claude's face. 'Is that right?'

Claude pulled back so she could focus on the paper. 'That's perfect.'

'How do you spell puzzle?' Natty said.

Claude smiled and spelt the letters slowly, Natty scribbling one too many zeds on the page.

'You look busy,' Madeleine said, holding out a cup.

Her eyes looked tired, puffy and dark, and restless, Claude thought. 'You look... weary,' she said. She took the drink and sipped.

'A little.' Madeleine said.

Claude noticed Madeleine rubbing her arm, her posture flaccid; she was trembling. Even when she had shown up with Natty soaking wet from the lake, Madeleine hadn't looked this weak; not like this at all.

'Is everything...?'

'Please don't ask me that,' Madeleine interrupted.

Claude put the drink down and went to Madeleine with open arms, and held her until the trembling eased. Aware of the increase in tension before Madeleine pulled away, she squeezed one last time. She averted Madeleine's gaze, feeling her own sorrow sink more deeply and expanding, drowning her.

'I'm sorry,' Madeleine whispered. She glanced from Natty to Albert.

Albert shifted his gaze from them and joined Natty on the floor. 'I can help with your spellings,' he said. He grabbed a piece of paper and a pencil and started to write.

Madeleine walked to the kitchen and stood to face the sink, aware of Claude's presence behind her.

Claude forced her to turn. 'I've missed you,' she said, knowing the words would drive more tears. They did. Strong hands stilled Madeleine's shaking head, drawing the dark eyes to focus on her. Taking the swollen lips to her own, Madeleine responded with tenderness. Claude felt the vibration rise within her and start to take hold. She pressed soft kisses to Madeleine's cheeks, her eyes, and then back to her lips, and sensed Madeleine's fingertips on her skin. Madeleine was deepening the kiss; and time stood still in a moment of bliss.

The door to the restaurant kitchen sounded, and both women jumped apart. Madeleine's hand covered her mouth as she stood back; Claude's hands shifted in her pockets and her eyes darted to her feet.

Regina stood for a moment before entering the room. 'Good evening, Claude,' she said.

There was softness in the voice that drew Claude's gaze from the floor. 'Good evening, Regina,' she said.

'I'm sorry to interrupt you both,' Regina said. 'I wanted to check you were alright, Madeleine.'

Claude studied Regina's concern, Madeleine nodding in response.

'I am fine, maman,' Madeleine said.

Regina nodded with small movements. 'I'll leave you be then,' she said. Turning, she left the room, the door clicking softly behind her.

Claude looked to Madeleine. 'She knows about us,' she said softly and watched a new wave of tears slide down Madeleine's cheeks. Reaching out, she pulled Madeleine into her arms.

Natty ran into the kitchen. Madeleine jerked but then settled limply in Claude's arms. 'Maman, I'm hungry, and so is Albert,' she said then ran back into the living room.

Claude eased Madeleine's head from her chest and placed a kiss to her lips. 'I'd better go,' she said.

'Please don't. He won't be back until late, and I need your company. I'm sure the children would enjoy a bedtime story, too.'

'Can Claude read to me?'

Natty's voice carried through to the kitchen and Madeleine released an involuntary chuckle through snuffles.

They hear everything, Claude thought, her eyes never leaving Madeleine. 'Yes,' she said, for Natty to hear. She has a beautiful smile, Claude thought. She held Madeleine's gaze with a racing heart until Madeleine eventually broke away and started to prepare food. Then, she watched, captivated by a time they once shared together.

*

Madeleine sat in the chair, drinking Cognac from the short glass as Claude descended the stairs. The bottle open by her side, she poured another drink. 'Would you like one?' she said.

'I think I will,' Claude said. She sat, feeling the warmth of Madeleine even though their bodies didn't touch. 'Thank you,' she said. She tipped the glass, emptying it, and swallowed quickly, the sharp sensation exploding and then a powerful heat burned the back of her throat. 'Gosh, that's strong,' she said. She held out the glass and Madeleine filled it.

'I feel so lost, so powerless.' Madeleine said.

Madeleine's voice was barely audible, yet the words penetrated with vivid acuity, a reflection of her own unspoken thoughts. 'I know,' she said. She emptied the glass, leaned forward in the seat and stared at the ever-shifting flames in the grate.

'I think about you all the time,' Madeleine said.

Claude studied the change in colours of the flickering flame. She stood and placed another log on the fire; it seemed the most natural thing to do. As she turned from the grate poised to speak, the front door burst open and Raoul staggered into the room. Tension squeezed the air from her lungs and her fists clenched; she hoped he hadn't woken the children.

Madeleine's eyes darted to the noise as she stood, her hands frantically brushing the front of her dress.

He gazed from one woman to the other. 'Well this is cosy,' he said.

His words slurred, but there was also an edge to his tone, reminding Claude of one time with Yvette's husband. It had been the time when Charles realised Yvette meant something to her, and she guessed he had sensed she held a place in Yvette's heart too. Madeleine's posture had shifted, as Yvette's had back then. 'I was just leaving,' Claude said.

Raoul seemed surprisingly capable she thought, given his intoxicated state, as he moved towards Madeleine. His cane absent, his limp barely noticeable, she averted her gaze as he took Madeleine's mouth with his own.

Breathless, rigid, she had never felt such an urge to attack another human being, the feeling of helplessness warring with rage, crushing her chest. Her voice broken, 'Good night, Madeleine,' she said. He released Madeleine's lips, or maybe she pulled away, Claude couldn't tell. Madeleine was wiping at her mouth, and Claude sensed her detest of him. Yvette had done the same thing back then too. Claude lowered her eyes from Madeleine and went to the door.

'Good night, Claudette.'

Madeleine's voice held a quality Claude didn't recognise, and she shut the door quietly behind her.

Kicking up the snow she walked into town, the numbing effect of the alcohol a distant sensation. Her thoughts sharp, her concern palpable, she entered Café Noir. She stepped up to the bar and ordered. Pierre, eyebrows raised, nodded and passed a large pastis across the wooden surface. She repeatedly turned the glass in her hand, the obsessive movement a reflection of her thoughts about him. The tingling that had made the hairs at the back of her neck rise at the steady stare he levied at her, persisted. The tight grip that the tone of his voice had on her chest tightened further. And the nauseous feeling that had risen and destabilised her, as he claimed Madeleine like a vulture defending its prey, ate at her. Madeleine's vulnerability had called to her she was sure, and a wave of guilt swept through her. She hadn't wanted to leave. She took a hefty slug of the milky liquid, and even its fire didn't warm her, instead, fuelling an unnatural desire in her – she wished Raoul dead. Anger gripped her so powerfully, and she watched her hands shaking on the surface of the glass. She slid it with precision across the bar, meeting Pierre with a knowing glance.

'Claude!'

Mentally fitting the image to the voice. 'Xavier,' she said, her eyes on the drink being pushed across the bar, and she reached for the drink with uncharacteristic unsteadiness.

'Xavier, what can I get you?' Pierre said.

'The same.'

He sat next to her, observing her as she stared at nothing, fingertips running around the rim of the glass. He nodded his thanks to Pierre, lifted the drink to his lips, sipped, and swallowed. He mumbled something, finished the drink and ordered another.

A warm streak trailed down her cheek, and she flicked at the wetness with the back of her hand, picked up the glass and gave it focused attention; a feeble attempt at fighting the stinging in her eyes. She didn't welcome the arm around her shoulder but found herself leaning into his masculine strength nonetheless. Her breathing slowed, her eyes closed, and the spinning sensation caused her stomach to churn. She opened them quickly and staggered in the direction of the toilet.

'She's not in a good place,' Pierre said.

'No!' Xavier watched until she had disappeared then turned his gaze towards Pierre. 'She's in pain,' he said.

'Something's not right,' Pierre said.

Xavier held his gaze. 'Raoul?'

'Yes.'

Xavier nodded.

Pierre looked around the room then settled on Xavier. 'He was in here earlier, bragging about stuff. I didn't serve, but I know plenty of people who did, and he doesn't sound like a war hero to me. Heroes never boast,' he said, his head rocking back and forwards.

Xavier mumbled, sipped his drink, and glanced over his shoulder. 'I'll go and check on her,' he said.

Claude lifted her head from the bowl at the sound of Xavier's voice. She groaned as he picked her up from the floor. She mumbled incoherently, eyes closing, as he swept her up and into his arms. The last thing in her awareness was the feeling of safety, and then the sense of darkness came, and falling.

Her eyes opened, and she realised she lay flat against the firm mattress. She noticed the shadow vaguely familiar in stature though failing to register fully before her eyes closed again.

Xavier watched over her until the first light of day appeared. Her breathing soft, the thrashing calmed, he left the room.

24.

Madeleine busied herself, piling logs into the stove, chopping onions, carrots and potatoes, cutting the meat into cubes of equal size. She didn't look up, acutely aware of her mother's presence. 'We will need more potatoes,' she said, taking thicker slices of peel with the knife than would be normal.

'Would you care to talk, Madeleine?' Regina said.

Madeleine continued to work, unable to face the look in her mother's eyes, a rush of energy causing her to shake. Dropping the knife and vegetable, her hands coming to rest on the surface, Regina approached her.

'Talk to me, Madeleine.'

Madeleine looked at her; the pleading in her eyes, the crevasses in her skin seemingly deeper than she had noticed before. The soft fingers, brushing the hair from her face, felt comforting.

'I do understand, Madeleine.' Regina cupped Madeleine's cheeks, kissed her forehead. 'I'll make coffee, and then there's something I need to tell you,' she said, indicating for Madeleine to sit at the table.

Madeleine sat, gazing blankly into space. It hadn't seemed long enough for the kettle to boil, and suddenly Regina was sat opposite her handing out a cup. She took it, all the while consumed by the sense of being on the outside looking in and unable to influence the stream of events taking place.

Regina seemed to hesitate, looked down at her hands around her own cup. 'I loved your father very much,' she said, her eyes rising slowly and settling on Madeleine. 'But there was someone before him.'

The words didn't carry any meaning, and Madeleine sipped at the drink, allowing her mother to talk.

'I had a crush on someone when I was very young,' Regina said.

Madeleine drifted.

'We were fifteen. I suppose it's not that young for a crush.' Regina's demeanour changed, she smiled with fondness in her eyes. 'I met her at work, and we became quite close.'

Madeleine could feel the words forming coherence, her attention peaking.

'I know what it is like to feel attracted to another woman, Madeleine.' Regina said. She sipped at her drink, traced the lipstick mark on the china with a delicate touch. 'My trips to Paris….'

A strange feeling came over Madeleine as she watched her mother's features soften. The butcher, she thought.

Regina took a deep breath, released it, a soft smile appearing before she spoke again. 'Her name is Orelie. I have known her since just after your father died. She came here on holiday once; you won't remember her though. She lives in Paris. We have been… very close friends for a long time.'

Madeleine swallowed; registering, the number of times her mother frequented the city over the years, all this time thinking of her visiting old friends, extended family, and occasionally for business reasons. 'What about the butcher?' she said.

Regina chuckled. 'Let me just say, it suits us both for others to perceive us as they do.'

Madeleine inhaled sharply.

Regina smiled, reached out and took her daughter's hand. I probably should have said something before now; it's not the sort of thing to shout about, and honestly, I didn't expect my life would be relevant to any of you. Now of course, apparently, it is. You are in love with Claude, I can see that and believe me I am no more keen on Raoul than you are. I can tell you now, I never liked him very much, and there's something about him since he returned that doesn't sit well with me,' she said.

Soft thumbs brushing across her knuckles, Madeleine squeezed her mother's hand. She couldn't process fully, but knowing she had her mother's understanding, a weight lifted. It didn't solve the problem, but there was solidarity in the shared burden. 'But, you kept pushing me to Gustave, and the need for a father for the children,' she said.

'I don't know how you can live the life you want, Madeleine,' Regina whispered. She reached out and swept the hair from her daughter's face, and looked at her. 'I had a life with your father; you always had a man to look up to. I am still torn by own upbringing Madeleine; I wish I weren't. I wanted you to feel the safety and support, the strength, that I had with your father.'

'Raoul cannot provide that for me,' Madeleine said, with a sharp edge to her tone.

'I can see that, and I also see how you look at Claude with such longing.'

Madeleine could feel the heat flushing her cheeks and looked away to escape her embarrassment.

'That feeling is the most powerful kind of love, Madeleine, and when we feel it, there is nothing else to compare. Nothing exists beyond it, and in the absence of it you are entirely lost and without purpose.'

Madeleine studied the hazy look in her mother's gaze, the conviction in her voice as she recalled from personal experience, becoming transfixed by the depth of emotion, through which Regina spoke. 'I didn't realise,' she said.

'You need to know you have the support of the town, Madeleine. People are quick to judge, but they are quicker to smell a rat. And, who wants a rat in their backyard? Raoul is too free with his mouth it seems, and some have found him uncouth and disrespectful. Claude is well respected. I have heard it was she who saved Gustave's life that night.'

Madeleine gasped. 'I didn't know that,' she said.

'She loves you,' Regina said. 'You are lucky.'

Madeleine's lips parted as if to speak.

'I'm sorry, Madeleine. I know don't have the answers. I just hoped that you might feel more comfortable talking to me if you knew.' Regina pulled Madeleine into her, kissed her cheek. 'I love you, my darling, and I want you and the children to be happy.'

Madeleine remained motionless as Regina stepped away from her. 'Merci maman, you have given me courage,' she said. Images of the children with Claude the previous evening, in contrast with them hiding and silent in Raoul's presence, fuelling her determination, she strode out of the kitchen.

She was halfway to town before it dawned on her that Claude would be at the railway site. She hesitated, a shiver making her aware that she had left without her coat. She lengthened her stride, turned off the main road and went through the gated access.

'Excuse me, Madame?' the young man said giving her a half-glance.

She ignored him and carried on walking, aware that he was looking at her with a frown. He moved to stop her then halted.

'Madame Vietti, please,' he said, turning her attention. 'You're not permitted to walk through here.'

Madeleine stared at him vacantly.

'Is everything alright?' he said, his tone softer as he looked at Madeleine. 'You'll freeze out here,' he said.

She averted his gaze and searched into the darkness. 'I need to find Claude,' she said.

'She will be a kilometre or two down the line,' he said, pointing. 'But you can't go dressed like that. You'll fall foul to the weather.'

'Are you going to try to stop me, Henri?' she said, and her eyes narrowed to ensure he got the message.

'Wait a moment.' He entered the small cabin and returned with a thin jacket. 'Take this,' he said. 'It's not the best, but it's more than you have.' He tilted his head, studied the coat as she put it around her shoulders. 'Take care, Madeleine,' he said.

She set off in the direction he had indicated, unaffected by either the cold on her face or the ice at her feet. Numbness set in before she had walked very far, a strange sense of warmth coming over her, her feet carrying her forward in spite of any better judgement that had evaded her senses.

'Good heavens, Madeleine!' Claude had dropped the shovel and was running towards her, and her head felt suddenly giddy with relief. She fell, just as Claude stopped in front of her.

'Madeleine, Madeleine!' Claude held the limp body in her arms, swept the hair from her face. Xavier appeared quickly at her side and collected Madeleine into his arms.

'We need to get her into the warm,' he said. 'Your room is closer than the restaurant.'

'I'll let Gustave know and meet you there,' she said.

Xavier walked further up the line and took a shortcut through to the town. By the time he reached the guesthouse, Claude was right behind him. 'Was he alright about it?' he said.

'Yes, surprisingly so.' She unlocked the door to her room, straightened the covers on the bed and Xavier laid Madeleine down. He pressed his fingers to her neck.

'She will be fine. Body heat is the best thing,' he said, looking directly at Claude, his lips twitching, a slight twinkle in his eye.

Her cheeks flushed.

'I'll get back to work,' he said. 'You both need your clothes off, it's more effective that way,' he said, closing the door behind him.

Claude stared at Madeleine, the hint of blue shading her lips and around her eyes. She undressed, her skin reacting to the cold damp air. She eased Madeleine out of the jacket, removed her clothes and moved them both into the bed. 'Gosh, you're like ice,' she said.

Madeleine mumbled something through chattering teeth.

Madeleine had looked as though she just stepped out of the kitchen. What on earth was she doing at the railway? Claude tried to manoeuver, the narrow bed forcing the cold against her skin. She wrapped legs and arms around Madeleine, breathed her in and groaned. 'So cold,' she whispered into Madeleine's neck, chattering teeth loud in her ear. She moved completely on top of her, rubbed against the chilled legs and clamped the frozen feet with her own, the texture of soft hair diverting her attention. Lifting her head, she studied Madeleine's face, held her palm to the cold cheek then gently massaged across her eyes and temples. 'You are so beautiful,' she said. She placed a soft kiss to Madeleine's lips.

Madeleine stirred and her arms moved around Claude's muscular back.

Claude groaned and her body tensed. 'Cold hands,' she said.

Madeleine pressed more firmly with her hand in the small of Claude's back, her lips seeking and finding, drawing Claude deeper into the kiss. She shuddered when Claude left her lips. 'I love you,' she said. 'I came to say, I love you and I can't live without you.'

Claude silenced the words with a languid kiss.

Madeleine fell into the softness, the tenderness of the touch, the heat slowly thawing her; her own hands enticing goosebumps to rise on the hot skin at her fingertips. 'I need you,' she murmured, her teeth still chattering from the cold.

Claude shifted to her side, pulled Madeleine into her arms, and held her close, the packed suitcase at the other side of the room reminding her. How could she leave? She sighed. 'How can I compete with the father of your children?' she said.

Madeleine remained silent.

'What about what others think, and the impact on Albert and Natty?' she said. Claude had thought long and hard about how they might be able to make things work between them. Other than secret lives lived behind a curtain, about which no one could speak, she had no answers. She had seen the destructive nature of such an existence; she didn't want that, not for herself nor for Madeleine and the children.

Madeleine tensed against Claude's chest. 'I don't know,' she said. The sensation of Claude's soft skin against her cheek, the warmth arousing her, Madeleine turned her head and took the nipple into her mouth with the salt from her tears. 'I know I want this,' she said. Moving swiftly, she shifted on top of Claude. Her hand exploring, eliciting mumbling groans of pleasure, the arching of hips drawing her hand down to the soft hair, and silky wet soon covered Madeleine's fingers.

Claude jolted from the pillow, and she lifted Madeleine's head to see her.

As Claude's mouth met hers, electric pulses fired, and hunger rose within her. Teeth clashing, tongues tasting, teasing and devouring, Madeleine's body moved in a rhythm of its own, and then awareness of Claude entering her, stilled her. 'Oh God,' she said, her hips craving Claude. The feel of Claude, so exquisite and consuming her entirely, light vibrations gathered and orgasm took hold of her.

Claude placed soft kisses to closed lids, Madeleine twitching in her arms. 'You look so beautiful when you're... like this,' she said. She brushed the hair around Madeleine's ear, her tongue tracing its intricate shape. 'Beautiful,' she murmured.

Hot breath on her, gentle waves of ecstasy flowing through her, Madeleine lowered herself down Claude's body and traced circles around the nipple with her tongue. Her hand resuming and toying with the soft hair, the warm and silky wet sensation at her fingertips again, a groan of pleasure fell from Claude's lips. The scent of her so sweet, Madeleine eased lower. Claude clamped her shoulders, and she looked up, unsure how to interpret the reaction. A low groan hit her ears again, and then her own pleasure escaped her as she took Claude with her mouth.

25.

It had been dark when Madeleine had left her bed. Claude had listened with an aching heart to the promises made of a future together, a future in which she wanted to believe. In the cold light of morning though, doubt filled her, and the suitcase in the corner of the room, loomed. Emotions oscillating in waves, lightness competing with shadow, did she accept the pain of leaving or the anguish that would inevitably come with staying? Madeleine had felt so good in her arms; so right, and she could still sense the fingers burning her skin, the throbbing deep inside her. Madeleine had driven her wild with passion, and that truth had messed with her mind, fooled her into believing the illusion of a future together.

A week had passed since Madeleine had come to the site, with declarations of love, and Raoul seemed even more entrenched in Madeleine's and the children's life. She had wanted to go to Madeleine every day since that night, but she had known that her presence would cause problems and she had stopped herself. Raoul was volatile and especially when inebriated; the whole town knew that. She wouldn't give him cause to hurt Madeleine.

Raoul would never give her up; she wouldn't if she were in his position, or the children, of that she was sure. She gazed into the street below, thick snow on the ground, heavy flakes falling from the sky. Would it always be this way if she stayed? Wondering if Madeleine were safe, not knowing possibly for days on end, dipping into their lives as and when the opportunity presented. She looked again at the packed suitcase, insecurity testing her will, confusion grounding her.

She had packed and unpacked several times since her drunken incident and hadn't summoned the courage to leave yet. With Christmas just around the corner, she had paid for the room until the end of December. An image of Natty and Albert writing their list for Father Christmas brought the hint of a smile then her heart reminded her of their absence, and she sighed.

A couple walked arm in arm down the street. And another. She recognised them, as she did most of the townsfolk now and most of the men would dip their hat to her as they passed. This small town had become the closest thing to home she had known. Paris would never be that to her. Paris was a place to live, giving more freedom for her lifestyle, but there was impersonality there too that had always left her feeling a deep sense of isolation, in spite of the company of other like-minded women. Those women had faded into obscurity now, representing a moment in her history that she had no desire to repeat.

Madeleine would never fade to her. Claude realised she had never fallen for anyone until she first set eyes on Madeleine, and she knew there would never be anyone again. She tensed to suppress the swelling in her chest, to keep the feeling at bay, lest she should succumb to her broken heart. Pinching the top of her nose, moisture made its way to her fingertips. Damn it! She turned from the window, and the suitcase, pulled on her coat and walked into town.

Christmas lights adorned the snow-glistening streets, the air of excitement building, stallholders setting up along the main road through town, floral perfume and cooked food wafting in the air. She pulled her collar tight to her ears and made her way towards Café Noir. Pierre set a coffee in front of her, and she nodded.

'Good day, Claude!'

She hadn't noticed Gustave sat in shadow at the back of the room. He folded his paper and tucked it under his arm as he passed her, his moustache twitching.

'Good afternoon, Gustave,' she said. She smiled inwardly. How things had changed between them.

'Are you going to the Christmas market?' Pierre said, drying a glass and placing it on the shelf.

'I hadn't thought about it,' she said.

'It's a big event for the town,' he said.

His eyes shone, and his soft smile made her feel genuinely welcome. 'Maybe.' she said.

'Everyone will be there,' he said.

The inflection in his voice changed on the word, everyone, conveying significance, and he held her gaze intently.

'Maybe.'

'I'm sure you will be missed,' he said, picking up another glass, drying it, and placing it on the shelf next to the first one.

'Good afternoon, Claude.'

She turned her attention to Xavier. He sat next to her and coffee arrived in front of him.

'You going to the market later?' he said.

'Maybe.' she said. She released a long breath, two pairs of eyes smiling at her.

'They reckon there'll be no work 'til past Christmas if this snow keeps up,' Xavier said. 'Trains are struggling too.'

Claude mumbled inaudibly, holding both men's attention. 'Are you here for Christmas?' she said to Xavier.

He chuckled. 'I guess so. No one will be going too far in this,' he said.

She had never asked him about family. The guesthouse dining room with a smattering of tinsel came to mind, a handful of men toasting Christmas, and the New Year together. They were the only family to people like him; people like her, she corrected.

'Do you get lonely?' she said.

He shrugged. 'Sometimes.'

He was staring at her when she looked up. She mumbled, 'I'd better get going,' she said, rising from the stool.

'Have another coffee,' he said, nodding to Pierre.

Two cups were placed in front of them, and she settled back on the seat.

'You wear your heart on your sleeve, Claude,' he said. His smile held no criticism.

She turned the cup in her hand. 'Have you ever loved someone?' she said.

'Yes, it was a long time ago.' he said. 'She was a singer in a bar in Paris. Sounds weak I guess, but she made my heart sing for sure.'

Claude looked at him, the warmth in his gaze, the softening of the rugged appearance of his cheeks. 'I don't think that's weak,' she said.

'She broke my heart,' he said. Large fingers and thumb toyed with the small cup. 'He was wealthy, could give her a life I couldn't afford. They had a child, a girl. I saw her once. The daughter looked just like her. Damn near killed me watching them together, so I left and have never been back.' He picked up the cup and finished the coffee in one slug.

She reached out, placed her hand on his arm. 'I'm sorry, Xavier. I had no idea.'

'That's life, eh! Yours is harder,' he said, holding her gaze. 'Question is, whether you will fight for her, or not?' He shrugged with a thin-lipped smile and a tilt of his head. 'I didn't, and I'll live to regret it,' he said.

'How can I compete? He's the father of her children,' she said, staring into his eyes.

His eyes darkened. 'That man is no father. He's no hero either,' he said.

'What do you mean?'

'Nothing, just a hunch I guess.'

'More hunches about that man flying around here than birds in the sky,' Pierre said. He placed two small shots of a dark liquid on the bar. 'On the house,' he said.

Xavier tipped the glass at his lips and swallowed. 'I served in the war, I know a hero when I see one. That man, he isn't one of them.' He signalled for another drink, and Pierre filled his glass.

Hero or no hero, he was still here and in their lives. Claude contemplated the shot. It would be too easy to numb the feelings again. She pushed the glass across to Xavier. His gaze wandered before settling on her.

'Well,' he said, picking up the glass. 'I've been making some enquiries.'

She studied him, and the drink talking, feeling lighter for his words.

'Paris, I know a few people. Haven't heard back yet though.'

She felt her chest ache, the pressure becoming unbearable. The idea that any news might get through in this weather would be nothing more than false hope, and she couldn't entertain that right now.

'If there's something there, I'll find it,' he said.

She couldn't argue with the certainty in his tone. 'Maybe I'll see you at the market?' she said, standing to leave.

'Maybe,' he said, and then smiled.

*

The afternoon had dragged, and darkness hadn't come quickly enough. Eric Duval, the postmaster, had stared at Claude to the point that heat flushed her cheeks when she asked for the third time for the parcel to be delivered to Madeleine's house on Christmas Eve. He had pressed her for an explanation, and she had given none, so he had stared harder and asked her if she were sure at least three more times. You could walk it there, he had said. No, she couldn't, she had thought. No, she wasn't sure about leaving, but her mind was close to settled on the idea. She had spent the afternoon pacing her room, Xavier's words echoing in her mind – fight for her, he had said. Memories of fighting for Yvette had surfaced. Then, remembering the first time Madeleine had come to her room and they had held each other. She didn't doubt Madeleine's feelings for her, but feelings alone would never be enough. After Yvette, she had made that promise to herself. Never get involved with a married woman. And technically she hadn't. She stared at the ticket in her hand, watching as the words printed on it became a blurred mass, placed it in her pocket and clenched her fist around it.

Music drifted through the frost-lined windows and lantern-lights danced along the street. Laughter came and went. She observed the town coming to life, the aroma from street-food more intense now and filtering through the poorly fitting glass intermittently, coaxing her to join the party. She hadn't seen Madeleine pass by; she hadn't acknowledged that was why she was staring out the window, that was, until her heart skipped, and her stomach spiralled at the sight of her, then it dawned on her. She checked again, no sign of Raoul. Albert was swinging from one hand, Natty from the other. They looked happy, she thought. Madeleine looked up at the guesthouse window, and she darted out of sight, her heart racing. What was she afraid of? Why was she hiding? She waited, then watched Madeleine's back, and searched again for Raoul. He hadn't come with them. She threw on her coat and ran down the stairs.

Jogging through the snow, she slowed to a walk as she reached them. She called out to Madeleine, her heart thumping in her throat as Madeleine turned to face her. Madeleine looked at her through heavy lids and with a smile that held more pain than joy, piercing her with sharpness.

'Bonjour, Claude,' Madeleine said, and the darkness in her eyes seemed to darken.

Natty ran into Claude's waist and flung arms around her. She lifted the small frame into her arms, ruffled her hair and smiled. 'Hello pretty lady,' she said. She ruffled Albert's hair as he too wrapped an arm around her. 'How's the carving coming along?' she said to him.

He pulled back and shrugged. 'I don't have the knife anymore,' he said.

Madeleine looked at Claude through vacant eyes. 'Raoul thought it inappropriate, what with the war and everything,' she said.

Her voice sounded uncertain, and there was shading on her cheek that hadn't been there before. 'Is everything alright, Madeleine?' She lowered Natty to the floor, noticed the tight smile and a gaze that didn't reach her. The children ran toward the candy stall opposite the Café.

'I asked him to leave.' Madeleine stroked the bruised cheek as she spoke. 'It was an accident,' she said.

'Please tell me he didn't hurt you?'

Madeleine shook her head. 'Please don't ask me,' she said.

Silent pain ripped through Claude, she studied Madeleine's shifting gaze and the trembling that shook her. Pressure burst inside her and her throat clamped with such force she felt a choking sensation. She froze, on the verge of changing the decision she had worked so hard to commit to. I'm going to Paris tomorrow, she repeated to herself. She couldn't say the words. She watched Madeleine's discomfort and sharpness cut through her again. 'I'm sorry,' Claude said.

'I want him to leave,' Madeleine whispered.

'I know you do.' She looked to Madeleine. 'We can't live like this, Madeleine, him, me, the children. It's too confusing,' she whispered.

Madeleine swept the tears with the back of her hand, looked down the street in the direction of the restaurant. 'I can't leave here,' she whispered. 'Not right now.'

Claude lowered her eyes. 'I know that.' The urge to touch Madeleine was too strong, and she rammed her hands deep into her pockets.

Natty ran towards them. 'Pierre gave us sweets,' she mumbled, a bonbon swelling her cheek.

Claude puffed out a short, sharp breath, her attention on the young, lively face. 'How about we get some proper food?' she said. 'They have sausages and steak.'

Natty nodded, rolling the sweet around her mouth. They joined Albert as he gazed at the bookstall.

Tension lingered between them as they walked, conversation muted. The jolly, festive atmosphere becoming lost on Claude, her thoughts drifted to the packed suitcase in her room. And then, in a blink, it seemed as if time had passed and she stood on the street in front of the guesthouse, watching the Vietti family as they sauntered towards home.

She turned from the departing family, hoping she hadn't given away the sadness that tipped warm wet tears onto her cheeks as she approached the front door. She could hear Natty's voice just before she closed the door behind her, and as she climbed the stairs her legs weakened and her heart thumped. Only when she closed the door to her bedroom did she allow herself to sob uncontrollably.

26.

Claude blinked into the darkness, the shadows cutting into glistening snow and revealing steel tracks; tapping the boards at her feet, the suitcase by her side. Her breath shallow, small puffs hung in the frozen air, and she rubbed at her eyes. Returning her hand to her pocket, she turned the ticket around, her shoulders hunched, the collar of her coat raised around her neck. She took two paces in one direction and then went back to her suitcase.

The night had been long; sleep evading her, and she had tossed and turned, the bed complaining loudly with every movement. Every cell in her body calling to her to stay, begging her to go to Madeleine, she had almost caved into her desires. She could live in the town with Madeleine at the house, as long as she was a part of Madeleine's life, she had told herself. It was just Raoul. Nothing was possible with him around and getting rid of him was proving impossible. Xavier meant well, but she didn't believe anything would come of his enquiries. In Paris, she could forget. In Paris, she could be herself again. And maybe, one day, Madeleine and the children could come and live with her. She would work hard, buy her own place and then come back and get them. The plan had fuelled her with hope, and increased her determination to leave, to make a future for them all. She was sure Madeleine would come to her if she had the means to look after them.

The long whistle drew her attention, the yellow light growing bigger and brighter, large puffs of steam extending across the rear carriages. She picked up the suitcase, aware of the ache in the pit of her stomach. She couldn't look back, if she did, she might return to the guesthouse. The future, she told herself. Look to the future. Create a future for Madeleine and the children, she repeated. If she worked hard in Paris she

233

should earn enough to support them quickly, maybe within a year, though it would take a lot longer to buy a place, she thought. She stood back to allow the old man off the train. As she stepped into the carriage, a young woman struggling with a large bag and a baby swaddled in her arms, edged passed her. The woman looked a mix of worry and beauty, her dress reminding her of Paris fashion, though a few years out of date. 'Here, let me help,' she said, taking the bag down the steps to the platform.

'Merci,' the woman said.

She had a distant smile, Claude noticed, though her eyes looked soft and bright. Claude went into the carriage, the smell of stale tobacco that lingered in the upholstered chairs. She took a seat and glanced out the window for the last time. The train inched slowly forward; away from Génissiat, gathering speed; away from Madeleine Vietti, racing into the darkness; away from a life that might have been.

*

The young woman studied the piece of paper again, looked across at the street name and walked into town, the baby sleeping soundly against her chest. The bell tinkled, drawing Pierre's eyes as she entered the Café.

Pierre noticed her. Fashionably dressed, in highly polished, laced boots; the snuffling noises emanating from the swaddled child. 'Bonjour Madame, what can I get for you?'

'Bonjour Monsieur.' Long slender fingers cradled the baby's head with tenderness. 'May I have a coffee please?' She looked around the empty room.

Her accent wasn't local, possibly not even French. 'Please, take a seat,' he said. He indicated with his arm, and she went to the table at the back of the room and sat. He studied her through the corner of his eye as he prepared the drink. Her pale complexion and distracted focus, shifted when she settled her gaze on the baby, becoming softer, warmer, and a warm smile appearing. He placed the drink and a croissant on the table in front of her. 'It's on the house,' he said.

She glanced up, her pain evident in the moment of accepting his generosity. 'Merci,' she said.

He returned to the bar, and she rocked gently until the snuffling noises settled. She sipped the drink. The bell rang, and she didn't look up.

'Morning Pierre,' Xavier said, sitting and leaning on the bar.

'Morning.'

Xavier yawned, rubbed at his eyes then scanned the room while he waited. 'Thanks,' he said, biting into the croissant. He indicated with his eyes to the corner of the room. Pierre shrugged. Xavier's brows rose, and he sipped his coffee.

'More snow today.' Pierre said. 'They say the telephone lines will go down.'

Xavier shrugged. Few people had a telephone in town. 'Certainly going to be a white Christmas,' he said with a chuckle.

'Always is here, my friend.' Pierre smiled.

Xavier looked towards the window, light creeping into the day. 'Has Claude been in?' he said. He had seen her at the market but worried all night at her demeanour.

'Earlier,' Pierre said. 'Caught the train to Paris first thing,' he said. His lips thinned, and he made a kissing sound. 'Shame, I liked her, a lot of people did,' he said.

Xavier slammed his hand down on the bar. 'Merde!' He pinched the bridge of his nose. Merde! Merde! Merde!

The woman looked up, sharply, then down at the baby who had started to stir with the sudden noise.

'I know. She was a good person.' Pierre said, shaking his head back and forth. 'Madeleine's children adored her too.' He let out a long breath.

'Bastard.' Xavier mumbled.

Pierre mumbled something incomprehensible, made another coffee and passed it across the bar.

Xavier nodded, palming the coarse stubble on his cheeks. He watched the young woman stand from the seat. She approached the bar and pointed at the crumpled piece of paper.

'Excuse me, could you tell me where to find Restaurant Vietti please?' She looked from Xavier to Pierre and back again.

Xavier noticed the light shade of her eyes, reminding him of Janette with her young daughter the one time he had seen them, and his heart skipped. 'Just follow the road that way,' he said, indicating. 'Won't be open 'til eleven though.'

'Merci,' she said, lowering her gaze and folding the paper. She left the Café and crossed the street, heading in the opposite direction.

'She must have just arrived from Paris,' Pierre said.

'Maybe.' Xavier finished his drink, placed the change on the bar, and pulled up the collar on his coat. 'Have a good day, Pierre,' he said.

He stood in the street and watched the woman enter the hotel. Turning, he went back to the guesthouse, sure that the newspaper cutting she had been holding was a photograph of the opening of the dam.

*

Madeleine looked up from the sink, Raoul staring at her, leaning on his cane. His gaze looked distant, red-rimmed puffy eyes from the after-effects of alcohol, the scarring on his face, shinning, spoiling his naturally chiselled features. Her heart pounded in her chest as he limped towards her.

'Coffee?' he said.

236

'I'll make some,' she said, tension reaching the back of her neck. She hadn't expected him to be out of bed so early, and his presence left her with a feeling of susceptibility.

He lifted the cane and pointed it at her. She caught it, gripped and pulled it from him. 'No Raoul,' she said, glaring at him. He didn't stumble as she had expected; instead he stepped towards her and pulled her into his arms. His wet lips pressed hard to her before she could pull away.

She pushed him backwards and wiped at her mouth. 'Don't!'

'I'm your husband, Madeleine,' he said.

She looked at him, and wondered not for the first time, how much the war had affected him, and then there was the alcohol too, and it had dawned on her that the war hadn't changed him that much. She had heard of others turning to drink after their experiences, but for Raoul, the war had just provided him with an excuse. He seemed to oscillate between kindness and anger at the flip of a coin and for no apparent reason, and his warmth when it did come felt wrong. She studied the man she had married through the abyss between them, and realised she sensed nothing but coldness towards him.

'I want you to leave,' she said, pulling the kettle from the stove, the water spilling as she poured it into the cup.

'I can't do that, Madeleine,' he said. 'The children need me; I'm their father.'

His tone was sharp determined, and pierced through her bravado. The children don't need you, she thought. She handed him the cup. She moved to speak, but the words caught in her throat and tears blurred the image of him.

He turned his back and walked with alarming capability into the living room, Albert and Natty's voices silencing in the same instant. She could see them in her mind's eye, playing, careful to avoid his displeasure, him sitting in the chair staring into space, slurping from the cup. She wiped at her cheeks with trembling hands, Claude's image, and an aching heart. One hour and Antoinette would come and look after them, and he would go to the bar for the rest of the day. Just one hour, she told herself as she went through to the restaurant kitchen and stoked the oven.

*

'A woman is asking after you,' Maude said. The tray clattered as it landed on the kitchen bench, Maude's head indicating the restaurant. 'I've explained that we're not open yet, but she insisted on speaking to you personally.'

'Did she say what about?' Madeleine said, wiping her cheek against her shoulder, her hands buried in a bowl of flour.

'No. Got a young baby pinned to her chest though,' Maude said.

Madeleine rinsed her hands in the sink and wiped them on the apron around her waist. Walking into the restaurant, 'Can I help you?' she said. She looked up, locked eyes with the stranger, and held the woman's pained expression with her own.

'Are you Madeleine Vietti?' the woman said.

The woman's voice seemed deeper than she had expected, given her youthful demeanour. She must have been no more than twenty-five years old. 'Yes, I am,' she said, her own voice unrecognisable. 'I'm sorry, I don't know who you are.' She caught brief sight of the newspaper cutting in the woman's hand, the photograph of the dam and the message relaying details about the opening ceremony.

'I am Florence. This is Jacques,' she said, her hand on the baby's back. In a firm yet calm voice, 'I think we have the same husband,' she said. 'I know him as Louis Moreau.'

Madeleine's lips parted then closed, her heart racing. Confusion lifted with realisation, and a sense of lightness came to her. 'Would you like to come through?' she said. She wondered if the woman might think her response strange; she certainly did.

Madeleine walked past Maude's quizzical gaze and through to the kitchen in her home. She turned to Florence and smiled. 'Can I get you a drink?' she said.

'Thank you,' Florence said, looking around the room.

'He's not here,' Madeleine said. 'He will be in town now, in the bar. My children are out with my sister. Please come through.' She made two coffees and went into the living room.

'You have a lovely home,' Florence said, her eyes on the flames leaping around in the grate, the homemade decorations dotted around the living room. The smell of sweet-pine, clove, and burning wood filled the space.

'Please, do sit.' Madeleine said, patting the seat next to her. 'I have to confess, I don't quite understand,' she said. 'Raoul has just returned from the war. He suffered an injury to his brain that affected his memory.'

Florence sat, sipped at the drink. 'He has lived with me for almost three years,' she said, staring at the fire. When she looked to Madeleine, her eyes were bright with tears.

Madeleine noticed the hand cupped around the drink beginning to shake. Florence's words didn't make sense, and yet, she wanted to believe the young, distressed woman. Three years would be just after she had been informed that Raoul had been killed in action. Had he been discharged from the army because of his injuries, then? How did the army not know this information? 'Gosh!' Madeleine turned her eyes to the fire, pondering the timings, his injuries; the crackling of wood, the sharp scent of it stinging her nose. Then, it dawned that there was only one conclusion. Raoul must have deserted.

'He left us suddenly, just after Jacques was born,' Florence said. 'I met him in Paris at a dancehall during the war. He was working in sales and doing very well. He told me he had served his time and got off for good behaviour; he always joked about that. One day, he humoured the wrong people and got into a serious fight in a bar. They followed him home and attacked him.' Her voice became timid. 'It's how he got the scars,' she said. Florence seemed to drift with the recollection and stopped speaking.

Madeleine felt the words blurring, incoherent to her sense of the truth. She watched the tears trickling down Florence's cheeks in a steady stream, out of the corner of her eye, then looked at her directly, placed an arm around her shoulder and whispered, 'I'm so sorry.'

'He was never the same after the incident. He lost his job and started drinking more regularly. I thought the baby would bring us closer, give him a sense of purpose,' she said. 'But I was wrong.'

Madeleine held the shaking body. 'I think we've both been duped,' she said, stroking the beautiful hair, the soapy scent drifting into her awareness.

Florence pulled away. 'I saw the article and couldn't believe it was him. The name puzzled me, but the scars must be unique to him. I don't really know what I'm doing here,' she said. Sobs rattled her chest. 'I don't even know if I want him back, I feel so out-of-sorts. So, let down, so abandoned. And I see what you have here; he's been living a lie all this time. I feel so angry; he's a disgrace.'

Madeleine flinched at the passion in her words. 'Yes,' she said, suddenly aware that Florence's summation of her husband might be the one thing they agreed on.

Snuffling noises diverted their attention.

'He's getting hungry,' Florence said. She wiped at her cheeks and smiled at Jacques.

'Would you like something to eat?' Madeleine said. 'I can make a sandwich while you see to Jacques,' she said, catching his soft fair curls and minded of Albert as a baby.

Florence eased Jacques from the sling. 'Would you mind?' she said, holding him out.

Madeleine took the featherlike weight into her arms, watched as he scrunched up his mouth then opened it wide and started to scream. Florence was unbuttoning her dress, and Madeleine looked away, heat taking her by surprise. Avoiding eye contact, she handed over the baby and went to the kitchen. 'I'll leave you to feed him. I'll be in the restaurant kitchen, but please take all the time you need.' Florence looked at her with sadness, and Madeleine nodded. 'I'll bring lunch through in a short while,' she said. When she stepped into the restaurant, her heart racing, her only thought was a pleasant one. Claude.

'Is there something we should know?' Regina said, eyes narrowing at Madeleine's broad smile.

'That woman, maman, is Raoul's other wife and from what she has just said, not only did he abandon us both, but it seems he deserted the army too,' she said, her head shaking back and forth as she spoke. Her hand covered her mouth, excitement bursting through her. 'Can you believe it?'

'Well, that settles that,' Regina said.

Madeleine watched her mother's eyes darken, her lips thin, the energy rising within her and colouring her cheeks. She felt sure that if Raoul had been stood in the kitchen at that moment, it wouldn't have been for very long.

'That good for nothing... hero! Pah, hero my arse!'

The gasp escaped Madeleine and then she chuckled. 'I can't believe it,' she said again, her hands trembling as she worked the flour in the bowl with renewed vigour.

'Did I miss something?' Maude said, returning from the restaurant.

Regina stood with her hands clamped to her hips. 'That young woman here to see our Madeleine is only the other wife of that good for nothing alleged war hero!' she said.

'Good heavens! Are you sure?' Maude said. She studied Madeleine. 'How can you be so happy about that?' she said, her eyebrows pinched.

'I think there's something I need to tell you,' Madeleine said.

'Yes!' Regina said. 'There is something else you should know,' she said, winking at Madeleine. 'I think it's about time we had an honest conversation, don't you?' she said, addressing Madeleine.

'Yes, but right now I need to look after Florence and her baby,' Madeleine said, 'She's terribly distressed.'

Glancing from her mother to her sister, Maude's frown deepened.

*

Claude approached the three-story townhouse, both hands balled into a fist and pressed deep in her pockets, tension in her shoulders. She hadn't ever thought she would be knocking on this door again. It had changed; the glossy black paint had lost its shine and dirt clung to the bottom third of the door. Yellow stained net curtains lined the inside of the windows, the subdued lighting barely visible through the blackout curtains that hadn't been fully closed. The weakness in her legs went to her stomach, and her hands trembled against the lining of the coat. She hadn't warmed up the whole day, wandering from café to café, familiarising herself with a city she had known well. It hadn't taken long. Memories had flooded her, adding to the chill in the air. The temperature was a few degrees warmer here, and the snow had dispersed, forming slush that squelched under the weight of her boots. It had soaked the bottom of her trousers, and the cold settled in her feet.

She hesitated, looked around her, smiled at the familiar entrance to the park across the road. She had sat on a bench many a summer evening watching the comings and goings of the house with the black door, burning excitement accompanying her thoughts. Women might arrive alone and leave with another on their arm, or with a radiant glow that would energise their pace. She reached up to the brass knocker and rapped it three times, her heart pounding in her chest. Voices drifted and faded behind the door, and she pulled the collar tight to her neck.

The door opened, and the stranger's predatory gaze wandered up and down her body, the smile growing and the woman's tongue sweeping across her upper lip as if pleased with her assessment of Claude. 'Well, hello!' she said, her voice husky. She drew down on the end of the long cigarette filter, the red glow appearing brighter, and opened the door. 'Do come in; is Yvette expecting you?'

Claude cleared her throat. 'No, is she in?' She glanced over the woman's shoulder, laughter emanating from the rear of the house.

'Naturally,' the woman said.

The woman waved the cigarette nonchalantly as she walked and Claude followed her. She could barely hear the music from the gramophone through the laughter and chatter, and her throat constricted in the smoke-filled room. She flicked her gaze from one woman to another and interested eyes settled on her, some with amusement, others with curiosity. Some warm, some dismissive. Chatter continuing, she followed the woman further into the room. The apprehension she had felt at the door disappeared suddenly, as her eyes fell on the familiar face. 'Yvette.'

It wasn't the name, spoken in barely a whisper that attracted the older woman's attention, but as her head turned the laughter transformed into a smile that held depth. 'Well, I never, Claude!' She reached out, taking Claude's hands into hers as she looked at her.

Warm softness reassured Claude, and she felt her shoulders relax as she released a long breath. 'Hello Yvette,' she said. She knew she had tried to smile, but her muscles had resisted, and Yvette was frowning at her, eyes full of concern.

'Is everything all right, my darling?' Yvette said.

Dismissing the two women she had been talking to with a wave of her hand, she led Claude through the room and into the quietness of an adjoining room.

The scent of leather, Claude remembered the library with fondness. It was here in this room that she had read *The Well of Loneliness* for the first time. Soft hands reached out to her, as they had back then, and she jerked involuntarily.

'What is it, Claude? Are you in trouble?'

Claude shook her head. 'It's not what you think. I need to find work and wondered if there might be something going at the factory.' Yvette was frowning at her.

'Rumour had it you were working the railways now?' Yvette said.

Yvette's hand clasped her arm, and she noticed the lines that aged her face. 'It doesn't pay enough,' she said, aware that Yvette's gaze held more questions. 'I can earn more at the factory,' she said, looking anywhere but at the eyes that penetrated her, seeking the truth. Yvette had always been able to read her, and Claude had always felt it in the heat in her chest. Now was no different, that heat rising to her cheeks.

'It's a woman isn't it?' Yvette said.

Claude watched the lines increase around Yvette's shining eyes, and sighed. 'Yes,' she said.

Yvette grinned broadly. 'Well, I'm very jealous,' she said, her tone matronly. 'You are clearly in love with her, and she is one very lucky lady.' She squeezed Claude's arm with affection before letting go. 'Now, can I get you a drink?'

Claude looked to the rows of books that spanned the wall, stopping at the point where she had pulled *The Well of Loneliness* from the shelf. It was still there, she noted, and smiled briefly. She turned back to Yvette. 'No, thank you, I'll leave you to your party. I'm staying at a bed-and-breakfast in town, until I find work.'

'Claude, I insist. It is the least I can do. Please stay here until you get a job arranged,' she said. 'Accommodation is expensive, and I have this house all to myself.' She indicated with her arms.

Claude felt intensity in the loneliness she sensed in Yvette's eyes.

'We separated,' Yvette said, reading Claude's mind. 'We both agreed it was time to live our own lives. He has another woman, and so do I.' She laughed without happiness. 'And I will ask about a job, though times are hard for everyone at the moment.' Her eyes drifted in thought. 'There is a spare room you can use, if you want it,' she said.

Claude moved to speak then stopped, the sadness behind the soft eyes touching her deeply. She had loved Yvette once, a long time ago. In some way, perhaps she did still.

'Your company would be appreciated, even if only for a few days,' Yvette said.

Claude nodded almost imperceptibly. 'If you are sure?'

'Of course,' Yvette said in a whisper.

'I'll come back tomorrow,' Claude said.

Yvette nodded, the faintness of a weary smile appearing briefly. 'I'll see what I can find out about the factory, and other work. You always were a hard worker, Claude.'

Claude felt Yvette's eyes drift across her body and tried not to feel exposed. She turned away, opened the library door and went to the front door, Yvette following her. Turning, she held the warm gaze with tenderness. 'Thank you,' she said and stepped into the cold, dark night.

Claude stood in the street staring at the house for a while, knowledge of the party in full swing on the inside, thoughts of Yvette separated from her Charles. How things had changed, for them all.

Her thoughts jumped to being here with Madeleine, and being able to touch her freely in the company of other women like them, and the hollow feeling that came to her stayed with her until she lay on her bed in the dank hotel room and sleep eventually overcame her.

27.

Florence had left the restaurant late in the afternoon with a large food parcel and a promise that Madeleine would send Raoul to the hotel when he arrived home. They had talked at length, and Madeleine had been honest about loving another, and about the fact that Raoul was no longer welcome in her home or her life. She had talked about his gambling and drinking before the war and Florence had nodded with her own experience of him. The difference between them, she had realised, was that Florence was in love with Raoul. She had noticed the small birthmark at the base of Jacques's neck, leaving no question as to his heredity. Raoul had one just like it. Excitement had built as reality had formed a concrete plan. She would be free of him for good and sooner than she could have imagined.

She had refrained from telling the children that their father would be leaving with his other son, though every ounce of her had wanted to shout it from the rooftops for the whole town to hear. They would all know by now, she thought, the hushed silence that had filled the restaurant during a brief moment at lunchtime had told her so.

She placed Raoul's suitcase on the front doorstep and shut the door. Grateful for the offer from Xavier and Gustave to deal with the situation, she had no desire to face him ever again. She climbed the stairs and looked out from the bedroom window. Stars filled the clear dark sky; snow glistened in the moonlight. She wondered briefly how Florence would cope with Raoul in the future and felt a wave of sadness. She pulled herself under the bedcovers and swept away the emotion with the memory of Claude's skin against her fingertips, and the sweet taste of her on her lips. She would go to Claude in the morning, just as soon as Raoul had gone.

Xavier stared at his scarred face from across the bar, fists clenched.

'Leave it be, Xavier,' Pierre said, sliding another shot in his direction.

Xavier stood, downed the drink, and walked up to the table in the corner of the room. 'Louis Moreau?' he said.

Slow recognition narrowed Raoul's gaze as he tried to focus. His head swayed then tension pulled him to sit upright. 'You must be mistaken,' Raoul said. The words slurred, and his eyes wandered with apparent disinterest. He picked up the drink in front of him and sipped.

'I don't think so, my friend,' Xavier said casting a shadow across the table. 'Got those scars on the back of a fight over a gambling debt,' he said, pointing at Raoul's face. 'And, the bragging about a war you didn't play a part in.'

'Must be someone else, you're drunk,' Raoul said.

Xavier's mouth twitched, and he brushed off Pierre's arm on his shoulder. 'Rumour has it you're a deserter,' Xavier said.

'Xavier, leave him be, he's not worth it,' Pierre said.

Xavier grunted.

'That's the last drink you'll take in here,' Pierre said to Raoul.

'Florence seems like such a lovely woman, too,' Xavier said. 'Beautiful baby boy looks just like his father from what I have seen.'

Raoul's eyes widened and he tried to stand, staggered and gripped the table.

'Yes, Louis Moreau, your wife is in town. Hadn't you heard? Your other wife that is.' Xavier said.

Raoul's eyes darted around the room, and he went to move, tripping over the stool at his feet. Losing his balance, he fell to the floor with a groan.

Xavier pulled him up by the collar of his coat and dragged him through the Café's door. 'You piece of shit,' he said. Hot breath fell onto Raoul's ear as Xavier bundled him up the street. 'Your wife is in that hotel,' Xavier said, forcing Raoul's head towards the stone building in front of them.

Raoul groaned, murmured something incomprehensible, but didn't resist.

Xavier had never thought he would. Cowards, in his experience, never had the balls to fight, instead, preferring to talk-up a big story and then run when things turned sour. Well, this man would be doing some running first thing in the morning, that was a guarantee.

'I took the liberty of collecting your things from Madeleine's. Your suitcase is in the lobby, waiting for you,' Xavier said. He stopped walking, released the scruff of Raoul's neck, studying him with disdain.

Raoul doubled over and retched, and Xavier turned away. Raoul tried to stand up straight, wiped at his mouth and staggered as he tried to walk towards the hotel.

Xavier grabbed Raoul's arm and hurried him to the hotel door. 'Now, this is what will happen, so listen up hero. Gustave will escort you to the railway station at five in the morning. You will leave on the first train out of here with your new wife and baby, and I don't care where you end up. But, you will never set foot in this town again,' he said. Raoul's glassy and vacant gaze suggested he wouldn't remember the instructions, but Xavier knew Florence had every detail firmly fixed in her mind. She had been more than delighted when Gustave had handed her the two hundred Francs, and two train tickets back to Paris.

Raoul mumbled something and Xavier glared at him.

'I suggest you go as far away as you can. Leave the country before the army catch you. Deserter. Let me tell you, you come near this town, Madeleine, or the children again and it will be the last time you take a breath in this world. Have I made myself clear?' He threw the limp body through the hotel door and watched as Raoul stumbled, gathered himself, and staggered towards the reception desk without looking back.

*

Madeleine woke to the sound of children's voices. She leapt from the bed and threw on her robe. Albert had stoked the fire, and both he and Natty sat writing, next to each other on the rug. They didn't turn their heads as she approached and she watched them quietly for a short while with a warm feeling and a soft smile. 'Would you like a drink?' she said.

Albert continued to scribble. 'Yes please, maman,' he said.

'How do you spell Christmas?' Natty said.

Madeleine chuckled, spelt the word slowly and went to the kitchen, ecstasy drawing more unprompted laughter. The carefree feeling became lighter as she stirred the drinks and she noticed with sharp clarity the soft vibration building inside her. She took the drinks to the living room and returned to the kitchen to make breakfast.

'Morning, Madeleine,' Antoinette said.

'Morning, Antoinette.'

'You look radiant,' Antoinette said, and her smile turned to a yawn.

'I am, very happy. I know it's going to be difficult being with Claude, but I couldn't be more delighted.' Antoinette was frowning at her. 'What?' she said.

'You haven't heard?'

Madeleine's heart skipped a beat. 'Heard what?'

'Claude left for Paris yesterday morning before the news about Raoul came out.'

Madeleine gasped, and her hand covered her mouth. 'Where in Paris?' I'll go to her, she thought.

'I don't know. I don't think she left an address,' Antoinette said, still frowning.

Head shaking with determined movements as Madeleine processed the words, the light feeling assuming density and fire, 'No, she can't have gone like that. I need to find her,' she said.

'Where will you go? Paris is too big to just walk around looking for someone.'

Madeleine paced the kitchen, running her fingers frantically through her hair. Xavier. Surely he will know something, she thought. He knew people; he had told her so. 'I don't know,' she said.

Antoinette lowered her eyes. 'They all thought you knew about Claude,' she said. 'They were talking in the bar last night. Everyone thought Claude must have told you.'

'No... No... No!' Madeleine stopped pacing and clasped her hands to her head. There must be places people like Claude would go, she thought. She could feel the tension rising within her, a wave of heat so powerful and with nowhere to go. She wanted to scream.

Antoinette pulled her into a strong embrace. 'I'm so sorry,' she said.

Madeleine moved away. 'No, Antoinette! Sorry, means I'll never see her again, and I can't think that way or I shall surely die. I need to find her,' she said.

Natty came running into the kitchen and launched a folded piece of paper at Madeleine. 'I made a Christmas card for Claude,' she said.

Madeleine gasped, fighting the sudden pressure at the back of her eyes. She studied the green tree with red balls, tinsel-like squiggles bounding the image, and wiped at the warm stream running down her cheek. 'It's beautiful, 'I'm sure she will love it, darling,' she said, and glared at Antoinette.

Natty ran into the living room. 'I'm going to make one for Nana,' she said.

'I will find her,' Madeleine said to Antoinette.

Antoinette hesitated, 'Maybe we should ask maman,' she said, the words coming hesitantly. 'Maybe she will know… or, or her friend might know where to look.'

Madeleine lifted her head, eyes widening. 'Of course!' she said. Hopeful thoughts came to her, quickly dampened by the reality of finding a needle in a haystack. Just because their mother had a friend in Paris didn't mean they would know where to find Claude. The idea felt quite absurd, and yet it was the only feasible option she had.

'We can at least ask,' Antoinette said.

'What are the chances?' Madeleine said.

'Did Claude not mention anyone? Anyone at all, from… from the past?' Antoinette said.

Heat suffused Madeleine's cheeks, recalling Claude's revelation, the woman at her father's house who lived in Paris. 'Yvette,' she said. 'I know there was someone called Yvette once, and I think she and her husband lived in Paris.'

Antoinette's eyes smiled and her face flushed. 'Goodness!' she said.

Two pairs of eyes turned to the opening door.

Regina gazed at her daughters with a shine in her eyes. 'I couldn't resist it,' she said. 'I went with Gustave to see off that piece of good for nothing at the station. How dare he use my name! Needless to say, he won't be coming back,' she said. Her wide, satisfied smile faded as the pleading gazes registered. 'What is it?' she said.

28.

'How long are the telephone lines going to be down?' Madeleine said, pressing the thumb of one hand into the palm of the other. She stared at the man behind the counter, who stuttered, and turned on her heel before he had finished trying to say, for the third time of her asking, that he didn't know. The door rattled loudly, and the bell continued to ring long after she left the post office.

She went into the Café, crossing the space to the bar before Pierre lifted his eyes. 'Damn telephone lines are down with no idea of when they will be working again, and with this snow that could be the middle of March,' she said.

He nodded, blew out a long sigh. 'Going to be a harsh winter,' he said. 'Coffee?'

'Yes please.' She sat and leaned on her elbows. The one slim chance of being able to get to Claude via Yvette had been thwarted by the harsh weather.

That her mother had known of Yvette had thrilled her, and only later had it occurred to her the extent of her mother's secret life in Paris. The moment of optimism had passed quickly when Regina hadn't been able to speak to Orelie. There was no way to get to Yvette, and even if they did, there was a strong chance that Claude hadn't gone to her. Why would she? It wasn't as if they had ended their relationship on good terms. The strong coffee aroma caught her attention. 'Thank you,' she said, taking the drink and sipping.

The doorbell tinkled, and a cold flurry swept through the small space. 'Good day, Madeleine,' Xavier said, and took the seat at the bar next to her.

'Good day, Xavier.'

'Any news?' he asked.

She shook her head. 'Lines are down.' She sipped at the coffee.

'Merde!' he said.

She rubbed at her eyes.

'How are the children?' he said.

'They miss Claude,' she said. 'We all do.'

'Yes, we all do,' he said.

The idea of travelling by train to Paris to find Claude had occurred to Madeleine, but that had raised more questions than it had provided a solution. What if she didn't get back before Christmas? What about the children? What if she couldn't find Claude? She dismissed the thought again, and sipped at the coffee. 'Do you have anything stronger?' she said to Pierre. 'I owe this man a drink,' she said, indicating to Xavier.

'What for?' Xavier said.

'For getting rid of Raoul,' she said.

'It was nothing,' he said. 'I just wish I had realised sooner, and then maybe Claude wouldn't have left,' he said.

She studied him. 'Realised what?'

'I made his acquaintance once in Paris, though he introduced himself by a different name, and it was before he got the scars; that's why I didn't recognise him. He talked freely about the war, the medals he had received, and how he had been discharged because of his injuries. When he turned up at the dam opening, it seemed like too much of a coincidence,' he said. 'We were playing in a card game, and I remember him becoming very drunk. I left the bar and found out later that he was a rogue. He frequented a lot of bars, telling his stories and there were a lot of women. He was in a landmine incident that much was the truth, but it turned out he escaped almost unharmed. The man they discovered wearing Raoul's tags clearly wasn't him. Raoul must have swapped them over. I hope you don't mind, I did some digging, Madeleine.'

Pierre passed two shot glasses across the bar.

She tipped the glass back and swallowed, Xavier's eyes on her. He mirrored her, and indicated for the glasses to be refilled.

'He was a coward and a deserter according to my contacts in Paris, and he got the scars following a brawl over a significant debt he couldn't pay. They tried to set fire to him, Madeleine. If it hadn't been for Florence, he would have died. She nursed his injuries because he refused to go to the hospital and she gave him a place to stay.'

Madeleine frowned. 'That wasn't what Florence said. She said they met at a dance hall.'

'She lied, Madeleine, of that I am sure. I trust the man who gave me this information. She was a lady of the night and happened to be passing the alley where they had taken him. He was screaming, and she extinguished the flames with her coat. She is a very smart woman, but I fear as much of a crook as he is. They seem well suited.'

She indicated to Pierre to fill their glasses again.

'I'm sorry, Madeleine.'

'It isn't your fault, Xavier,' Madeleine said. She had suspected as much from Raoul, but hearing Xavier talk about him swapping his ID tags with a dead man turned more than her stomach. Her heart had ached for Florence and Jacques, and she even wondered whether she should have offered them more than she had. Now, she felt a wave of betrayal settle in her. How could another woman be so dishonest?

'Another coffee?' Pierre said, filling the glasses in front of them.

Madeleine gazed at the door, the words coming to her slowly. 'No, thank you, Pierre.' She held the glass to her lips, the aniseed aroma awakening her, sipped and swallowed.

'At least they won't be back,' Xavier said and downed the shot in one hit.

She stood. 'I need to get back to the house,' she said.

'Madeleine?'

'Yes.'

'There was nothing you could have done to help Florence,' he said.

'I know,' she said.

*

The beep of a horn jolted Madeleine as she walked down the road. The car pulled up to the curb, and Gustave leaned across the passenger seat and wound down the window. 'Good day, Madeleine, would you like a lift?' he said. The windscreen wiper shot across the screen and a burst of snow flew at her. 'Sorry about that,' he said.

She looked at him, seeing respect and kindness in his gaze. 'That would be very kind,' she said. She stepped aside to avoid the car door and climbed inside. The air seemed no warmer on the inside, but at least the wind didn't bite. 'Thank you,' she said.

'I imagine the children are very excited about Christmas,' he said.

'Yes, they are,' she said.

'Are you planning your usual Christmas Eve spread at the restaurant?' he said.

'Yes, we are,' she said.

'Very good,' he said. 'I will be there. Will you be attending mass?' he said.

Please don't ask to escort me, she thought. 'I expect so,' she said.

He paused as if thinking of how best to phrase what he wanted to say. 'And, would Antoinette be attending?' he said.

She glanced through the corner of her eye, noticing the colour shift in his cheeks, his moustache twitching. She turned her head to face him, and his cheeks darkened further. 'I do believe Antoinette will be going, Gustave, yes,' she said with a smile in her eyes.

'Do you think?' He paused. 'If... If I asked her, maybe she might...'

'Yes, Gustave,' she said, noticing a sheen forming across his eyes.

'Do you think so?' he said.

'I'm sure Antoinette would be delighted to have you escort her, Gustave. Just ask her.' She watched him, his obvious bashfulness amusing her. 'You like Antoinette?' she said.

He cleared his throat. 'She is a fine young woman,' he said.

'Yes, she is,' Madeleine said.

Silence filled the space, the car crawling down the snow-laden road, the windscreen wiper flicking across the glass at random intervals.

'I need a new foreman, Madeleine,' Gustave said.

Madeleine frowned and turned to face him.

'When Claude comes back, would you let her know please?' he said.

Madeleine swallowed, and heat coloured her cheeks. She cleared her throat. 'Yes, of course,' she said, aware of the tingling sensation in her stomach.

'The job is hers, if she wants it,' he said. 'She's highly regarded. And.' He stopped, tweaked at his moustache, pulling both sides down. 'And, I'm not alone in saying I'm very pleased that Raoul has...'

He couldn't get the words out, and she reached out and placed her hand on his arm.

'Thank you, Gustave.'

'And, I'm very sorry about how I behaved, Madeleine,' he said. He glanced across at her and then to the road, and they continued the journey in silence. The windscreen wiper jumped across the glass again and swept the snow clear, replaced by the next flurry.

He pulled the car up at the curb, and she turned to him. 'Thank you, Gustave,' she said.

'I hope she comes back soon,' he said.

'Me too,' she said.

Suffused with warmth, Madeleine stepped out of the car and entered the house.

'We got the tree in, maman,' Albert said, rushing to greet her.

His face alight, Madeleine smiled warmly. Eyeing Antoinette and mouthing thank you, she shook her head.

'I'm sorry,' Antoinette whispered.

'The lines are down for who knows how long,' she said. She had felt quite desperate at the thought of getting a message to Claude, but knowing that Gustave had a job for her when she did return had made the situation seem less disturbing. Maybe the lines would be back up tomorrow, she told herself.

'Maman, can we put the lights around the tree now?' Natty said.

Madeleine nodded. She lowered to her knees. 'Can I help?' she said.

'Come on,' Natty dragged her to the pile of tinsel, and the baubles and string of bubble-lights that were strewn across the floor. 'Like this,' Natty said, pulling at the heavy wire that connected the large lights.

Madeleine watched Natty struggle to position them, then smiled at the tutting and frowning on her daughter's face. 'Here, let me help,' she said.

'I'll make cocoa,' Antoinette said.

29.

Claude sipped at the hot drink, entranced by the glowing fire, oranges and yellows dancing around black coal, her mind replaying the images of the previous days; the shaking heads and quizzical gazes, few showing compassion, most contemptuous of her for daring to ask for work. 'Work is hard to come by these days. We're still struggling from the war,' most had said. She had turned from the factory gates the words ringing in her ears. Every workplace had given the same response; no one was hiring before the New Year, and any available jobs after that would first be offered to the men, with or without families. She had pulled up her collar, finding it inadequate against the chill.

She leaned her head back in the chair and closed her eyes.

'I'm sorry, Claude,' Yvette said.

Yvette's hand touched her shoulder, and she opened her eyes, the flames now flickering in Yvette's gaze.

'Charles says there's no work for women now.'

Claude nodded, shifted her gaze and sipped at her drink. 'I don't know what to do?' she said.

'I take it you can't go to your father?'

Claude shook her head. 'No.'

'I'm sorry, Claude.'

Claude sensed the words tinged with sadness and regret. Maybe things could have been different for her and Yvette, she thought. 'It wasn't just about us,' she said softly. 'He couldn't accept me being this way. As good a father as he was, he only got me the job in Génissiat because he thought being there would keep me away from this lifestyle. If he knew I was looking for a job to support another woman and her family he would disown me.'

'You really are in love with her,' Yvette said.

Yvette sat next to her on the couch, the familiar scent of her perfume reminding her of the times they had spent together. She looked directly into Yvette's eyes. 'Yes, I am,' she said.

'Is she in love with you?'

'Madeleine, yes she is,' she whispered.

'Hmm.' Yvette leaned back, sipped at the wine, and turned the glass in her hand. 'We were good together, Claude,' she said. 'And I have always loved you, though I know you have no reason to believe me.' She sipped from the glass again and Claude noticed the distinctive shape of her lips, wet from the drink. 'It damn near killed me to see you with those other women; to know they had a part of you that I couldn't have because I had to let you go,' she said.

Claude lowered her eyes.

'I loved you, Claude, and I didn't fight for you. I let you go, and I have to live with that. Don't get me wrong, I know we couldn't be together now, and I am happy. You left Madeleine because a bully returned from the war?' she said, her tone caustic. 'To claim a wife he then disrespects. And, whose children live in fear of him to the point of withdrawing and adopting a position of silence to avoid his wrath.' She sipped at the wine giving time for the words to settle with Claude.

Claude pinched the bridge of her nose, the truth, twisting in her gut.

'You left the woman you love to a man like that, Claude. Good God, what were you thinking?' Yvette took a long slug, rose from the chair, filled her glass and sat again.

Burning heat pressed at the back of Claude's eyes and tears burst onto her cheeks in gasping sobs.

Yvette moved with precision, placed her glass on the arm of the chair and took Claude's hand in hers. 'You are such a strong, and wise, young woman, Claude, you always have been.

But in matters of the heart, you can still be so... naïve and bloody chivalrous! You formed a plan in your own mind, to create a future with Madeleine and the children without speaking to Madeleine about it. You left without telling her. How do you think she is feeling right now? And the children?'

She wasn't sure whether the screaming voice in her head hit Yvette's ears as well as her own, the warm wet flow continuing down her cheeks, her head buried in the comfort of the soft breast, and the arms that wrapped around her.

'Sshhh!' Yvette said, rubbing Claude's back.

Wave after wave, despair flowed through Claude, each bringing a new flood of tears. 'I miss them so much,' she mumbled.

'Sshhh.' Yvette said, pulling Claude closer, holding her tighter.

The whispering sound repeated, and Claude allowed the rocking motion to soothe her. Then her eyes closed and with the comforting movement the sobs eventually calmed. She eased out of the warmth and shuddered. 'I've been such a fool,' she said. Yvette was studying her with a soft gaze and warm smile, touching as profoundly as the light fingers that caressed her face.

'This can be fixed, Claude.'

Lips pressed briefly to Claude's forehead, before Yvette released her. Yvette picked up her wine and sipped. Claude slumped heavily in the seat. She had been a complete fool. Was she really that terrified of love? Madeleine had accused her of as much. 'Madeleine must be feeling so hurt,' she said.

Yvette squeezed her arm. 'This can be fixed, Claude,' she said, again.

'God, what have I done?'

They must be devastated, she thought. Madeleine had come to her that night, risking near death walking through the icy-cold snow half-dressed to be with her, and this was how she had repaid her. A fire ignited, and she wanted to scream. 'I've been such a bloody fool,' she said.

'It's Christmas Eve,' Yvette said. 'The trains might not be running in a couple of days if the weather deteriorates.' She gazed out the window at the snow, graceful in its descent.

Claude stood and paced the room. 'What will I do about Raoul?' she said.

'Men like him can be bought, Claude. Everyone has their price my darling.' Yvette fitted a cigarette into a long holder and lit it, drawing deeply.

'How much?'

'I would guess a thousand Francs, though there is no guarantee he wouldn't return. Men like him usually need to feel threatened. He said he had spent years in recovery, there must be a record of him at a hospital,' she said. 'I can ask around.

Claude shook her head. 'I don't have that kind of money.'

Yvette walked to the mahogany bureau and pulled open the drawer. She removed the long book, scribbled, tore out the leaf and held it out in front of Claude.

Claude stared at the paper for some time. 'I can't take that,' she said.

'It is the least I can do, and I would like to help. Please take it, Claude. I have the money.'

Claude couldn't get her hand to move, the cheque waving in front of her.

'Take it, please.'

Yvette pressed the paper into Claude's hand, took a long drag on the cigarette and released the smoke slowly.

'I...'

'It's sorted,' Yvette said. 'Discussion closed. I will see what I can find out about him and get word to you in case you need further leverage. Now get out of here. You've got a train to catch if you want to get back in time for Christmas,' she said

The trembling in Claude's stomach flowed to her hands as she reached out and pulled Yvette into her arms. 'I don't know how to thank you,' she said. She released the soft warmth for the last time, and gazed through her tears into Yvette's glassy eyes.

'I would do anything for you, Claude. If you can't get rid of him, you are all welcome here until you can sort something out,' she said.

Claude nodded. The gesture wasn't an empty one, but it was wholly impractical, and she knew it would be a last resort. 'I'll try and reason with him before giving him this,' she said, waving the cheque.

'Good luck with that my darling. In my experience, drunks and gamblers are better with bribes than reasoning. I am going to make a call,' she said, stubbing out the cigarette in the ashtray, reloading the filter and lighting another one. She picked up the glass and sipped. 'Now go!' she said.

Claude thought she had seen a tear fall as Yvette had turned away and cleared her throat. The wave sweeping through her caught her by surprise, and her eyes welled up again. Love has many forms, she thought as she brushed at her cheeks, pocketed the cheque, and headed for the stairs.

*

Staring into the dark sky, she watched her breath cloud, the cold squeezing her chest. She looked down the line, aware of the hands of the clock moving too slowly on the station wall. She didn't need to hear it tick for her worries to tumble. The idea that the train might not get through to them moved her to pace the platform. There hadn't been an announcement, but then again sometimes there wasn't. She glanced towards the station office, laughing faces the other side of the counter. The station would shut in a few hours, and the staff would be preparing for an evening of festivities. With any luck, she would be in Génissiat before midnight mass. She wondered briefly about Madeleine, the children, Christmas, the money, and Raoul! Turmoil fuelled the excited feeling in her stomach. She didn't have all the answers.

The yellow light appeared in the distance before the long whistle sounded, and she felt a rush of exhilaration, her heart racing. She moved closer to the platform edge, suitcase gripped firmly in her hand.

A heady mix of tobacco and sweat struck her; the carriage empty but for a young couple huddled together at one end. At least it was a few degrees warmer than on the outside. She settled into a seat, her reflection in the glass, her focus on the shadows against the landscape as the train started to move. Easing back her eyes closed, the rhythm of noise and vibration enticing her to drift in thought.

The sense of soft warm skin under her hands reacting sensually to her touch, and a soft sigh falling from sensitive lips. She shifted in the seat, leaned her head against the cold window, allowing the images of Madeleine to caress her. Madeleine's fingers burning her skin, goosebumps tingling up her spine, the hairs on her neck rising. Tender kisses, playful and then provocative, luring her in, stealing her heart. And Madeleine had done that. Her heart had reached out, and Madeleine had touched it with every part of her. She had been held with such exquisite tenderness and love it had felt beautiful and painful in equal measure.

She could feel the warm trickle sliding down her cheeks, and clamped her eyes firmly shut. If she were honest, she had run away. Even if she couldn't see Madeleine and the children every day, and if Raoul refused to leave, she had acted selfishly by leaving them. She had cut them out of her life, under the illusion of creating a future that they would all share together. But, Madeleine had wanted her not him. She drew her knees up to her chest and wrapped her arms around them, squeezing into a tight ball in the corner of the seat. Giving her attention to the rattling wheels against the track, the images faded into darkness, the occasional long-whistle drawing her back to awareness as they passed through each station.

Maybe it was an inner sense of time having passed that caused her eyes to flash open? Or, perhaps it was the change in tone and sensation of the wheels on the track? Even in the pitch-blackness, she recognised the railway site as they passed through it, the new rails buried in snow, running alongside the main route. She sat up, releasing her legs, and shivered. She rubbed her hands up and down her arms, stood and stamped her feet. The carriage shunted her forward, and she grabbed at the seat in front, steadying herself. The carriage lurched again, and she looked out the window at the approaching lights. Bracing herself, she reached for her suitcase. The carriage lurched again, finally coming to a halt. With stiff legs and cold that penetrated through to her bones, she stepped onto the station platform, took a deep breath, and headed for the guesthouse.

She placed the case in the corner of the room, breathed in the damp aroma and smiled. She rubbed at her neck, ran her fingers through her hair, and stared out the window. In half-an-hour or so people would be heading to church for midnight mass. She would go and find Xavier; they could go together. She puffed out a deep breath, unable to release the tension that gripped her, the folded cheque in her pocket providing a slither of comfort. Hope. You can do this, she told herself. She opened her door and climbed the stairs, banged on the door to Xavier's room, waited, then pounded again. When he didn't answer, she ran down the stairs and into the street.

Pierre was locking the door as she arrived outside the Café. She watched him until he turned. 'Hello Pierre,' she said.

His hand rose to his chest, and a beaming grin lit up his face. He grabbed her shoulders and pulled her close. 'You came back,' he said.

She pulled away and gazed at him. 'Yes,' she said, and smiled. He was staring at her with wide eyes.

'Did you hear the good news?' Pierre said.

Claude shook her head.

'Claude, how good to see you back,' Voices echoed as they passed her on the street, warm smiles deepening the frown on her face.

'What news? I haven't seen Xavier,' she said.

'He's at Madeleine's, getting ready for mass,' Pierre said.

'What's the good news?' she said.

'Claude!' She turned to face Gustave's twitching moustache and couldn't help but notice the shine in his eyes. 'How wonderful to see you back,' he said. He reached out and patted her on the back. 'Did Madeleine pass on my message?'

She studied him with mute fascination, words spilling from his lips at a pace she couldn't comprehend.

'There's a supervisor job going at the railway, and I was hoping you would take it,' he said, puffing his chest out and rising another inch in stature.

Claude closed her mouth, gazed from Gustave to Pierre. Both men smiling back at her. 'I feel as though I am missing something,' she said.

'Raoul's gone,' Pierre said.

Claude's mouth opened and didn't close, and Gustave slapped her on the back, again.

'Right, if you will excuse me, I need to go and collect Antoinette for mass,' he said, twisting the end of his moustache.

She had never seen his feet move with such dexterity. She turned to Pierre. 'I don't understand,' she said.

'It's a long story, but the day you left a woman showed up who happened to be his wife.'

'What!'

'Yes. He deserted the army, stole another man's identity, and started another life, with another wife! Who would have thought it?'

Claude stood, gathering her thoughts as he continued to speak.

'Young baby too, not more than a couple of months old. She had seen his picture in the newspaper, came from Paris to find him.'

Claude frowned.

'The opening of the dam! It was all over the news, and she turned up with the clipping – his face all over it. He won't be coming back, Regina and Gustave saw to that,' he said, shaking his head. His voice softened. 'Madeleine wanted to get hold of you, but the telephone lines have been down,' Pierre said.

'I need to go,' she said.

'Yes, of course.'

She started to run. 'I'll see you in church,' she said, over her shoulder.

He waved, but she didn't notice.

*

Claude slowed to a walk, stopped, and gathered her breath, smiled at the lights glowing in the window. Delirious and dizzy she could feel the chuckle bubbling in her chest, sore from breathing heavily in the cold, the crumpled cheque damp in her fisted hand. With unsteady legs, she walked slowly up the path. Her heart trying to escape through her chest, she banged on the door, squeals from the inside melting her further. By the time the door opened her throat was clamped and her mouth dry.

Madeleine's hand shot to her mouth as she gasped.

Claude stood, struck by her beauty and the sudden inability to coordinate any part of her body. 'I...'

Madeleine reached forward, grabbed her arm and pulled her into the house. Gazing into Claude's eyes, her own wet with tears, 'You came back,' she said.

'You look beautiful.' Claude said.

'Claude!' Xavier said. He smiled broadly, stepped up to her and pulled her into a fierce embrace.

'Claude's back!' Natty screamed and launched herself at Claude's waist wrapping her arms around her.

Claude pulled her up, and tiny arms squeezed around her neck. Putting on a strange voice. 'You're choking me,' she said and Natty laughed.

Natty released Claude and studied her with a broad grin. 'I made you a card,' she said, wriggling and climbing down.

'Hello Albert,' Claude said, holding out an arm to him.

He leaned into her, wrapped his arms around her. 'Merry Christmas, Claude,' he said.

'Merry Christmas to you all,' Claude said, her eyes settling on the stream of tears trickling down Madeleine's face.

Albert released her and stared into her eyes. 'Are you staying for Christmas?' he said. 'We're going to mass in a minute.'

Claude addressed his sparkling gaze, so full of expectation, and ruffled his hair. 'I certainly hope so,' she said. 'Would that be okay with you?' she said to him, her eyes shifting to Madeleine.

'It's better now that man has gone.' Natty said, tying the laces on her shoes. She picked up the card by her feet and ran back to Claude, holding it out in front of her. 'This is for you,' she said.

'I didn't like him either.' Albert's voice was a whisper.

'Thank you,' Claude said to Natty.

'Will you come with us to mass?' Madeleine said.

Four pairs of eyes waited on her words, and she smiled at the intensity in their gaze. 'I would be delighted to join you all,' she said.

She watched, Madeleine wiping away the tears with the back of her hand, the trembling fingers that had touched her with such tenderness, the warm glow in her cheeks, and the light that danced in her eyes. I love you, she thought. 'Shall we go,' she said. She held out her arm and Madeleine hooked her arm through it as they walked, and warmth filled her.

'I thought you didn't like church,' Madeleine whispered.

The hot breath tickling her ear caused a shiver to chase down her spine. 'I don't,' she said. The words came out hoarse, and Madeleine's smile had her throat constricting such that she couldn't swallow. 'There are things that I do like, that would entice me to go to church,' she said.

'Perhaps we could talk about those things later,' Madeleine said.

'What things, maman?' Natty said.

'Nothing!' Claude and Madeleine said in unison.

'I want to open presents later,' Natty said.

'Yes, after mass,' Madeleine said.

'I don't like church either,' Natty said.

'They hear everything,' Claude whispered.

'No,' Natty said. 'Only the important words.' She skipped on ahead with Xavier at her side.

Madeleine squeezed Claude's arm. 'I can't tell you how happy I am.'

'You can show me later,' Claude said.

Madeleine stopped walking, pulling Claude to a halt, and stared at her. 'Will you stay with me tonight?' she said.

Claude smiled. 'Yes,' she said.

*

269

Claude stood, watching Natty and Albert with a small pile of presents in front of them on the floor. She caught Madeleine's gaze, the warmth in her smile. 'Thank you,' she said, accepting the glass of Cognac. 'Merry Christmas, Madeleine.'

'Merry Christmas, Claude,' Madeleine said.

Madeleine leaned towards her and she felt soft lips burn her cheek, and an electric current fire through her. The kiss lingered, and she wanted more. As Madeleine pulled away a groan fell from her lips. 'Too much,' she whispered.

'Never.' Madeleine said. She turned towards the children. 'Right, who's ready to open presents?' she said.

'Me!' Both children screamed together, selecting a present and unwrapping it carefully.

'Wow!' Thank you, Claude,' Albert said. His hands followed his eyes across the detail of the hand-carved, painted train. 'It's amazing.'

'I've got another doll. Look, look,' Natty said, holding it out to Albert.

'That's great, Natty,' he said, pulling away and continuing to inspect his most prized gift. 'I made you something too,' he said, handing over his carving of a car to Claude. 'It's the second one I did, at the lake.'

'Yes, I recognise it,' Claude said. 'Thank you so much! It's the best present I've ever had.'

His grin widened, and he returned to the floor and started opening another present.

'You've been very generous,' Madeleine said.

'Not at all.' Claude's eyes lowered to the carving in her hand.

Albert opened the large box and looked with wide eyes at his mother. 'A train set!' He leapt to his feet and ran into Madeleine's arms. 'Thank you so much, maman, it's just what I wanted.'

Madeleine's flushed smile filled Claude with warmth. She watched Madeleine stand and go to the kitchen, wondering whether she should follow her. When Madeleine returned, pushing the small pram, Natty leapt into the air squealing.

Natty looked up with her widest grin. 'Thank you, maman,' she said.

'I had to hide it,' Madeleine said, but Natty hadn't heard a thing and was already fitting her new doll into the pram.

Albert opened a second gift from Claude, studied the writing on the cover of the leather-bound book.

'Tom Sawyer was one of my favourites,' Claude said.

Albert opened the hard cover, leafed the pages with care.

Claude's gaze shifted from the children to Madeleine.

'What is it?' Madeleine said.

Claude tilted her head towards the children. 'There are things we need to talk about and things they will find out sooner rather than later,' she said.

'Later,' Madeleine said, closing the space between them and taking Claude's hand in hers.

She would never know how the briefest contact could have such meaningful impact. Her eyes closed and the melting sensation of Madeleine's lips on hers swept away all concern. When she opened them and held Madeleine's gaze, the words fell from her lips. 'I am so in love with you,' she said.

'I feel as though I have always loved you,' Madeleine said.

'I love you, maman,' Natty said, removing the dress from her new doll.

Claude chuckled.

'Come on, it's time for bed, you two,' Madeleine said.

'Claude can read me a story,' Natty said.

'Not tonight, Natty, it's Christmas Day already,' Madeleine said.

Albert clasped his new book to his chest. 'Thank you,' he said to Claude. 'Will you be here in the morning?'

'Yes, Albert, I will.'

He nodded. 'Good,' he said and ran up the stairs, Natty following closely behind.

Claude turned to Madeleine and paused.

'What is it?' Madeleine said.

'I'm sorry, I didn't get you anything,' Claude said. Madeleine continued to stare at her, her eyes softening, darkening, a smile forming.

'Claude, you have given me more than I could ever have dreamed of,' she said, and closed the space between them.

About Emma Nichols

Emma Nichols lives in Buckinghamshire with her partner and two children. She served for 12 years in the British Army, studied Psychology, and published several non-fiction books under another name, before dipping her toes into the world of lesbian fiction.

You can contact Emma through her website and social media:

www.emmanicholsauthor.com
www.facebook.com/EmmaNicholsAuthor
www.twitter.com/ENichols_Author

And do please leave a review if you enjoyed this book. Reviews really help independent authors to promote their work. Thank you.

Other Books by Emma Nichols

Visit **getbook.at/TheVincentiSeries** to discover The Vincenti Series: Finding You, Remember Us and The Hangover.

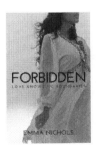 

Visit **getbook.at/ForbiddenBook** to start reading **Forbidden** and **getbook.at/Ariana** to delve into the bestselling summer lesbian romance Ariana.

Thanks for reading and supporting!

33289985R00159

Printed in Poland
by Amazon Fulfillment
Poland Sp. z o.o., Wrocław